CRUEL AS A QUEEN

KENDRA MORENO

COPYRIGHT

Please do not participate in piracy.

Copyright © 2019 by Kendra Moreno

All rights reserved.

No part of this book may be reproduced in any form or by any electronic or mechanical means, including information storage and retrieval systems, without written permission from the author, except for the use of brief quotations in a book review.

This is a work of fiction. Names, characters, businesses, places, events, locales, and incidents are either the products of the author's imagination or used in a fictitious manner. Any resemblance to actual persons, living or dead, or actual events is purely coincidental.

Edited by Michelle Hoffman

Proofed by: Dani Black

Cover art by Ruxandra Tudorica with Methyss Art

Formatted by Nicole JeRee at The Swamp Goddess

ISBN:9781081919955

*This one is for all those who are struggling, whether physically or mentally.
There is hope even when it doesn't feel like it.
You are loved. You are loved. You are loved.*

FALL DOWN THE RABBIT HOLE
ONE LAST TIME...

Four stories. Four adventures. The past will meet the future in this final companion installment of the Sons of Wonderland.

Once upon a time, there was a curious little girl ...

KENDRA MORENO

... then she grew up and became a monster.

CRUEL AS A QUEEN
BLURB

Villains are made, not born. Alice knows that better than anyone, her story starting with an accidental fall down a rabbit hole. She experienced wonderful things, but when she returns home, no one believes the mad imagination of a little girl.

Doctors tried everything to make her admit she's wrong, to make her forget, but nothing will ever take away her memories of Hatter, White, Cheshire, and Alex. No matter what they do to her, she will not bow.

Alice will make everyone pay for what they did. They thought she was a monster before. They haven't seen nothing yet.

AGED EIGHT

"Come, come, Alice. Would you like a spot of tea?" the Hatter asks, gesturing towards two double doors. I smile at him, excited to be included. It's been an odd little world I've fallen into, completely mad and illogical. I can't believe a world like this exists, and it's all my wildest dreams come true. A world with Mad Hatters and Late Rabbits. Why, all it's missing is a Grinning Cat.

"Tea sounds lovely, Mr. Hatter."

"Dormouse! It's time for tea!" he shouts into the open doorway.

"It's always time for tea," a voice calls back, whom I suspect is Dormouse. Really, is he a mouse?

I follow the Hatter inside the room, staring at everything in awe. Mommy and Daddy never let me near the fancy china at home. Here, it's as if every possible fine china is set on the table, some glistening in pristine condition, others chipped and missing pieces. Some have delicate floral pictures on them, others are black with skulls. I dare not ask what the difference is and suspect I will be drinking from a flower teapot rather than any of the others.

Though I'm quite intrigued by the skull teapot. What sort of tea pours from its spout?

"Have a seat next to me, pick a chair and have some tea," Hatter chimes. There's a small twitch in the corner of his eye, barely discernible, but I'm very good at watching things. I'm about to ask what's the matter, but he turns away and moves towards the far end of the massive table.

Some of the chairs have creatures in them, rather funny ones. There's a woman who looks at me with goat eyes, delicate ram horns curling from her hair. She beautiful, interesting; she's some impossible thing I would like to study. How curious she is, just like everything else about this world.

Another creature has a head full of spines, like that of a hedgehog. His nose is a little bulbous, just like the creature his hair reminds me of. There are tiny ears on his head that twitch at my entrance. He lifts a teacup and salutes me with it, the way daddy's friends do at parties. I nod hello, but I don't smile; he's a little unnerving.

Sitting at the far end of the table, beside the Hatter, is a man with rat-like ears. I wrinkle my nose. I'm not fond of rodents, but I stride forward and take a seat opposite him, taking in the numerous piercings along his ears and the odd look on his face. He's sizing me up, no doubt taking in my simple blue dress and the apron mommy had made me wear, which I have yet to part with.

"What kind of curious creature are you?" he asks, tilting his head.

"Why, I'm a little girl. What are you?"

"'What are you?'" He snorts, insulted. "Who am I? I'm the Dormouse."

"You don't look like a mouse. You look like a rat."

Dormouse gasps in outrage before turning to look at the Hatter. "What sort of game are you playing, Hatter, bringing this heathen into our home?"

"She's just a child." Hatter smiles at me gently. "Behave, Dormouse. I found her wandering in the forest. She must have slipped inside the rabbit hole."

"What's a rabbit hole?"

"Oughtn't you know?" Dormouse sneers. "You're the one who used it."

I sniff at him. I don't like the Dormouse. He's rather rude.

Hatter pours a teapot on end, and I watch as a sweet-smelling yellow liquid fills a teacup. He hands it to me, and when I take a sip, the taste of lemons dances on my tongue. I wish tea tasted this good at home. Mommy always makes me drink Earl Grey, and I'm not fond of it. The Hatter's tea is far tastier.

"The Rabbit Hole is how you got to Wonderland, Alice," Hatter answers, ignoring Dormouse's rude remarks and pouring himself tea from a black teapot. Curiosity eats away at me, and the urge to try that one fills my body. What is in the black tea pot? "You must have followed White through when he came back."

"You mean the rabbit? The rabbit is from Wonderland?" I'm astonished. It looked just like an ordinary rabbit, even if I kept hearing a ticking every time I drew near.

"That was indeed White, or the White Rabbit. He's the Time Keeper. You'll meet many interesting creatures here. That's why you're meeting me. I'm the most interesting of all."

Dormouse snorts, and I shoot him a quelling look. I could listen to Hatter talk all day, and I wish he would tell me more about his world. Dormouse, I want to wring his neck. I shake my head the slightest amount. No, that's not a polite thought to have. I'm a guest in this home. I should act like one.

"Hatter is a dense caboose, letting all his madness loose. He'll dance a jig and pour some tea, but he's no better than you or me," Dormouse chants. Hatter grins.

"A raven flew inside a writing desk and asked me for some bread. When I fetched a snack and then came back, it was to find the raven dead."

"He suffocated!" Dormouse shouts so loud that it makes me jump. "You suffocated the raven!"

"I would never! He died of unnatural causes!" Hatter presses his hand to his chest, as if he's completely insulted.

"Lies!"

Hatter looks at me then, a wide grin on his face. When he sees my furrowed brows and the confusion in my eyes, the grin drops. He pushes his hair out of his eyes.

"My apologies, young Alice. I'm afraid the madness takes over sometimes."

"What kind of madness?" I ask. At the same time, I reach for the black teapot, but the Hatter stops my hand.

"You mustn't drink that tea, Alice. It's not made for creatures not of Wonderland."

"Why?" I glare at him, a bit of anger flowing through my blood. Who is he to tell me what I can and can't do? If I want to drink the tea, I will.

"It isn't safe."

I jerk my hand away from the Hatter and grab the teapot anyways, before pouring the tea into an empty chipped teacup. It splashes out of the sides, my hand too quick. Momma would have scolded me for that, for staining her white linens, but the Hatter only watches in fascination as the blood-colored tea fills the cup. Daddy would have beaten me for the slight, but I don't dwell on that too long.

"Is the tea what makes you mad?" I ask, setting the skull teapot back down and lifting the cup. "Will it drive me insane?"

Curiosity drives me, urging me to take a drink. I take a whiff of the liquid, inhaling the perfume. Roses. It smells like Roses and Chocolate.

"It might. It might kill you, or it might make you powerful."

Powerful. That word catches my attention. What is worth gaining power? Am I willing to risk dying for it? Am I curious enough to drink tea the Hatter says is not safe? Do I even care what he says? A powerful lady wouldn't care. A powerful lady would drink it all and smile afterwards.

Hatter watches as I take a sip, the flavor coating my tongue. I hum in appreciation before tipping the cup all the way up, draining it. Dormouse sports a frown on his face, his eyes squinting at me. He's not pleased. The urge to hurt him claims me again, and I stand up before I know what I'm doing. I pull back my arm and throw the empty tea cup right at his face. It narrowly misses his ear, my aim askew.

"What the fuck?" he snarls, picking up his own teacup and hurling it at me.

I laugh as I dance out of the way, the china shattering across the tiled floor. Red tea splatters, and for a moment, it looks like blood. I pick up a plate and throw it like a Frisbee, wildness flitting through my veins. I want to play like this every day, live without rules and only worry about madness and Hatters. Hatter snatches the plate from the air before it can hit my target and frowns. I pout, pressing out my lip. I was certain that one would strike the Dormouse right in his ugly mug.

"That's enough, Alice."

"Oh, it was just a bit of fun."

Both stare at me as if I've grown another head. Spoil sports, the both of them. I sigh and look towards the door.

"Perhaps, we should take her to see the King and Queen," Dormouse says, glancing at the Hatter. "She's a curious girl."

"Curious, very curious." Hatter pulls out a knife and I tense, watching it. "What are you doing here, Alice?"

"What do you mean?" I ask, confused. "I followed a white rabbit, of course."

"But, why are you here?" he snarls. I whimper and look at the door again. Maybe if I run fast enough, I can escape. "Why are you here?" he shouts, the plate he held in his hand smashing onto the table top and the anger in his eyes forcing me to take a step back. The anger is so sudden, so unexpected, it sends panic through me, and I worry I did something wrong.

"I don't know!" I cry, turning towards the open doorway. "I don't know!"

I run. I run away from the angry man in a top hat. I run away from the Rat who watches my every move with skepticism.

"Alice! Wait! I didn't mean that! We can help you!" the Hatter shouts behind me. But I don't stop.

I run. I run. I run.

Daddy never likes it when I run. But the Hatter, the Hatter follows, and he makes me feel better because he tries to understand. Daddy never tries. When the Hatter kneels before me and wipes my tears away, I throw my arms around him, hugging him, needing his mad warmth.

"It's time we took you to see the King and Queen, Alice. Perhaps, they can find a way to send you home," Hatter whispers, standing up and offering me his hand.

I don't speak.

I don't tell him I want to hit the Dormouse as he watches with knowing eyes.

I don't tell him I don't really want to go home, that I don't want to see my mommy and daddy ever again.

I don't tell him I can hear the violent sound of his heartbeat beneath his ribcage, or that it's so loud all I want to do is silence it.

No, that wouldn't be polite, at all.

AGED EIGHT

"Where in Wonder did you find her?" I hear the White Queen ask for the thousandth time. For a Queen, she really seems quite dense. I'm certain Hatter has mentioned he found me in the woods at least three times prior.

"In the woods, Your Majesty," Hatter dutifully answers again while I sit prim and proper on the stairs. "She was just wandering around alone."

"Do you think she's a threat?" The sweet Red Queen asks, glancing over at me. She doesn't even whisper, the cow. Oughtn't that be something discussed behind closed doors and not where I can hear?

"She's a child." Hatter smiles when I catch his eyes and then returns his attention to the royalty before him.

I don't understand what good they can do. None of them seem too privy on talking to me. They only want to discuss me. I'd heard one of them mention finding White and opening up the portal again. I'm not ready, hoping to stay here for as long as possible. If I have it my way, I'd never leave.

The bushes rustle in front of me, and I furrow my brow. What on earth is making that noise? I lean to the side, trying to catch a glimpse of what it is, only to see a shoe that's there, and then it isn't.

"Hello?" I call, bringing the attention of the monarchy and the Hatter. "Is someone there?"

"That's probably Alexander, dear. You are welcome to go play with him." The sweet Queen smiles at me when I look towards her.

"Is that wise?" the White Queen asks. "We know nothing about her."

The sweet Queen scoffs. "Sister, she's a child. What harm can she do?" When she looks back at me, her eyes are kind, even if they're condescending. I might be a child, but I'm not daft. "Run along, dear."

I stand only because I'm tired of listening to their voices discussing ways to get rid of me. The rustling comes again, and I move towards it, peeking around a topiary of a giant horse. No one is there, but a boyish giggle finds my ears from another direction. For the first time since we came to the castle, a tiny smile curls my lips, and I move as silent as a mouse—far quieter than the Dormouse Oaf—towards another topiary. This one is shaped like a swan. I catch the briefest sight of him before he's gone. Blond hair. He has blond hair like I do, although mine is much paler.

"Hello?" I call again, because he's obviously a skilled hider. I bet he plays the best game of tag. There's no one here to tell me not to get my dress dirty. It's refreshing.

"Who are you?" the voice asks, echoing from a short distance.

I turn towards the voice, those of the Hatter and monarchs already too far away to hear. He's led me away from them.

"I'm Alice," I answer, looking around for him. "Who are you?"

He jumps out from behind a bush so suddenly, I would have jumped had I not known where he was. He puts his fists on his hips and stands there like a king, although not as regal.

"I'm Prince Alexander." He puffs up his chest. "I will be the Red King one day."

I raise my brows. "You don't seem very princely."

He's wearing dark trousers and a shirt, both covered in dirt and smears of green. He has smudges on his face where he's wiped his filthy hands across it. His hair has bits of sticks and leaves in it. But his eyes, his eyes are so blue that it draws me towards him. Even with dirt covering him, those eyes give far more away.

He snorts, the sound grating on my ears. I don't think that's very good manners for a Prince.

"Regardless, I'm the Prince, so you must do as I say."

I bristle. "No one is going to order me around. I'm not your subject."

"I order you to play hide and seek," he continues, as if I hadn't even spoken. "I'll hide. You seek."

"That isn't very fair. I'm a guest. Shouldn't I get to choose?"

"But I'm a Prince, and so what I say goes." He looks at me, a childish grin on his face. How odd that I both want to wallop him and do as he says.

"Fine." I sigh. "But I get to choose what game we play next."

"Deal. Count to twenty, Alice." Alex winks at me, and it makes my heart dance inside my chest. Curious. It's never done that before.

I turn towards the closest topiary, this one of a giant diamond, and place my head against it. "One . . . two . . . three . . ." I've always hated hide and seek. I don't want to look for someone, and I certainly don't want to find them. I'd prefer to sit alone and read my books. At least then I can keep the thoughts at bay. "Seven . . . eight . . . nine . . . ten . . ." I count the rest of the numbers in my head, already annoyed at the turn of events. When I speak twenty, I turn from my spot and squint my eyes, searching. The faster I get this over with, the faster I can change the game. "Ready or not, here I come."

I move deeper into the garden, realizing fast that it's carved to be a maze. Inside the maze, it's almost unnaturally quiet, the air moving with vibrations rather than sound. A fog hovers in the maze, making it a little hazy, and a little frightening.

"Alex!" I call. I can't help the slight quiver in my voice. *Strong girls aren't scared. Strong girls aren't scared.* "Come on. This isn't funny."

I spin in a circle and look the way I came, already turned around and unsure which direction I should go. Blast! I'm going to lose, and Alex will have to come find me himself. I growl and hit the closest bush. There's an answering squeak, and a tiny chipmunk runs out. I gasp. Another rodent! This world is filled with them, apparently.

I squat down and hold out my hand to him.

"Come on, little chipmunk," I coax. "I won't hurt you." The creature stares at me before moving a little closer. "That's it. Come on."

The chipmunk climbs inside my hand, and I immediately clamp my other one around him. He screams and bites me. I flinch, anger filling my body.

"That wasn't very nice," I snarl, and squeeze. He screams in panic, and I hesitate for a second, my mind saying I shouldn't do what I want to. It doesn't last long before I'm squeezing harder, until his little screams cut off, and the maze falls into silence again. I look around me and see a bucket sitting forgotten on a stone bench. I'm about to drop the little body inside and pretend as if nothing happened, when an idea strikes me. I'm not a fan of the white roses the garden has at the entrance. I want to paint them red. I look down at the limp body of the chipmunk. I want to paint them as red as blood.

I begin my work.

HOURS LATER, I FIND MY WAY FROM THE MAZE. THE WHITE Queen's eyes immediately zero in on the bucket in my hands, where the scent of pennies wafts. She can't know my secret, so I put the bucket behind my back and smile at the sweet Queen.

"I found some red paint, your majesty. May I paint some of the roses red?" I make sure to smile sweetly at her. As a child, it's important to make the adults think that they're in charge, to make sure they think you're just an innocent. I learned that with mommy and daddy, and it's a lesson mommy taught me well. I get whippings at home if I don't do as I'm told, but if I smile and play sweet, especially around guests, they forget all about the punishments.

"What an imaginative child!" she coos, smiling at me. "Of course, you can."

I skip off towards the rose bushes and start painting with my fingers, a brush nowhere to be found. I try my best to ignore the murmurs behind me. I don't really care what they have to say about me. I'm going to enjoy my time here while I can.

Oh, how lovely the roses look painted red.

CRUEL AS A QUEEN

I've been invited to the Red King and Queen's table, where the entire length is filled to the brim with food. It's surrounded by dozens of odd creatures, and I've finally met the White Rabbit in person. He sits across from me, a smile on his face, as he talks to the king of something or other. I haven't been listening if I'm being honest. I've been trying to tune out the sounds of the eating around me. It seems many of the creatures sitting with me have never had to sit through etiquette classes. They've never had their knuckles bruised because they used the wrong utensil. They slurp and burp, hum and clatter; it makes my ears hurt and my stomach turn just listening to them. I don't touch anything on my plate.

"May I be excused?" I ask suddenly, and those around me stop what they're doing and stare.

"But you haven't touched any of your food, dear Alice." The sweet Red Queen points to my plate, concern on her face. I don't want her concern. I don't want anything from a woman determined to get rid of me.

"I'm not hungry."

"Let the girl go," the king says, already dismissing me. I like him even less than the Queen. "She can find something to entertain herself with, surely."

Her Majesty nods her head and meets my eyes. "Very well. Just be careful, child. And if you see Alex, tell him his mother is looking for him please."

I nod my head and stand, fully intending not to speak to anyone while I'm roaming the halls. This castle must have a library, certainly. What else is the point if it doesn't?

I stroll through hallway after hallway, peeking into rooms only to be disappointed each time. When a boyish chuckle reaches my ears, I turn towards it, searching for the source. One more doorway to look into; this time it bears the fruit I'm looking for. I step inside the massive room, the walls lined with bookshelf after bookshelf, each filled to the brim with leather-bound books. I turn in a circle, taking it all in. I would kill for this library, to have free reign of such a thing.

"Aren't you supposed to be at supper?"

I whirl at the sound of the voice and grimace when I find the

Prince lounging on a seat in the corner. He's laying down completely at odds with his Princely title, his legs spread in a way that makes me blush. There's a book open in his lap.

"The Queen was looking for you," I say while I'm staring up at the ceiling.

"Why are you looking at the ceiling?" I can see him looking up, too, out of the corner of my eye, curious as to why I could be staring at the plain brown paint. I gesture towards him and his spread legs, my blush no doubt growing brighter on my face. "I can sit how I like. I'm the Prince."

"That doesn't mean the rest of us should suffer for your unfortunate title." I can't help the slight growl in my voice. He's insufferable.

Out of the corner of my eye, I see him move and reposition himself. "Is this better?" he asks.

I risk glancing at him, and I'm relieved to see that he's sitting normal again. "Much."

"You're a curious creature, aren't you?"

"I wish everyone would stop saying that." I rub my hand along my dress and, for the first time, realize there's a splatter of red on it. Oh, mommy will be very unhappy about that. "I'm not the odd one here. At home, I'm quite normal."

"But that's why you're so very odd, see? This world is mad. And here you are, logical in an illogical world. I find it intriguing."

"Well, you can just keep your intrigue to yourself," I sniff.

I glance at the books again, reading the spines. Some are in languages I know nothing about, others have names that make me cringe. When I come to a book titled *The History of Wonderland*, I pull it from the shelf and study it.

"I used to study that book when I was younger. It's rather bland."

"I don't think it's bland at all." I flip open the book and start to flick through the pages. "I think it's wonderful."

"You like to read?"

"Yes, but my parents don't allow me to read books outside of my studies."

I can feel his frown from my position, and when I look up, it's still there. "That's very sad, Alice. You're welcome to read anything in this room." A smile. "That is, if you can read some of the languages. I think we have one written in Jabberwock somewhere. Harsh language, but it's important to study everything."

"You would give me free reign inside the library?" I ask, surprised. I'm a stranger, and one that they keep referring to as curious. They should want to protect their books, not allow me to read them.

"Of course. Why not?"

"Well, aren't you worried I'll ruin them?"

There's that sadness again, his eyes looking down at the book in his lap. When he meets my eyes this time, the sadness is gone, and a smile lights his eyes. "Here," he pats the seat beside him, the large chair big enough for two. "Sit down, and I'll read to you."

"Read to me?" I can't help but parrot his words. He's being so kind, and it confuses me. Before, he had been horrible, teasing, and full of himself. This new attitude makes me hesitate; I'm uncertain how to handle it.

"Come on, Alice. It's alright. I think you'll like this one. It's an adventure story about a Knave and his Princess."

I hesitate for a moment more before I move towards him with jerky movements, completely uncertain if I should be doing as he says. When I sit down beside him, he smiles and chuckles under his breath.

"Relax, Alice. Don't think of me as a Prince. Think of me as a friend."

I don't correct him, that I don't care if he's a Prince, but it's uncommon for a girl to be sitting so close to a boy alone. It's not proper at home. But I suppose I'm in a different world, so I can act differently. I force myself to relax my spine and lean back in the chair. We're close enough that our shoulders touch, goosebumps trickling up and down my arm. Alex turns to look at me, his bright-blue eyes meeting my own pale ones, and for a moment, my heart starts that irregular beat again, so loud I can feel it in my ears. I've never felt so nervous.

A friend, I don't think I've truly had one of those before.

Alex reaches up, and I tense as he touches my wild hair around my shoulders, his fingers running down the gold.

"You have the prettiest hair. I don't think I've seen anyone else with our colored hair. Yours is much paler than mine."

"It's common at home," I say, more to remind myself than to correct him. I'm trying to get my heartbeat under control, taking slow measured breaths. I keep expecting my momma to appear out of nowhere and berate me for sitting so close to a boy.

"Well, in Wonderland," he says, "you're not only curious, you're unique." He grins. "I like that."

Then he turns to look at the book in his lap, unaware of just how much his words mean to me. For the first time, I don't think impolite thoughts. I don't question things or feel the need to find answers.

For the first time, I feel at peace, as Alex begins to read.

"Once upon a time, there was a Knave and his Princess, soon to be Queen...."

AGED EIGHT

"I don't really want to go home," I tell the Hatter, staring at the swirling green and white tunnel in front of me. White had explained that the rabbit hole will spit me back out where I fell in—the woods near my home.

"You're a part of Wonderland now, Alice." The Hatter squats down in front of me, a half smile on his face. "One day, when you're ready, you can come back. But you must go home first and figure out if that's what you want."

"Of course, I want that." I've been here a week and already know I want to live here forever. I will be counting down the moments until a white rabbit shows up at my doorstep and tells me I can come back. "I don't want to leave."

Alex stands next to his parents, a thin gold circlet around his head. He's revealed to me he hates the thing, that it's uncomfortable on his brow and pinches his ear. I don't think it's so bad, but I don't have to wear one all the time, so what should I know? He'd given me the book to take with me, *The Knave and The Princess*. Now, I clutch it in my hands like a treasure. I'll have to hide it when I return home. Momma and Daddy won't allow me to keep it.

"See you around, Alice," he says, a smile on his face. He waves at me, and I know, I'll remember him best. Alex and the Hatter. The others I can do without, really.

"You promise you'll come back for me, that I'm a part of Wonderland?" I ask the Hatter, frowning. My newest fear is they'll forget all about me, and I'll live out my life dreaming of white rabbits, Hatters, and a Prince.

Hatter takes my hand, a simple smile on his face.

"I promise one day you'll return, but to come back here you must learn that things must happen as Wonderland deems, and then you'll return as if in a dream." His eye twitches.

I nod my head and turn to the rabbit hole, to the pretty swirling colors. I only glance back one last time at Alex, to see his smile and another little wave of his hand, before I jump inside with a squeal.

I'M THROWN OUT OF THE SPINNING LIGHTS RATHER QUICKLY, AND I land on the forest floor with an oomph. The leaves and dirt run along my blue dress, no doubt making me even filthier, but I smile anyways and stand up, brushing myself off.

There's a chill in the air that hadn't been here when I'd first left, and I frown. It feels like snow, but that can't be right. It was summer when I slipped inside the rabbit hole.

Furrowing my brows in confusion, I push my way through the trees and out to the house. My worry only grows when I see my home. The garden has died. Not a single plant is left alive for my mother to tend to, and she loves her gardening.

I make my way towards the door and try the knob. Locked. I knock, feeling odd for doing so on my own home. I've never been locked out before.

"Momma, daddy," I call. "I'm home."

There's a thump inside the house, as if someone dropped something very heavy, and then hurried footsteps towards the door. Something shatters. The locks are clicked, and there's a furious scuffle before the door is yanked open, and I meet the sickly eyes of my mother. Her face is thinner than I remember, dark circles under her eyes.

"Momma?"

She grabs me and yanks me inside, enveloping me in a tight hug.

"Oh, Alice. We thought you were dead. Where have you been? We've looked everywhere for you! Richard! Richard, come quick!"

Steps upstairs and then my daddy is coming down, his eyes confused when he sees me. There's no relief in his eyes as there was in momma's. There's no love there, either, but I don't think about that.

"Where have you been, girl? It's been months."

"Months?" I frown. "It's only been a week."

"You went missing in July, Alice," momma says. "It's November."

"That can't be right. It was only a week! I swear! Perhaps, in Wonderland, things are different."

"What is this Wonderland?" daddy asks.

"I fell down a rabbit hole and ended up in this curious world. There was a Mad Hatter, and a White Rabbit that wears a wrist watch, and a Cheshire Cat. The King and Queen were a bit rude, but the Prince was lovely." Daddy shares a look with Momma over my head, and I clench my jaw. "You don't believe me, do you?"

"We believe you, Alice," Momma whispers, but Daddy doesn't agree. He doesn't believe me. Neither does Momma. They're looking at me as if I've grown a second head. "Your dress is filthy, Alice. What have you been doing?"

"Adventures, Momma. I went on an adventure."

This time, I ignore the look they share. It's okay, because I have Alex's book tucked safely inside my apron.

"Can you explain this Wonderland again?" Daddy asks, and I know I will be punished for daring to speak of such things.

But it's true. It's all true.

And I refuse to dismiss the memories as if they're nothing more than mad ramblings.

"Come along, Alice. We're late."

"Where are we going, Momma?" I glance up at my mother, see her restlessly twitching, which is unlike her. Momma is always calm and relaxed.

"Don't ask questions, dear. Hurry up."

"Okay." I frown. "I will just go grab my coat."

She clenches her jaw like she wants to say more, but she doesn't speak, so I go grab my jacket and pull it on. I come back to the doorway and Momma gets down on her knees to wrap her arms around me. I'm surprised for a moment, confused as to why she's hugging me so tight just to go out, and it puts me on edge.

"Momma, are you okay?"

"Of course, dear. I'm just so glad to have you back at home."

It's only been a week since I returned from Wonderland. Momma and Daddy had been asking me repeatedly about my time there. I've told them the entire story at least a dozen times and even took Daddy to the spot where the rabbit hole appeared. Of course, it's nothing more than a regular spot now. It won't be a rabbit hole without White's magic. I tried to explain that to him, but the frown-lines on his face only grew deeper. He's been acting strange since I returned, stealing glances at me when he thinks I'm not looking, and the worst thing of all is the overwhelming disappointment I sense from him now. It had been there before Wonderland, but now, it's so strong, it makes me flinch.

My parents usher me into the automobile, not giving anything away. My confusion only grows when we turn a direction I've never gone before, down streets I don't recognize. The trip takes around thirty minutes, and my confusion grows when we pull up outside of a plain brick building.

"Where are we?"

They don't answer me, but they don't have to. The car door pulls open, and a large hand reaches inside to clasp around my bicep. I squeak and try to pull away, but the hand pulls me from the car quickly. I scream and grab a hold of the door, clutching it like my life depends on it.

"Momma! Daddy! Help me!"

But their betrayal hits me hard. I see it in their eyes, in the tears dripping from my mother's, in the disappointment in my father's. They've done this. They've sent me here.

Frantic, I fight against the hold, kicking out with all my might, a ferocious scream on my lips. Another hand reaches in and yanks me from the door, latching onto my other bicep, until I'm lifted in the air and carried in between two large men dressed in white.

"Stop! Stop! Let me go!" But no one listens. My parents slide from the car behind me and follow us inside. I stare at the word stamped onto a plaque in the bricks. "Davis Institute for the Insane." Committed. My own parents are having me committed. I snarl in outrage as they carry me into the building, my legs swinging in an attempt to knock their hold loose. If I can just get away, I can run. I can run and never look back and wait for the moment White comes back for me.

"I'm telling the truth!" I scream, one last effort to make my parents believe me. "I saw them! I went down a rabbit hole!" Momma covers her face and turns into my father's chest, unable to stomach seeing her daughter carried off to the crazy house. "I saw the White Rabbit! I saw the Hatter! Momma! Daddy! Don't send me away! Please!"

Desperate, I fight against their hold harder but I'm no match for the large men carting me towards the double doors, carrying me to my prison. I'm only eight, not nearly as strong as I hope to be. I'm useless. I can't free myself.

Out of the corner of my eye, I see a flash of white, and I turn, hopeful, and find White standing in the corner. He's holding so still, no movement, but I see him clear as day, and I reach out for him, even though my movements are restricted by the hold on my biceps. Relief fills my body. It's time already. Thank God! Thank Wonder! But something in me wants everyone to believe me, too. I want them to see.

"White! Look right there! It's the White Rabbit! See him!" Every eye turns at my words and stares at White in the corner, but not a single one reacts as if he's there. Not a single person nods, or apologizes, and they don't let me go. "White!" I scream. "Save me! Help me, White!"

His face is solemn. He doesn't move to help me, or respond, or acknowledge he's here for me at all. He just watches as I'm finally dragged through the double doors and into my prison. My screams grow louder, more piercing as I scream for him, scream for anyone to save me. And then I remember the book, the book that Alex gave to me. It's tucked inside my apron, the only place safe from momma and daddy, and I pray they don't take it away. A book does no harm. It's only a book.

"White!" I howl, just before someone sticks a needle into my arm. It works immediately and my body grows limp, but I'm aware as they carry me to a padded room and strap me down to a table.

"Should we use a straight jacket?" one of the men asks a doctor who walks in the room.

"No, straps are fine. We don't have a straight jacket small enough to fit her."

A tear leaks from the corner of my eye, and the doctor watches it fall before sighing and leaving me alone in the room. I can't move, can't speak, can't give in to my emotions, but my brain is aware and running in circles.

Hatter. White. Cheshire. Alex.
You promised.
Where are you? Where are you? Where are you?

AGED THIRTEEN

"Tell me about your visions, Alice."

I stare out of the window, watching as a raven sits on a thin branch. His beady eye meets mine, studying me, and he gives out a squawk of understanding. A bird knows when you're inside a cage.

"Alice?"

I turn away from the raven as he takes off in flight, my jealousy of his wings bringing a glare to my face. The man on the other side of the desk sits without a care in the world, his fingers steepled in front of him as he looks over his glasses at me. He's new, trying to make his mark on this place. I don't tell him making a mark here isn't a good thing, that it's already so marked up, its indistinguishable between an asylum and a prison, even if it's white as snow, white as fur. Dr. Taylor will learn soon enough.

"I don't have visions."

I'm not afforded the same liberties as the doctor is. I'm sitting in a chair far harder than his comfortable desk seat, my back forced ramrod straight against the hard metal. I can't move, my wrists and ankles strapped to the chair. They used to only strap my wrists . . .

. . . until I kicked an orderly's teeth out.

"My notes say you've spoken about a place called Wonderland and seeing various characters you claim are from there."

"I don't have visions," I repeat. *No, I have memories.*

"It's in your best interest to work with me Alice," Dr. Taylor sighs, his penetrating eyes looking at me in a way that makes me uncomfortable. "I can get you out of this place if you only cooperate."

It's the same speech I've heard before, where a new doctor comes in and promises to get me out, if I only do as they say, if I only pretend as if my memories are false. I know the score. When I first came to this place, they'd told me the same thing. So, I'd been a good girl, smiling when they told me, agreeing that my memories were nothing more than a fanciful imagination. *Wonderland wasn't real*, I said at least a thousand times. *There's no such thing as Mad Hatters or White Rabbits or Cheshire Cats.*

Nothing changed.

My parents never came back for me. The last time they visited was when I was nine, and mom had been heavily pregnant. They were trying again for a child less damaged, less insane, than me. It had hurt at first, feeling as if I was being replaced, but after a while, I understood. I wasn't a part of this world anymore, anyway. It was okay if they pretended I'd never existed. It's okay they probably forgot they have a child named Alice shut away inside an asylum. It's okay that I have a sibling somewhere I'll never know.

I realized after a year of pretending, of being who they wanted me to be, that no one gets out. No one ever does, not unless it's in a body bag.

"Alice, are you listening to me?"

I'm getting really sick of Dr. Taylor.

"No," I answer honestly. "Anything you say will be the same as I've heard before."

"I don't think that's true." He frowns, and I roll my eyes.

A lock of hair slides over my face, and I blow at it, trying to move it out of my eyes. They rarely let us get our hair cut nicely, and it's usually a bad sign when they do. My hair is unruly now, and down to the base of my spine. I've considered hanging myself with it, but I honestly think that's what they want me to do. Most patients don't have long hair, so I have to assume it's a test. It's a useless one, because I don't want to die, but it's still one they've been trying for a long time.

"You're here to get my statement, to see if it's any different from the last doctor. You'll make promises, you'll tell me I'm gonna get out of here as long as I can show you I'm not mad, that I'm normal. So, I'll smile and tell you, 'Of course, oh, what I've seen is just my wild imagination, just the silly thoughts of a teenage girl.' And you'll say, 'Good girl,' and stick me back in my cell, day after day after day." I look back out the window, soaking in the sunlight. We hardly get to go outside. The view will have to do. "No one gets out. We die here. Your job is to determine how quickly."

He stares at me in silence for long minutes. I can feel his penetrating gaze, studying me like an insect under a magnifying glass. I hate the feeling, but there's nothing I can do. I'm strapped down so tightly that the leather cuts into my wrists, and I'll no doubt have punishing welts when I'm sent back to my room.

"Do you want to die?" Dr. Taylor finally asks.

I don't turn to look at him. Sometimes, the doctors like the power of their position, of playing God with patients too helpless to fight it. Other times, they seem almost bored. The worst ones are the ones who have pity in their eyes, who have grand dreams of saving every patient. I can't stomach the pity.

Every night, Dr. Taylor will get to go home, to leave this place and have a nice dinner, kiss his wife if he has one, smile at any kids he might have, and then he gets to slide into a nice bed after a warm shower. I would kill for any one of those things. We don't get to leave. We don't get to go outside unless we've been well-behaved, and even then, we're strapped to a chair or laced into a straight jacket. When I get sent back to my padded walls, I'll get a metal tray of oatmeal for dinner that is always bland and too thick to eat without feeling like you're swallowing paste. The shower I get will be so frigid, it'll make my teeth chatter and threaten to send me into hypothermia. And then I'll get to curl up in the corner of my padded room. Beds aren't for the insane. Too many things on them can be made into a weapon. No, we get a thin mat and a holey blanket, and even those get taken away if we cause trouble.

"Of course not." I meet Dr. Taylor's eyes. "I want to live more than anything. But I'm told I'm living wrong, and I've been imprisoned in this hell and forgotten. I haven't accepted my fate, Doctor, and I refuse to."

He scribbles something on his notepad, and I have the urge to spring across and rip it to shreds. I've actually done that before when I was younger. It's why I'm no longer allowed to be without the straps.

"Do you see yourself ever leaving here?"

"Does anyone ever answer yes?" He nods his head. "Then they're idiots. No one leaves. We're nothing more than experiments."

"It says in your file you answered yes when you were younger."

"And I learned my lesson."

Dr. Taylor sighs and stands from his chair, pushing the hair back from his face. I watch warily as he circles the desk and leans against it. It's a power position, one that forces me to tilt my head up in order to meet his stare.

"Perhaps, there's another way I can help you?"

His words make me tilt my head, my brows wrinkling. That's a new line I've never heard before. Curious, I say, "how?"

He squats down in front of me, his face too close, so close I want to reach out and take advantage. If not for the restraints, I would.

"There are certain liberties allowed to the doctors here," he mumbles, his eyes dropping from mine and trailing down my body. The hair on the back of my neck stands on end, and I suddenly feel unsafe. When his clammy fingers touch the skin at my exposed ankle and begins to trail up my pant leg, I jerk in my restraints hard enough shake the chair. "I could set you free, if only for a moment."

"Get your fucking hands off of me," I snarl, jerking at the straps around my wrists.

"Now, Alice, I'm only doing my job. If you're a good girl—"

I don't let him finish. He gets too close, his face leaning into mine, assuming that I will be pliant and helpless. I rear my head back and slam it against his hard enough to make stars dance in front of my eyes. I hear a satisfying crack where my skull strikes his nose, even if black dots dance across my vision.

He falls backwards, his back hitting his too-clean desk, blood spurting from his nose.

"You fucking psycho!" he grunts. "What the fuck is your problem?"

I smile as the orderlies slam through the door. A small chuckle slips from my lips as they swarm me, restraining me further. Someone grabs hold of my skull, their hands large, and keeps it straight, so I can no longer look around.

Dr. Taylor holds a tissue to his face, trying to catch the blood that isn't slowing. He deserves every bit of that.

"Doctor?" One of the orderlies stares at Dr. Taylor expectantly, waiting for orders.

His eyes meet mine, and I see the evil lurking there. "This patient needs to be medicated."

My chest seizes. "No. Please don't."

But he continues as if he doesn't even hear me. One of the men around me leave the room for a moment before coming back inside, a tiny cup in his fingers.

"Take the pills," he orders.

I pinch my lips tightly shut, my eyes wide with panic. I've seen what the medications do to the other patients. The pills take away their ability to function, their ability to react. Some of them are so drugged up, they can't even move, their eyes open to a never-ending horror show.

"Take the pills, Alice," Dr. Taylor sneers, his face smeared with blood in such a way, it makes him appear insane instead of me. That's the reality, after all, isn't it? I was never the crazy one here.

I clamp my jaw hard, but it's no use. The man holding my head wrenches me backwards, my neck twinging at the sudden movement. Another squeezes my jaw hard enough to bruise until I'm forced to open my mouth. As soon as I do, they drop the pills inside and force my mouth shut, another plugging my nose. I struggle underneath my restraints, my face turning first red, then purple as I fight against the lack of air.

No, no, no. I won't lose who I am. I can't. I silently beg anyone who can hear me, God, Wonderland, my parents, but no one comes to my rescue. No one comes to save me. I swallow.

I'm alone, forgotten, and when the pills kick in, I forget myself, too.

AGED FOURTEEN

The doctors are so surprised the pills they shove down my throat everyday haven't made me forget my memories. I'm so drugged up most of the time, I don't know what I'm saying, but their names cross my mind every single moment.

Hatter, White, Cheshire, Alex . . .

I'm going mad with worry, trying to be strong. Hatter said that I'll always be a part of Wonderland. They'll come back for me. They have to. *Please come back.*

Dr. Taylor is still here, and he's still the same asshole he'd been from our first meeting. He doesn't actually meet with me anymore, not often. I get the "privilege" of listening to him drone on once a month. It's mostly a discussion about how many people I've managed to hurt, even while drugged. They never seem to time the next dose correctly, so before they can shove more pills down my throat, I'm usually able to kick someone in the groin or bite them if they get too close. I like when they get too close.

Our discussions are almost always one-sided. The drugs don't let me talk much. They scramble my brain to the point where it's a struggle to function, but I see and hear everything, much to my dismay. There are some things I wish I couldn't see.

It's time for my monthly meeting with the idiot today, and as usual, the orderlies are off on their medication schedule. I don't understand why the asylum keeps them around. They're useless really. They deserve what they get, every single one of them.

I'm sitting in the corner of my padded room, my white pants and shirt dirtier than ever. They've stopped giving me clean ones as a type of punishment, I think. Another trick to take away my humanity. No showers for the insane.

I keep my arms wrapped around myself tightly, as if I can squeeze hard enough to keep everything from spilling out of me.

The door opens on silent hinges. No matter how dirty they allow me or this place to get, they take care of the doors. Can't have us escaping our prison. No one wants that in the headlines.

"Alice, it's time for your meeting with Taylor." I don't like the orderly who's speaking. He's always too rough, a sick grin on his face as he bruises my pale skin. He gets off on fear and pain, taking this job so that he can torture innocent people.

I don't move, staring up at him with glazed eyes. The drugs have worn off enough that I can move and function, but there's always a glaze across my eyes now that never seems to go away. One day, maybe they'll give me too many pills, and I'll go out that way.

"Stand up," the orderly commands. Still, I don't move. Fuck him.

He flicks open the stick he uses on difficult patients, the one that I've felt kiss my spine and the back of my thighs. I tense.

"What are you doing, Jeff? Just pick her up and take her. We don't need the stick."

The other orderly, Daniel, is kinder than the others. He's newer, hasn't been warped by this place yet. His green eyes meet mine, so pretty compared to the shit-brown of Jeff's. In another world, I would have smiled at him, coy and demure, but I've already been corrupted. I squeeze my arms tighter around my middle.

"Shut up, Danny boy. She's being difficult, so I can use the stick if I want to."

Jeff moves towards me, and my arms start to shake. I can already feel the stick hitting my calves, my back, my thighs. The pain that comes with it will be immeasurable, and I won't be able to walk without a limp for days. At least the drugs help in that aspect. I won't feel the pain after they shove the pills down my throat.

Jeff moves a little closer, and Daniel tenses at the same time as a small whimper escapes my throat. I hate the sound immediately, wishing I could take it back when the smile spreads across Jeff's face.

"Get up, Alice."

I curl tighter, trying to shrink as small as possible, wishing I can just disappear. *Where are you? Where are you? Where are you?*

"That's enough, Jeff," Daniel tries again, taking a step forward.

"Shut up!" Jeff raises the stick above his head, and I prepare myself for the impact, knowing it's going to hurt bad enough to make me bleed. He's in a mood today, and his anger is always transferred to the patients.

Daniel rushes forward then, and I flinch when he steps in front of me—in front of the stick—and stares down Jeff. No one has ever protected me before, and I don't know how to react.

"I said, 'That's enough.'" Daniel blocks my view the slightest amount, but I can see the rage that fills Jeff's body, and I know that this is going to be bad.

Instead of Jeff backing down, he swings the stick at Daniel's face instead. I react before I know what I'm doing, flowing to my feet and jerking Daniel out of the way just in time. Instead of striking Daniel, the stick flies through empty air. Daniel stumbles and catches himself against the padded wall and ducks just in time to avoid another swing.

My eyes dart towards the still open doorway, unprotected and open wide. I can escape.

I hear a sickening crunch behind me, and I turn to see Daniel stumble back, a hand clamped over his jaw, a harsh cry ripping from his lips.

"No one will blame me for this," Jeff snarls. "I'll just tell them you got too close to Alice. They'll believe it, like they always do."

Daniel slides to the floor, and I look between the open doorway to my freedom, and the only person who has ever stood up for me. I take a step towards the doorway.

Another mottled groan rattles me, and I turn back to see Jeff raising the stick again, high above his head, what will no doubt be a killing blow. My heart stops. Daniel's green eyes meet mine again where he lays slumped against the wall. They're filled with pain, anger, and acceptance. He nods his head at me the slightest bit, giving me permission to run, to escape from this place.

Leave, his eyes tell me. *Be free.*

But all I see is that stick swinging down, and I'm reacting before I know what I'm doing. I turn and rush at Jeff, a fierce scream ripping from my lips. His swing pauses midair, and he turns to look at me too late. I latch onto his back like a monkey and wrap my weak arms around his throat. I'm still too small, too fragile to hurt him like this. I can't get my hands around his throat.

Jeff swings the stick over his shoulder and connects with mine, sending a bolt of pain through the bone. I may not have the strength to take him down, but I have teeth. I wrench my head around and latch onto his ear, blood welling in my mouth the moment I clamp down. The metallic taste almost makes me gag, but I clamp down harder before ripping away, the meat of his ear coming away with a sickening noise. Jeff screams in agony, announcing to the entire asylum that I'm attacking, and more orderlies swarm into the room, sealing my fate, stealing my chance for freedom. I spit the flesh from my mouth as they yank me from Jeff's body, pinning me to the floor, never gentle. There's a knee in my back that makes it hard to breathe, and someone has their hand clenched in my hair to keep my face pressed into the padding beneath me. In this position, I can meet Daniel's eyes, can see him struggling to breath, his jaw at an odd angle. Still, he meets my eyes, and there's an apology there, one I don't understand.

We're all just here to survive, after all. It was my mistake for being human in a place robbed of its humanity.

"The medicine isn't working."

I can't breathe; the straps across my chest are too tight, too restricting. I can't move at all, my wrists latched down, my ankles, thick leather straps keeping me immobile. There's even a strap around my forehead.

"I've received permission from her parents to start electroshock treatments." I recognize the voice. It's Dr. Taylor. What do they mean 'electroshock?'

"Are you sure that's wise? She's still a child."

"Which is why we had to have their permission. She bit the ear clean off of Jeff's body, and she broke the jaw of the new kid. Even now he's in the hospital. They don't think he's gonna make it. Infection, apparently."

"Poor kid."

"What are you doing to me?" I try to ask, but my throat isn't working. I must have been sedated. I can't feel my toes.

"Are we starting now?"

"Yes, prepare her for the treatment. Connect the electrodes."

An orderly comes into my field of vision, a woman I've never seen before. She gently connects something around my head, something with wires. It's cold like the touch of metal, heavy. What is this? What's happening?

"We're going to start at a lower setting, see what has an effect."

My mouth works up and down, begging without sound. I can't speak, can't scream. Panic fills my body.

Hatter! White! Cheshire! Alex! Where are you? Where are you? Where are you?

"Alice, patient zero-zero-four-two, electroshock treatment one. Begin test," Dr. Taylor orders.

There's a sound that fills the room, as if a livewire is hanging from the ceiling, and then my body is lifting off the table even with the straps, my mind going blank with pain, my heart freezing inside my chest. I scream in agony, silent, my eyes tightly shut, and then it's gone, my body weak and filled so full of pain that tears leak from my eyes. Something wells inside my mouth; I think it's blood.

Dr. Taylor leans over me and meets my leaking eyes, a tiny smile curling his lips.

"Again."

LATER, WHEN I'M DUMPED INTO MY ROOM IN A HEAP, MY CLOTHES

still dirty and torn, my heart hurting, I hear someone outside my room talking.

"Did you hear? Daniel, one of the orderlies she attacked, died today. Poor thing. Infection they said. The girl's a monster."

For the first time, I believe them.

AGED SIXTEEN

Freedom is a thing so easily taken away. We're born at the mercy of our parents, and as we grow, we're at the mercy of the world. All it takes is a single snap of a finger for your life to be changed irrevocably. A mother who can't take care of her child gives her baby away, tears in her eyes, aching heart, angry at the world that won't let her earn her money in a way that doesn't involve her opening her legs. A child that lives in a home with his seven siblings only knows a tightening cord, their mother doped up, their father unknown, his life spent taking on the job he shouldn't have to; he's twelve. A little girl is spoiled and pampered, told she can be anything, until she opens her mouth and tells a story, and they tell her she can't be crazy, she can't speak such things, she belongs somewhere else, she should be forgotten; she's eight.

Freedom is so easily taken away.

"Tell me about your visions."

I don't answer the new doctor sitting across from me. Dr. Taylor had finally left this shithole for greener pastures, after his years of tyranny. The moment he left, the electroshock treatments slowed, and they've only given me one since he left. It's been months since that time. I've almost forgotten the pain of it, the shame, the helplessness.

"Alice?" The new doctor's name is Marcus Flint. He's insisting I call him by his first name. He told the other patients the same from what I understand, so I'm not special in that sense. A few of the others talk when we're allowed out in the garden. A few of them have more freedoms than I do. Those are the ones who belong here, who think this is some sort of holiday or retreat. Those patients make me sad.

Dr. Flint is middle-aged, his temples greying prematurely, his nose crooked in a way that speaks of bar fights rather than medical school. His eyes are kind most of the time, but every now and then, there's this evil light that enters them, and I know not to underestimate him. I know not to assume that he will be different.

"Alice, tell me about your visions."

I meet Dr. Flint's eyes and consider not answering. What will that get me? Another night without food? Another electroshock treatment? I decide that holding my silence isn't worth those things. I've learned to pick my battles.

"They aren't visions," I whisper, clenching my fists. I'm strapped down to the metal chair as usual, the leather straps too tight. I have permanent marks on my wrists from the leather, because they fear me, a sixteen-year-old girl.

"Ah, yes. Tell me about your memories then." Dr. Flint's eyes gleam as he watches me, his glasses at the end of his nose. He scratches at his notes, useless really. My story hasn't changed in the eight years I've been here. It never deviates, and still they ask me the same question.

"I'd rather not." I clench my jaw. "They exhaust me."

"Your cooperation is essential to your recovery."

"There is no recovery to be had, Dr. Flint. My story will not change, because it's the truth." My voice lacks the power it used to have. It's raspy, and weak. Screaming has damaged my vocal cords beyond repair.

Dr. Flint stands, and I tense automatically. It's never a good sign when they feel the need to stand, to assert their dominance.

"You are far different from the other patients, Alice."

"How so?" I ask, humoring him. My fingernails bite into the palm of my hand as I clench them.

"The other patients play along. They try to convince me they're sane, that they've already recovered. And here you are. Your story never changes. You don't ask to be released."

"I'm not stupid." *And I'm not crazy.* I turn and look out the window, the green grass and sunshine outside beckoning me. It's been too long since I've been out of this building. I miss the sunlight. "No one escapes this place. No one is let go."

"Perhaps, your family will come back for you."

I laugh at his words and shake my head. "My family will do no such thing. They have a new child, another little girl. Hopefully, this one isn't crazy."

Dr. Flint stares at me. I can feel his eyes peeling back my layers and trying to figure out what makes me tick. I'm an anomaly in this place. My hope doesn't rest on my family coming back for me, or for this place to suddenly get shut down, or for them to grow a conscience and let me go. My hope rests on a White Rabbit returning.

"Maybe, there are other ways you can be free," Dr. Flint suggests.

I tense at his words, knowing them to precede something I really won't like. "I don't want any more drugs," I mumble.

The asylum likes to prescribe new pills all the time, trials, medications that haven't been proven to do anything. Doctors pay for us to be guinea pigs, and if one of the pills cause the patient to go completely insane and kill themselves, well, that's alright. There's a room in the back of the asylum where the dead bodies go. The are pushed in whole, and come out as no more than ash, used for fertilizer in the gardens. I've seen it happen far too many times.

"Not pills, Alice." Dr. Flint squats down in front of me, and I finally meet his eyes, that evil flicker there causing me to dig my fingernails in further, no doubt drawing blood. "There are ways you can be free, if only for a moment." His fingers wrap around my skinny knee, an attempt at a caress that feels more like steel wool on my skin.

"No." I don't snarl. I don't threaten. Just the simple word. It should be enough. In another world, it would be. His hand doesn't move. I've been down this path before, but Taylor deemed me too dangerous to try the act again, and the orderlies are afraid of me. I've managed to escape the fate that Dr. Flint is now offering.

"Come now, Alice. You know there's no reason to fight it." His fingers trail up, up, up, and I panic.

"Get your hand off of me." This time I can't help the snarl that slips out. He smiles, as if it pleases him, as if he gets off on it. I grit my teeth when his fingers slip under the edge of my shirt to touch on my pale skin. "I said, 'get your fucking hand off of me!'" I jerk hard against my restraints, the leather cutting deeper into my skin, irritating the already scarred flesh. The metal chair doesn't even rock with my movement, too heavy for me to impact.

Dr. Flint chuckles, and I know I'm in trouble. My heart thumps hard enough in my chest that I can feel it in my throat, my eyes, my ears. Fingers scrape against my skin, searching, defiling, hurting.

He gets closer, pressing his body against my knees, his face too close to mine. I immediately react, snapping at his face, prepared to bite off whatever I can close my teeth around, but he's faster than I expected. Dr. Flint jerks away with a grin.

"That wasn't very nice," he chides before loosening his tie and pulling it from his neck. Before I can figure out what he's doing, he wraps it around my head, the silk going between my teeth tightly. I jerk violently, trying to keep him from tying it, but it's too late. I breathe hard through my nose, almost hyperventilating, my panic getting the better of me. "There now, that's better."

Those fingers trail to places they shouldn't, and I begin to scream, and scream, and scream. My voice is muffled by the silk between my lips, and no one comes running. No one comes to save me.

Hatter, White, Cheshire, Alex. . . .

My mind shuts down.

AGE EIGHTEEN

Dr. Flint only lasts a year before he's fired. He doesn't get dismissed because of his treatment of the patients. Someone found out he was Jewish, and this asylum is strictly a Christian organization.

I was happy to see him go, but as how things always go, he's only replaced with someone else just as bad, just as evil.

I've stopped fighting it, only reacting when I know I will see results from my outburst. Almost every time I'm a bad girl, I receive an electroshock treatment again. I have to make sure my fight is worth the pain of electricity flowing through my body.

I've developed a stutter when I talk, I'm assuming from the treatments. It sounds clear in my mind, but when I speak, my words don't flow like they should. The doctors seemed happy about the development. They've been keeping the machines on a low voltage to extend the amount of time they can test on me.

I've envisioned killing everyone in this building many times, ripping the heads from their bodies, bathing in their blood. But I'm growing weaker. If White doesn't come for me soon, I won't be here for him to find.

This office has become the place I dread coming to. Dr. Stevens is the newest doctor, and he's much worse than Dr. Flint had been. He takes liberties, does what he wants, all in the name of science. There's a cross hanging on the office wall, a mockery really. Dr. Stevens like to bring up bible verses in his conversations. That hasn't stopped him from touching me, though. No, he can always just ask for forgiveness from his God.

"I don't think the electroshock treatments are doing much to curb your madness, Alice." Stevens looks over the notes in front of him, the file thick after being here for ten years. Every time I see the file come out, it's bigger, as if I'm some sort of lab rat they have gathered more information from. I'm waiting for the day they decide to dissect me.

I stare at him, no expression on my face. I don't trick myself into thinking he actually wants a response. No, the last time I had spoken out of turn, I'd been slapped across the face, blood welling in my mouth after biting my tongue. He'd smiled afterwards and taken great pleasure in watching the red liquid drip down my chest.

"Perhaps, we should try another avenue. You're of age now. We don't need your parents' permission. It says, in your file, they have vetoed the lobotomies, but unfortunately, as an adult, they no longer have any say over your treatments."

I'm tempted to perk up at his words. Maybe my parents actually cared after all, but then his other words settle in, and I realize I haven't suffered the worst this place has for me. I've seen the patients who had lobotomies, their heads shaved, their eyes empty. They don't survive long after the "treatment".

"W-why would you-you do that?" I ask, meeting his eyes. Stevens has dark-blue eyes, almost dark enough to be black. Normally, I would call them pretty, but on his face, they're harsh and terrifying. They're the eyes of a monster.

"We have seen slight success with the electroshock therapy, but I'm curious to see if other avenues will prove beneficial. A lobotomy could cure your madness."

"It will kill-kill me. There is-is no cure for m-memories." I curse the stutter that only seems to thicken under the realization White will be too late when he returns. I will already be dead, whether my body is or not. "I will not be-be your lab rat."

Stevens smiles. "We don't need your permission, Alice. You're a ward of the asylum. You have no family anymore, and you have no rights here. Whatever treatment I prescribe goes."

"P-please don't." The words taste like ash in my mouth. Saying please to this man makes my stomach turn, but I can't help the feeling that a lobotomy means my death, my freedom forever out of reach.

He doesn't humor me or make me beg more. Stevens dismisses me with a flick of his wrist, and the orderlies come inside to begin loosening my straps. They're usually trained to never let my wrists go unbound, but one of the orderlies is a split second too late. The fear of having the new treatment makes me react before I can think on it. I jerk my hand away and grab the stick form the orderly's waist. Before he knows what's happening, I've already bashed it over his head, knocking him out cold. I swing the stick towards the other one. He's a little faster on his feet and manages to dodge it, but he doesn't account for the other chair behind him bolted down to the floor. He trips, and I'm bringing down the baton across his face hard enough to hear something crack, blood spurting from his nose as he collapses to the floor. I turn on Dr. Stevens who sits at his desk calmly, as if I didn't just take out two large men. He steeples his fingers and looks at me.

Two years ago, I would have thrown myself at him and ripped him to shreds, disabled him, make sure he can never do what he's done to me again. I'm no longer that girl. Fear drives me now, and I've learned my lesson. I don't beat him until he no longer breathes; I don't approach him at all.

I turn on my heel, and run through the open doorway.

I sprint through the hallways of the asylum, heading for the exit and my freedom. A few orderlies try to get in my way, but when I swing the baton, none of them expect it, and every single one of them goes down, whether from shock or something else, I don't know. I don't stay to find out. I take the last turn and come face to face with the gate, the newest addition in security for the asylum. We'd had a patient escape a few months ago, and they weren't taking any more chances of losing their test subjects. I slam into the gate, but it doesn't move. Their new process means the person behind the desk has to press a button to release it. I turn towards the thick glass window where an elderly woman sits. Her eyes are wide as she takes in my appearance, the frantic rise and fall of my breath.

"L-let me out, please!" I cry, slamming against the gate again. Still it doesn't budge. "P-please, I beg you. Please."

The woman's eyes flick to the camera screens and then back to me. Her arm twitches.

"Open the-the gate!" I beg her, tears flowing down my face. I'm so close, a press of a button away. If only she would press the button. "They're going to-to kill me." I sob against the gate, banging my fist against the metal until my hands start to bleed.

Her hand twitches again, this time raising up enough to lay her hand against the release lock. Hope fills my body.

"Please," I sob. "P-please open . . . please open the gate."

Shuffling sounds behind me, and I start to yank on the handle in earnest, screaming at the top of my lungs, begging, pleading. Something buzzes, and the door releases so hard I stumble backwards. I recover quickly and throw myself through the door.

"What the hell are you doing?" the guard shouts at the woman behind the desk. Her eyes are watery as she watches me. I don't have time to thank her as I barrel through. I shriek as the guard tries to grab me, swinging the baton as hard as I can. I miss, but it gives me the opening I need. The doors are fifteen feet in front of me. All I have to do is get out those doors and run until I can't run anymore, and I'll be free.

"Someone stop her!"

I pump my arms harder, pushing myself as fast as I can go. My bare feet slide across the tile as I scramble for the door. Freedom, I can taste it.

I slam through the double doors just as something pricks my neck. I lose my footing and slam to the ground, the concrete skinning any flesh exposed. My chin suffers the worst of the damage. I immediately try to push myself up, but I've lost feeling in my arms, my body growing as heavy as a sack of sand. I manage to roll myself over onto my back with a grunt, trying to get up.

Get up! I scream in my mind. *Get up and run!*

But I can't. I can't move. *No, no, no, no, no.* This can't be it. I can't be so close and fail.

I stare at the man who steps forward out of the shadows, a syringe in his hand, the thing that had pricked me on the throat. Dark-blue eyes look me over, a grin on his face. When he kneels next to me and trails his fingers over my breast, I sob in my throat.

"So close to freedom, Alice. How does it feel to be so close only to lose it?" A sinister grin crosses his face, and I know.

Stevens had been playing with me all along.

He let me get this far. He told the lady at the desk to open the gate. He wanted me to taste the freedom and then take it away. Black spots crawl across my vision.

"Y-you're a, a monster," I whisper as the drug takes effect and I start to slip under.

It doesn't stop me from hearing his last words, or feeling his fingers push the hair from my face.

"Oh, Alice. We both are."

THE BUZZING IS WHAT WAKES ME UP. SOMETHING IS BUZZING, AND then I feel a tug on my hair. I open my eyes to hazy white; wherever I am is new to me. I've never been in this room before. I jerk my wrists against the restraints, but it's useless as usual. Tears prick my eyes. I look around frantically and find a man next to me. There are clippers in his hand, the source of the noise, and I jerk harder against my restraints.

"P-please, no," I sob, but he ignores me.

I lean my head away from him when he draws close, and he tsks. "Hold still, or I'll take off more than hair, girl."

More tears fall as he begins to shave my head, blonde locks falling to the floor slowly in graceful rivulets. My head grows cold as more and more of my hair is taken from me. I sob into my chest as the man takes away the last thing that belonged to me, as it coats the floor in a sheen of pale yellow.

The man doesn't waste time. He takes my dignity in five minutes, and then I'm being moved from the chair to a gurney and strapped down before being wheeled through the asylum, heading for my doom.

I know how this will end. I know how this works.

"Patient number zero-zero-four-two," Stevens says, stepping up beside the gurney as we roll down the hallway. "Treatment one."

"Alice," I sob. "My name, name is Alice."

Stevens looks down at me and grins. "Not anymore. You're patient zero-zero-four-two."

He takes away everything that I am, my hair, my name, my freedom, until I'm a body trapped inside a hell, until I'm no longer a human at all.

When they slide me to the table and begin to put me under, the sound of a drill somewhere far in the distance, tears drip down the sides of my face.

Where are you? Where are you? Where are you?

My thoughts race wildly as I try to fight the darkness closing in around me, but then the anesthesia kicks in, and they steal those, too.

You promised. . . .

AGE NINETEEN

"Patient number zero-zero-four-two. Caucasian female. Aged nineteen. Suffering from delusions, hallucinations, and bouts of hysteria. Dangerous. Biter."

I don't even react to the statement. Sometimes, it's a struggle to get words out, or to get my body to listen to my commands. I'm strapped to a table, my new normal. My skull holds a constant buzzing, as if I can still hear the drill, but there's nothing there. They've only done one lobotomy before studying me. I'm remarkable, they say. I didn't lose my functions, didn't go comatose. What they don't realize is the inner fight. For all appearances, I've become docile until I'm not.

I'm labeled dangerous for a reason. I seem to have gained some sort of strength from the procedure, the drill tapping into something "miraculous". And the treatment had cured my stutter. I think it's from the trauma.

Stevens talks in a monotone voice, pissed he's here on a Saturday. I'd collapsed this morning when I tried to stand. I don't know what happened, but the orderly had panicked and called the newest doctor, Dr. Morgan, who then called Dr. Stevens because he's never been in contact with me before. I can't help but be amused by the clear annoyance on Stevens' face.

"Hatter, White, Cheshire, Alex, Alex, Alex," I mutter. I've been unable to stop the bouts of word vomit that slip from my mouth. In my mind, I don't want to be saying them out loud—they only make my predicament worse—but still they slip free, taking the choice from me.

"What is it that she's saying?" the young Dr. Morgan asks, moving closer. I barely tense, ready for when he comes too close, ready to take advantage.

Stevens sighs and grabs Dr. Morgan before he gets close enough. I clench my teeth at his interference. "Dr. Morgan, please refrain from getting too close."

"But she's strapped down, Dr. Stevens. What harm can she do?"

Stevens removes his glasses and rubs the bridge of his nose, completely done with the younger doctor. His years here are wearing on him. I can't wait to see him break.

"There's a reason there was an opening here, boy. She's marked dangerous."

"Hatter, White, Cheshire, Alex, Alex, Alex." My voice grows louder without my permission, almost turning into a growl. I yank at my restraints hard enough to bruise, adrenaline filling my body. Something tells me to fight, to make it more difficult for them.

"Should we call someone?" Morgan's voice is hesitant.

"We need to administer a sedative. Go grab the nurse."

Morgan rushes from the room, leaving me alone with the monster. He sets the file down on the examination table and moves towards me. I yank harder.

"Patient zero-zero-four-two. I am advising you to calm down, or else I will be forced to sedate you for your own safety." If I was able to, I would have snorted. It isn't for my safety at all. The closer he comes, the harder I pull at the restraints, until my body aches from the force.

"Hatter! White! Cheshire! Alex!" I scream at the top of my lungs, my voice piercing. Stevens cringes but doesn't step away.

"Alice!" His voice saying my name only makes me more violent. "Alice, you must calm down!"

Then he reaches up and touches my leg. I immediately tense and stop moving, my glazed eyes staring at the man above me, his fingers trailing along my skin. Destroyer, Stevens is a destroyer.

"That a girl," he murmurs, his hand moving higher.

A tear slips from the corner of my eye before I can stop it, and another follows immediately. I turn my head away, prepared to shut my mind off, when I see him.

A choked gasp escapes, and hope fills my body. He came back. White came back for me.

He stands in the corner, wearing his signature green waistcoat, those tall rabbit ears twitching on his head. I stare at him as he studies me, and I realize what he must see. I'm frail, far too thin. I no longer have hair, my head shaved, and there are thick scars there. I've never seen them, but I can feel the thick raised flesh where they had cut my scalp to perform the lobotomy. I must look like some sort of horrifying creature.

"White," I whisper, completely ignoring Stevens as he touches my body. "Help me, White."

The doctor follows my gaze, but he doesn't see the man standing there. No one ever can unless White wants to be seen. He returns his attention to my body.

"You can talk to your ghosts all you want," Stevens whispers. "Focus on your white rabbit."

I sob, my fingers spreading, reaching towards White, towards my only chance at freedom from this place. White glares at the doctor touching me, and I can see his anger there. He's going to help me; he must.

"Please?" I cry. "Please, take me back!"

White stares around the room, at the doctor, the sterile padded room, the sounds of other patients screaming and moaning out in the hallway. They're never ending, and sometimes, my own screams join their own.

"I can't do that," White whispers, and my heart stops. "I can't take you back, Alice."

"Please?" My voice grows a little louder. "I'm begging you."

He blinks rapidly, but before he can speak again, Dr. Morgan steps back into the room with a nurse carrying a syringe. Neither of them comments as Stevens jerks his hand from beneath my gown. Morgan clears his throat and takes up position, the nurse getting the sedative ready.

"White!" I scream, hysterical. No! He's here to save me. He has to be. "Help me! You promised! You promised I was a part of Wonderland!"

"I was wrong. You must not return, Alice."

The doctors move around me while I begin to thrash against my restraints as hard as I can.

"You promised! You promised! You promised!" I let out an ear-piercing shriek, and everyone covers their ears.

"I'm so sorry," White chokes before turning towards the door.

No! No! White was supposed to save me, to take me back to Wonderland. He isn't supposed to leave me here to die.

"Hatter! White! Cheshire! Alex! Alex! Alex! You promised!" My screams only grow louder as Stevens prepares to sedate me. In my hysteria, I jerk hard enough at the restraints for one of them to pop free. The leather strap flings away, and my first instinct is to wrap my fingers around Dr. Stevens' throat. I squeeze hard, my fingernails sharper than I remember. "Off with their heads!" I scream. "Off with their heads! Off with their heads!"

Morgan and the nurse try to pull my arm away, screaming for help from the orderlies, shouting a code red for everyone to hear. Another strap breaks, and I jerk, wrapping a second hand around Stevens' throat. His face turns red quickly, and then morphs to purple, as I choke off his air supply.

"Stop her! Someone get the sedative!"

Stevens had dropped it with my attack, and it had been kicked around in the fight, no doubt. Morgan drops to his knees and scrambles for the syringe.

Stevens claws at my hands, cutting deep grooves into my flesh with his nails. Blood begins to drop from the wounds, but I don't feel a thing. My eyes are locked on White as he stands at the doorway, his sad eyes watching the scene.

"You promised!" I snarl at him. "You promised!"

The nurse jabs a needle into my arm and squeezes the plunger own, filling me with the sedative. Stevens is no longer fighting, his body limp in my hands. I bare my teeth at the man with rabbit ears on his head, at my friend and my betrayer.

"Get the doctor away from her!" one of the orderlies shouts.

I feel the moment the drugs enter my system, my fingers loosening, losing my strength. Stevens slides to the floor with a thump.

"You promised," I groan as I'm pushed back down. "You said I would always be a part of Wonderland."

White's ears droop. Someone tries to resuscitate the doctor on the floor, but I can hear the panic. He's dead. At least there's some relief in that.

"I'm sorry, Alice," White whispers. "But you are not a part of Wonderland, and I cannot help you."

My eyelids begin to flutter as I give into the powerful drugs running through my bloodstream. I fight to remain awake, but the feeling of floating takes over.

"Then off with your heads." I force the words out, slurred and barely discernible.

"I'm sorry," White repeats one more time, before turning and leaving the room, leaving me behind in this hell, my last source of hope. My lips move, tracing the words I try so hard to keep in, try so hard to forget.

But memories are odd things. We never forget the ones we want to.

"Hatter . . . White . . . Cheshire . . . Alex . . . Alex . . . Al. . . ."

Chapter 9

AGED TWENTY-ONE

I'm trapped in the cage of my own body, a prisoner in my own brain, my limbs no longer my own. After Stevens's death, I was cleared for more lobotomies.

"She's insane", they said. "It's the only way to help her."

I've been subjected to two more treatments since then, and each time, it takes a little more from me. But I won't die. God help me, they won't kill me.

There's a rage inside of me that I can't control, the likes that I've never felt before. I don't know how to control it, and I'm not even sure I want to. My records hold a list of all the orderlies and doctors I've ever harmed, including ones that I've killed. The list keeps growing longer, and still they don't put me out of my misery. It's like they get a sick satisfaction from seeing me turn into a rabid animal. I don't understand why they keep me, why they don't just make me disappear in the night.

I've lost most of my ability to talk clearly. I don't stutter; I hardly speak at all. This world has become cloaked in rose-colored lenses, everything both fuzzy and clear at the same time. I don't talk to the doctors anymore, and they seem very pleased by that fact. Every morning, I scream inside my head, begging for someone to wake me up, to take me away from this place, to correct the mistake. There must have been a mistake! There has to have been! White will come back for me.

His words were just that: words. Hatter won't let him leave me here. Alex won't. I'm a part of their world.

"Alice, I want you to try to speak today. Does that sound like something you want to do?" The newest doctor is a woman. Any hope that she was better than all the men dashed out the door the moment she looked at me and asked, "what color is her brain tissue?" She's worse than any man, worse than any monster. The only consolation is that she never touches me in the way the other doctors would.

I don't answer her. I rarely do. I no longer get beaten. There's no point really. I can hardly move on my own when I'm not fueled by rage. The only time I can actually cause any damage is when my anger gets the better of me. Some sort of fancy brain function, the doctor had said. The adrenaline forces my brain to function for a short period of time, even though they drilled into my soft tissue and took from me.

I stopped crying about my life years ago. I don't even know what a life outside of these walls is like. My last memories are as a child, prancing through a make-believe world that somehow came to life. I focus on those memories when I can't take the reality.

"Alice, come on. You're going to miss it!" Alex shouts excitedly at me. I giggle and follow him through the forest, smearing dirt across my blue dress. Hatter had told me to stay close, but Alex was never one to follow rules. Neither am I.

"Where are we going?" I ask, dodging hissing flowers and angry tree roots. They don't seem to like me after I kicked one of them. Now, I'm their enemy more than anything. They hate me. But it's okay. I hate them, too.

"It's a surprise!" When we finally break through the tree line, I gasp. In front of us is a large waterfall, the water sparkling in the phosphorescent glow of the plant life.

"It's beautiful," I whisper.

"You haven't even seen anything yet," Alex grins, before he starts climbing the rocks at the side of the waterfall.

I follow him immediately, gripping the slick rock tightly. My foot slips once, but I manage to keep my footing, and we scale the small cliff together. At the top, we stare over the waterfall for a moment, watching as the sparkling water splashes into the pool below. Alex offers me his hand, and I slip mine inside his without hesitation. If there's anyone I trust in this mad world, it's the boy next to me.

"Are you ready?" he asks, a sly grin on his face.

"For what?" Alex has always been odd for a prince, nothing like I expected, but that's exactly what I like about him. He's unusual, just like I am.

He doesn't answer. He jumps from the cliff, our linked hands forcing me off behind him. I scream as we fall down, down, down towards the dark water. I hold my breath just as we hit the warmth, crash beneath the surface, and sink. Alex's hand is ripped from mine, and I kick for the surface frantically. When I break the water, I look around in a panic before Alex pops up beside me, laughing. His delight is so infectious, I can't help but begin to laugh, too.

I miss Wonderland with a depth of my soul that I never knew I possessed. It's those memories that comfort me as they poke me with needles, cut into my skull, or beat me within an inch of my life. Today isn't one of those days, though.

"Alice, if you can say three words, I will approve for you to go out into the gardens." I look up at the doctor, her words like music to my ears. The only problem is, I'm not sure if I can actually speak three words. My ability to speak comes and goes. But I want to try. I want to feel the sunshine on my face, even if I'm left out there too long and get sunburned. I would give anything to feel something so normal again.

"Out–" I swallow when the word doesn't come, but I try again. "Out . . . side."

The doctor nods her head and scratches notes on my thick file. "That's one. Two more."

"P . . . ple . . . please." My voice is so soft, I'm afraid she won't hear me, but she nods her head, encouraging me to continue. "Sss," my voice breaks off, and I want to cry. I need to get the word out. "Sun . . . li . . ."

"That's it, Alice."

"Sun . . . light." The word is dragged out and barely discernible, but it's enough for her. She smiles at me and steeples her fingers.

"Very good, Alice. I will tell the orderlies to take you outside after our session."

The doctor spends the next thirty-odd minutes discussing options and how great I'm doing. I suppose I probably am doing okay. After having three lobotomies, I'm certain I should be dead. Instead, I'm somehow managing to continue on. I think I'm some sort of anomaly to them. I've never heard of another patient surviving two treatments, let alone three. Even in the insane asylum, I'm a freak.

When she dismisses me, I breathe a sigh of relief. Sunlight. I'll get to feel the sun on my face again. I'm placed in a metal wheelchair, the leather straps buckled down without worry. They rarely worry when I'm being rewarded. My anger only comes out at the worst times, when I've been stuck inside every day. The fits are the worst after the treatments. It's as if something is triggered inside my brain that demands I draw blood, maim, kill if I'm able. Perhaps, that's how Wonderland changed me while I was there. I've become blood-thirsty without the ability to act on it. It's the worst feeling in the world. When the anger takes over, it's as if I'm a completely different person, as if I can't control my body at all.

The moment they roll me from the building and into the garden, I close my eyes and tilt my head up towards the sun. The warmth hits my skin and sinks in, making me smile for the first time in months. I don't get to come outside often, but when I do, I absorb as much of it as I can.

"Dr. Jones said to leave you outside until you're ready to come in, or until the end," the orderly comments. I don't know why he's speaking to me or telling me exactly what's happening. They don't usually spare me the courtesy. "When you're ready, just tilt your head down as if you're sleeping. I'll know to come get you."

I nod my head at him, and he leaves me there in the middle of the garden. There are a few other patients out here, most strapped to some sort of chair, but there are a few who sit or lay in the grass as if it's the best thing in the world. I would kill for the feel of the grass between my toes. I haven't felt that since I was a little girl. Something tells me I probably won't ever get to again.

My jaw begins to twitch, an unfortunate effect of the treatments. Sometimes, my muscles will start to move on their own, leaping or twitching as if I've been given another electroshock treatment. I hate when they do it. It's just another reminder that I'm not in control of my body, of my life, or of my future. My existence depends on someone else's whim, and that's the saddest thing I've ever heard. I've been completely forgotten, completely lost to the world. I don't exist anywhere else except for in my mind. My mind is a terrifying place sometimes.

I've been sitting in the garden for an hour, absorbing the sun, alternating between closing my eyes and staring at the fiery ball in the sky, when I see him.

He's sitting on a bench across from me, silent, watching. Our eyes meet, and a tiny bit of hope spreads through my chest. He came back for me. I knew it was just words. I knew they wouldn't forget me.

I open my mouth to say his name, frustrated when it doesn't automatically come. It's usually one of my easier words; all of their names are. White stares at me, taking in my appearance. Shame fills my body. I'm not the little girl anymore, not that they remember. I've grown up under the brutality of this place. My hair has barely started to grow back, still short enough that my scars are very obvious. It's growing in an odd tuft pattern and resembles a duckling's feathers more than hair. I have no doubt my body looks hollow and frail. I'm unable to eat as much as I used to.

White doesn't speak. He doesn't say my name or promise me he's going to get me out of here. There's an unbearable sadness on his face as he stares at me, as if he can't quite stomach the sight. That's my first sign that something is wrong. Why would he be sad if he's here to save me? Shouldn't he be happy?

None of the other patients react to the man in a waistcoat with rabbit ears on his head. No one ever does. White doesn't like everyone able to see him. He prefers to be a silent watcher, until he no longer needs to be.

My fingers clench into the metal of the wheel chair arms, the leather straps digging harder into the divets in my skin. Permanent now, I hardly have to worry about them bleeding. My skin is thicker there, used to the trauma that the straps have dug for the last thirteen years. My body is a mishmash of scars and punishments, branding me as mad more than my words ever did. I was never crazy. The White Rabbit sitting in front of me proves that.

I stare at White with hope in my eyes, begging him silently to take me away, to rescue me from this hell, to take me back to Wonderland. I'd give anything to go with him.

"P–", I try to speak, the muscles in my jaw twitching with the effort. "P-please..."

White doesn't react to my plea. He doesn't nod his head and tell me everything is okay like the Hatter would have done. My anger starts to grow inside of me, my heartbeat in my throat as he sits there, completely uncaring that I'm being tortured, that I'm dying. I try to hold it in, knowing that my outdoor time will end if I let it out, but I never have much control over the rage. My teeth snap together as a scream tears its way up my throat, so loud and piercing that it makes all the other patients cringe in agony. I jerk against the restraints hard enough to rock the metal wheelchair. Orderlies come from the building and rush towards me, ready with whatever sedative they have. I jerk again, another tortured scream slipping from my throat.

When White stands up and begins to walk away, I can't stop my adrenaline from spreading through my body.

I scream, and scream, and scream until they sedate me again, and I sink into inky blackness.

Where are you? Where are you? Who am I?

AGED THIRTY-THREE

"Hatter... White... Cheshire... Alex..."

The words tumble from my lips without restriction, as if I'm somehow hoping for them to come save me, as if they haven't betrayed me completely. Those four words, their names, are the only words that come easy to me after the years of medications and treatments. Anything else is such a struggle that I hardly try any more. It isn't worth it.

My last treatment had been years ago. They stopped doing them so frequently due to my deterioration. At least, that's what I heard the doctors say. I may not be able to speak well anymore, or move how I want to, but I can listen, and I hear everything. I heard when there was the fear of discovery from the authorities, the doctors discussing how they could hide the evidence of their treatment of the patients, including taking all of us to the fire room. I heard their declaration that I was no better than a piece of trash now, worthless, best forgotten. I heard each time the doctors changed, including the hushed whispers of a new one that now has the women fawning.

I hear everything.

The orderlies have stopped taking care of me, hardly remembering to feed me most days. I haven't been allowed a shower in weeks, and I smell like it. My white pants and top are smeared with dirt and grime, my skin clammy to the touch. If I were able, I would be disgusted by it, but I no longer care. I no longer have the motivation or the energy to rebel against it.

Since my treatments have been stopped, they haven't cut my hair. Now, it hangs in strings around my face, still the pale yellow I remember, but caked with grease and things I have no name for. It serves to cover the worst of my scars, where the hair no longer grows. My newest room has no windows, barely has any light at all. If I were to describe what hell is, this would be it. There wouldn't be hellfire and damnation, or a devil flaying your skin from your body.

Hell is being tossed into a room and forgotten.

Control of my facial features is difficult, and sometimes I feel as if there's someone else controlling my body while I sit in the back seat. Even as I think the thought, a smile curves my lips, a small giggle creeping out. I've truly become mad within this place, created with electricity and inhumanity. I was never a monster before. They've turned me into one now.

For years, I was angry at the world, at my parents for leaving me here, at the doctors for their "treatments," at the people who said they would come back for me and take me away. I'm still angry, a rage unlike anything I've ever felt swallowing me whole at times, but other times, I'm just numb. I can stare at the grimy padded walls of my prison for days, hardly blinking, barely breathing, barely living.

When the door opens, it startles me, but my body doesn't react in fright. It's been a while since anyone has come to check on me, days since I've been fed. I'm uncertain if this is a check to see if I'm alive or a declaration of a new treatment.

Slowly, I force my eyes from the wall towards the doorway. A man I've never seen before stands there, dressed in his white coat, contemplation on his face. He's attractive and that worries me. In my experience, the attractive ones are usually the worst when they come here. They think they can get away with more, and they usually do. He has the qualities of many movie-stars, a charisma that leaks off him even though he has yet to say a word. He rolls his wide shoulders as he takes me in, his bright eyes bouncing around the room, cataloging all the details.

Slowly, he walks inside, unafraid. "Ms. Liddell, I'm Doctor Blatherskite." His voice is deep and smooth, sending a bolt of longing through me. I've never had anyone cause such a reaction in me. Pity that it's when I'm gaunt and damaged.

The door closes behind him before he comes over to me. I tense, unsure where this is going. I want to glare but the only thing I can manage is an uneasy grin. Then he does something that I've never before witnessed, that no other doctor has done.

This man sits down on the grimy floor in front of me, cross-legged, right at my level. Doesn't he know my reputation? Is he not afraid? He's so relaxed, it makes me relax the smallest amount, too. They're always the same, wanting something, but I humor him for now. This one is acting different enough to catch my intrigue.

A tiny giggle slips out again, and I want to grimace. My face doesn't cooperate. "Hatter . . . White . . . Cheshire . . . Alex . . ." I speak the words as if he can understand me, as if they hold all the answers.

"I'm very interested in your condition, the hallucinations your file mentions."

My eye twitches at his words, the feeling unpleasant against my neglected muscles. I want to tell him that what I experience isn't hallucinations, that I could care less if he's interested in them, but he's sitting at my level, and I'm nothing more than a shell of the girl I used to be.

"Hatter. White. Cheshire. Alex." My voice is stronger when I say the words this time, more certain.

"Exactly." He nods his head. "I believe you've seen these people, these creatures. I don't think they're hallucinations at all." I freeze and focus everything I can on him. This is a new trick. None of the doctors have ever told me that they believed me. Perhaps, new research has been found, but it doesn't make sense. "What would you say if I asked you to take me there?"

I shake my head violently, the action far easier than it should have been, and far bigger than I planned for. I only meant to shake my head once. Instead, I come across as if I'm having a seizure. The words don't come as easily as the action.

"Im-imposs . . ." I give up. My vocal cords don't work correctly for words other than the four names. The doctor seems to understand me, though. A small, gentle smile pulls on his lips.

"Is it, Alice?"

The care in his words gives me pause. This new tactic is making me worry. I've never before felt as if someone cared about my well-being, not since I was a girl. No one cares about a woman who grew up in a madhouse, who speaks of nothing but Mad Hatters and White Rabbits.

I don't tell the doctor that there's no way to get to Wonderland without White. There's only one Key, and the White Rabbit wears it. It's clear to me that I'm not welcome there, not anymore. White has popped in over the years, and he never helps, never interferes, no matter how much I beg. I hate him, and I hate the Hatter for allowing him to leave me. Someone should have come for me by now, but even Wonderland has forgotten me.

Oh, how I long to remind them of who I am.

"You don't have to talk," the doctor continues. "I'm aware that it's difficult for you after what these people have done to your body. I want to help you be free of this hell, to take your rightful place."

What do you mean? I don't speak the words, but they must show in my eyes.

"You could be a Queen, Alice. You could make them all pay, make them all kneel before you and beg for your forgiveness. You could destroy them."

Is that what I want? I no longer know. I'm angry, so angry, but do I want to destroy them? Perhaps, Hatter doesn't know. Cheshire, well, he doesn't care for much, anyway. Alex is the prince. Would he even be privy to such information? Maybe only some of them are at fault. I want to destroy White certainly. And the other creatures of the world, I can do without. None were very welcoming towards me. Could I destroy them?

I stare into the doctor's eyes, searching for trickery or cruelty. There's none of the first there but plenty of the second. He can, no doubt, be brutal, but he doesn't seem to be directing that at me. I'll trust him for now.

CRUEL AS A QUEEN

Slowly, achingly, I nod my head. If I'm a Queen, I can do what I want, and no one can lock me up, or give me orders, or forget I exist.

If I'm a Queen, I will be free.

My meals begin to arrive every day, three times a day. I'm given food I've never tasted, more flavorful than anything I've ever been provided. The first day, I make myself so sick, I vomit, coating my white walls. I expect the mess to stay there, dreading the smell that will fill my room, but surprisingly, the mess is cleaned right away, Dr. Blatherskite coming in himself to apologize for the delay. It confuses me, but I don't question it. For the first time, I have a sense of hope, even if it's from someone I shouldn't count on. I don't know the doctor. I don't know his true plans, but I find myself easily allowing him into my mind, fixating on him as if he's some sort of God.

He's not, even if he has the looks of one, but still, my brain tells me otherwise.

The second day, I'm escorted to the showers. I've never been in them when they're empty, and I've certainly not had a hot shower in a long time. When the orderly shoves me towards the showers and steps out, I move towards the spouts jerkily. My body doesn't move like I want it to, not anymore. I resemble a creature that has risen from the graveyard rather than a woman.

Inside the showers, Doctor Blatherskite stands against the wall, his white coat stripped from his shoulders. He wears pressed slacks and a button-down shirt, rolled up to his elbows. I pause, staring at him, as he does the same to me.

"Go ahead," he says, gesturing towards the shower closest to him. "There is soap and shampoo for you, and I have someone bringing you new clothing." When I stare at him expectantly, waiting for him to leave, he shakes his head. "Sorry. I can't leave you alone. I don't know if you would take the opportunity to slice your wrists, so I'm not taking any chances. You'll just have to ignore my eyes on you."

I lost my sense of modesty long ago—communal showers are not some place to be shy—but I find myself feeling that way now. I'm far too thin, far too weak. If he sees how I look underneath, will he run away and pick a new Queen?

"There's no reason to be afraid, Alice." The doctor keeps his voice low for my benefit. I'm not a scared animal, though; I won't run even if I could. "I won't hurt you. I'm only here to help."

I turn my back to him, his eyes making me nervous even if his words are pretty. Such pretty words I've never heard before.

I grab the hem of my ratty top and yank it over my head. The movement is rough, strained, but I still manage to get the material off and throw it onto the floor. The cold air hits me and makes me even more aware of my body. My ribs are prominent, my skin shallow enough to count each one, my hip bones stick out in sharp relief. I'm a walking skeleton, and I've never felt more dead.

I try to push my white pants off, but I only succeed in pushing them down around my legs. My balance is so far gone that I teeter violently as I try to get them from my feet. It's the gentle hands on my shoulders that stop me, that make me tense so hard, I can't breathe.

"Here, let me."

Smooth hands deftly remove the material from around my legs, careful not to knock me over. And then he steps away again, leaving me naked in front of the shower head.

The showers are set on timers. Two minutes, and the water stops. Normally, we would be forced to wash in those two minutes and be done, but I don't think I'm capable of that any more. Movement is difficult, anyway, let alone the motions of washing my hair and body. I have the feeling that I'm not being rushed, though, that I can push the button as many times as I want.

The first blast of the shower is cold as ice, stealing my breath from me. It warms up quickly, steam rising from the water as it turns my fragile skin red. I close my eyes and just stand under the spray, unsure of how often I will be afforded this luxury. When the button clicks and the water cuts off, I press it again. There's no complaint from the doctor behind me.

I grab the soap and do my best to wash my body in hard motions, scrubbing the dirt from my skin. I wince internally when my fingers run over the sheer number of bones sticking from my body, the unnatural shapes that shouldn't be there. This is not how I ever imagined myself. This is not what I dreamed of.

Washing my hair is trickier. No matter how hard I try, my hands won't scrub the locks, won't work the shampoo in, and my frustration gets the better of me. I end up flinging the bottle of shampoo across the floor, furious at the direction my life has gone. Shampoo drips into my eyes, but I don't wipe it away. I can't even though they burn.

"I can help," the doctor speaks, coming to stand behind me. "If you want."

I don't answer, but he doesn't wait for me. He comes into the shower with me, fully clothed, and begins to work his fingers through my hair. Slowly, gently, he begins to work the lather until he's reached every inch. He doesn't comment when his fingers touch the scars on my scalp; he doesn't flinch or hesitate. He moves through the motions, and there's nothing sexual about it. For the first time, I feel like a human being.

When he turns me around, my eyes meet his, and I would have been speechless if I wasn't already robbed of my ability to speak. The water has plastered his clothing to his body, until I can see the well-defined muscles underneath. His hair hangs over his forehead, giving him a roguish appearance. There's no lust in his eyes, no ill-intentions. He's not asking for anything in return for his kindness, not yet, and his care makes my heart throb. Where did this man come from?

"Bla . . ." I attempt to say his name, the one he gave me, but he shakes his head, a small smile pulling at his lips.

"You can call me Jab, Alice. If it's easier."

I test the word in my mind, before attempting with my lips. "Jab." It comes easy, surprisingly, and I stare at the satisfied smile on his face. All these pretty words with a pretty face. When will the ugly part start?

His fingers touch my chin and encourage me to tilt my head back, until he's rinsing the suds from my hair, the water running murky with the grime sent free. Then he steps away and allows me to stand in the hot shower for as long as I want. He never once touches me without permission. He never once rushes me to get out of the shower. And when I'm done, he hands me a towel before drying my hair with another one.

For the first time in years, I cry.

AGED THIRTY-THREE

My body is filling out with the constant barrage of food and care Jab provides. My hip bones no longer stick through my skin, my ribs are harder to count. I still feel weak, the weight not helping in that aspect, but at least I don't look like a skeleton anymore. Small mercies.

Jab tries every day to get me to speak, and he's more successful than any other doctor who has been through these doors. There's something about him so persuasive, that I find myself doing whatever he asks of me, though he doesn't ask much. It's nice to feel cared for. I haven't felt this way in so long, I'm not even sure I truly recognize my emotions, but I find myself fixating on the man, hoping that he will be the one to free me.

"Visualize the words you want to say, Alice." Jab doesn't strap me down to the metal chair in his office. He doesn't sit behind a desk and stare at me. Instead, I'm laying on a brown couch, softer than anything I've felt, even though the material scratches at my skin. Jab sits close, in the metal chair I could never move. He dragged it across the room as if it weighed hardly anything before plopping it down in front of me.

I close my eyes and think hard about the words I want to say. *My name is Alice.* It's been so long since I've said them, since I claimed the name. I don't feel like myself anymore, and the name feels foreign even in my mind, but Jab calls me by that name. I like the way he says it.

"My . . . na—"

"Good. Focus. Force your lips to overcome your predicament. You are not what they made you. You are what you make of yourself."

"My . . . name is . . ." I grunt, focusing so hard I feel my veins bulging from my forehead, "Alice."

The words are stunted, harsh, but I still manage to get them from my lips, far more progress than I've ever made. I try to smile at Jab, at his excitement, but I can feel the unnatural pull on my face. Instead of something sweet, it comes across creepy and sad. Mentally, I sigh. Why does he even continue to push me? Why does he take care of me? I can't even smile correctly any more. A man like him would never be interested in something as damaged as I am.

"That was good, Alice. Very good." Jab trails his eyes over me, not in any way sexual. "You're gaining more weight. That's very good, too. I think you're ready."

"R-ready . . . for?"

Jab smiles and leans forward, touching his hand to the scarred skin of my wrists. The moment he touches me, I feel a jolt in my body, and it feels as if my chest opens, like I can breathe for a moment. What was that?

"The next step." Jab releases my hand, and the feeling fades, but something stays behind. I feel just a little bit less weak, just a little bit better. It's not enough to change anything, but, perhaps, I can sleep tonight. "We won't proceed until tomorrow. Tonight, you should rest."

He touches the button on the desk that let's the orderlies know that they can come in. The door opens, and I flinch, Jab's eyes immediately catching the motion. Roger is one of the newer orderlies, but he was here before Jab by a few weeks. He's in his late thirties, prematurely balding, but he combs his hair over in an attempt to cover up the evidence. His black eyes catch on me, and I can see his intent there. Jab isn't the only one pleased with my weight gain. Roger has taken liberties with me before, but since Jab arrived, they've been held to a minimum. Now, I know I won't be allowed to go any longer. I whimper when he steps into the room and push myself into the couch.

Jab doesn't say a word as Roger steps over to me. He just turns and closes the door behind Roger, sealing us all in.

Roger stares at Jab in confusion. "I'm sorry, Doctor Blatherskite. I thought I saw the button flash."

"It did, boy." Jab's face is stoic, no emotion. But his eyes? "I called you in here to take Alice back to her room. Do you want to tell me why she's terrified at the sight of you?"

Roger shrugs. "No idea. They all are. It's pretty normal with the crazy bastards. They fear the control."

I want to snarl at his answer, to disagree, but my lips won't work. I can't focus enough to force them out.

Jab's eyes meet mine, and I see a sickening yellow color swirl in their depths. My jaw clenches. Real or imagined? I'm never quite sure anymore.

"I don't think that's it at all." Jab takes a step forward, and Roger backs up, wary of the look in Jab's eyes. I recognize the intention there, can see the anger swirling in his gaze. The problem is, I don't know what Jab is angry about. "Have you been touching these patients against their will?" Jab's voice is calm, calculated. "Have you touched Alice against her will?"

Roger frowns, but he doesn't deny it. "All the orderlies do. We're instructed that it helps keep the patients in line, doctor."

True fury morphs Jab's face into a gruesome mask, and Roger stumbles back, tripping over the foot of the metal chair. It doesn't move even though he pushes against it. Jab reaches out lightning quick and grabs a fistful of Roger's shirt, pulling him close.

"Why is she afraid of you, boy?" he snarls. "You didn't just touch her."

"I didn't do anything," Roger whimpers. "She asked for it."

And then the air in the room freezes. It's as if we walk into a void, how it feels right after a blizzard. It's so quiet, I can't hear anything but the frantic heartbeat inside Roger's chest. Everything slowly begins to move again, a smile curling Jab's lips.

"Well, then, if she asked for it, I suppose it's alright then." Jab lets go of Roger's shirt, and I tense. I never asked for any of this. I never asked for him to touch me, to torture me, to defile me. I never asked for any of it. Jab gestures to the door. "Allow me to speak to Alice alone."

I watch, angry but unable to do anything. I'm still too weak. But Roger never makes it to the door. The moment he steps past Jab, the doctor reaches out and shoves him hard. Roger hits the floor with a thump, sprawling out on the rough, threadbare carpet. Jab drops and presses his knee into his back, holding him down as he begins to scream. Jab meets my eyes as he reaches down and grabs Roger's left leg. He doesn't look away as a loud crack rents the room, echoing in the small confines. I grimace as the orderly's screams grow shrill. Jab doesn't stop. He drops the useless limb to the floor, no mercy at all in his gaze as he reaches down and grabs his right leg, the good one.

"Alice never asked you to rape her," Jab snarls. "And I never asked if you wanted to die. But here we are."

Crack. I watch, enraptured, as the second leg falls to the floor, twisted at an odd angle, as Roger violently sobs into the carpet, begging, pleading for the mercy he never showed me.

"Come here, Alice." Jab holds out his hand for me to join him where he crouches on the floor, his knee still pressed into Roger's back. I hesitate. "Come on. It's okay. I won't let him harm you."

Slowly, I unfold myself from the couch and stand on unsteady legs. I shuffle forward, closer to the sobbing man and the doctor. That yellow sheen jumps across Jab's eyes again, and I know I didn't imagine it that time. Still, I slip my shaking hand into his steady one. I let him tug me down to my knees beside him.

"Are you angry, Alice?" I nod my head. "How many times have you wanted to hurt this man?"

I stare into Jab's eyes. Too many times to count. I can't get the words out, but Jab can see them in my eyes. He reaches into his pocket and pulls out a small knife, flipping it open so easily, I'm envious. He gently sets it in my palm and curls my fingers around the handle.

"Then hurt him."

My eyes widen as I look down at Roger, sprawled out on the floor, incapable of escaping. Even if I let him go now, he will never have a life again. It's almost poetic justice, to have him live the rest of his life as a cripple, much the same as I have been forced to do. But it isn't enough.

I'm not the only one he's touched. Roger is notorious for abusing the patients, some more than others. I even heard the other orderlies talking about how he brutalizes the male patients, too. He doesn't deserve any sort of mercy.

But I've never killed like this, not with the person helpless beneath me. It's always been in self-defense. Roger isn't hurting me at this moment, but he has hurt me far too much to get away with it. My fingers clench harder around the handle, but still I don't bring the knife down.

Jab curls his hand around mine, steadying the shaking. His eyes meet mine. "Make him pay, Alice. He doesn't deserve the mercy he never showed you."

"I-I . . . cannot."

"You can. You're stronger than you think." He pauses, his eyes softening the slightest bit. "Let me help you."

Without waiting for my answer, Jab brings our joined hands down onto Roger's back, a strangled, wet scream wrenching from the man's mouth. The blade slides into his skin like butter, blood welling out instantly from the wound to coat our hands. I don't get a second to register what I've done before Jab pulls the knife and my hand away and brings them down again. The sight of the blood excites me in a way I never expected, and the next time the knife comes down, it's by my hand alone. Roger's screams fade away as I stab and stab and stab, blood splattering the white pants and top I wear, staining it, until I'm covered in red. Jab doesn't stop me as I continue the attack long after Roger stops breathing. He watches, a small smile on his face, sitting on the floor cross-legged as if he doesn't have a care in the world. Small spots of blood dot his normally pristine clothing, too, but he doesn't seem to care.

The smile drives my madness forward, and I tire of the body beneath me. I turn without warning and go for Jab, even after all the kindness he's shown me, even after letting me kill my rapist, I turn the knife on him. I spring forward, but the smile on his face only grows. Jab grabs my wrist easily, holding me back from stabbing him, from brutalizing him. No matter how hard I try, I can't move the knife any closer to his jugular like I want.

"So beautiful," Jab whispers, studying my face coated with blood splatters, the savageness I'm sure that shows in my eyes. "So bloodthirsty."

I want to make you bleed, I think. If only I could move the knife forward.

"Will it make you feel better?" His other hand reaches up to cup my jaw, his fingers tracing patterns in the blood there. "How badly do you want to see me bleed, Alice?"

So badly. I ache with the urge, my body humming with adrenaline. I feel stronger than I have in a while, and I want to take advantage of it. Suddenly, Jab lets go of my wrist, and I fall forward, the knife sinking into his shoulder rather than his neck. He grunts in pain as it slices through muscle, his eyes flashing bright yellow. Panic fills me. I just stabbed the only person willing to help me escape. I just ruined my chances.

"I'm . . . s-sorry," I force out, staring at the knife protruding from his shoulder. A tear leaks from my eyes.

"Don't be," he whispers, his fingers still cupping my jaw. "Apologies are for the weak, Alice. And you are strong." Then he brings my face forward and presses his lips against mine. I freeze beneath the onslaught, my first instinct to fight, but it's overshadowed by the desire that crashes through my body. I've never felt like this, never felt truly wanted. Another tear falls as my lips begin to move against his.

Jab takes me back to my room himself. When I step inside the padded prison, there's a cot with a pillow and blanket for the first time since I came to this place.

The pillow catches my tears.

JAB DOESN'T COME TO MY ROOM AGAIN FOR TWO DAYS, EVEN though he said we were moving on before. I start to worry that whatever happened in the office got him fired, or worse, that he decided I'm no longer worth his time. I've replayed that kiss a thousand times in the past two days. Each time, I imagine something different.

Sometimes, Jab shoves me away in disgust. Others, he pulls me closer, and we go much further than a mere touching of lips. I drive myself crazy with the thoughts.

Even though Jab doesn't come for me in those days, the food arrives like clockwork. The second day, there's cake with the meatloaf, and I take it for the apology it is. It's been so long since I've had dessert. The first bite is decadent, almost too sweet, but I don't push away the chocolate treat. I shove more in my mouth, until I feel as if I might faint from the sugar rush.

Oh, how I've missed cake.

On the third day, I'm sitting in my room, staring at the notepad in front of me. Jab had given me a notepad and a small pencil to work on my hand functions. The lines are still shaky, but I'm getting better every day, even if it's in such small amounts, no one could notice but me.

Shouting from the hallway makes me look up in confusion from where I had been studying my letter A. The doors are thick to the rooms, meant to prevent escape, so I can't make out the words, but it's definitely a male voice shouting. I set aside the notepad and pull myself to my feet, moving towards the sounds. Before I can press my ear against the metal, the door is thrown open.

Jab stands framed by light, giving him an unholy garish glow. For a moment, his eyes flash bright yellow, the pupil changing shape, before they're normal again.

"Come with me, Alice. Hurry."

"W-what . . . is—?"

"I'll explain later. Just please, come quickly." Jab holds out his hand, and I slide mine into his. I don't understand what's happening, but I trust him just the same.

He yanks me through the door the moment I thread my fingers with his, pulling me off of my feet. I stumble into him hard, grunting in pain. He doesn't stop to see if I'm okay; he scoops me up into his arms and begins to run. More shouting comes behind us. I peer around his shoulder, curious, to see orderlies and nurses chasing us. Their shouts blend together, until I'm only able to pick out words rather than sentences.

"Imposter!"

"Killer!"

What are they talking about? Are they coming for me? Have they finally decided it's my time?

Jab doesn't run for the exit. That way is blocked by the angry group, anyway. He heads straight for his office, kicking the door open and slamming it closed behind us. He gently sets me down on the couch before he locks the door behind us and closes the blinds. The angry shouts get louder for a moment before they grow softer, moving in a different direction. My hair hangs in my face as I watch his hasty movements. He shrugs the white coat from his shoulders and tosses it aside, showing his sleeves up to his elbows.

"You're going to have to feed, Alice. I can only push so much power into you without the feed."

I wrinkle my brow, staring into his eyes. I focus very hard on my next words, searching for an answer.

"What . . . do . . . you . . . mean?" My words are weak and quiet, but Jab hears me. He always does.

"My blood," he clarifies, pulling the pocket knife from his slacks. I don't flinch as he lifts it and slices it across his wrist. Blood wells immediately, and he takes a seat next to me on the couch. He holds his arm out towards me. I curl my lips up in disgust. I'm not going to drink his blood. Jab doesn't give me any chance to lean away, to escape. His hand threads into my hair, gently but completely, his fingers touching my scars there, and pulls me forward until my lips are against the red coating his skin. I try to fight against his hold, the idea of drinking his blood is revolting, but I'm so weak against his strength, I accomplish nothing except to force some of his blood into my mouth.

The flavor of it isn't what I expect. I assumed blood would taste like pennies, like hell if I'm being honest, but it tastes nothing like the hell I know. Jab's blood tastes like chocolate and roses, like something so other, I can't comprehend it. My tongue darts out for a moment, and then I seal my lips against the cut.

"Drink, Alice," Jab groans above me, the sound sensual, causing something to stir low in my belly. "My powers will fuel you, strengthen you, and you will become something so much more."

His hand relaxes against my hair when I grab his wrist in my own hands, pulling more of the sweetness into my mouth. With each pull, I feel stronger and stronger, as if I can do exactly what he says.

Finally, I pull away from his wrist and stare up into his eyes, my sight so clear, I blink a few times as if I can't believe it. The fuzziness that I've always felt on the edges of my vision, the edges of my brain, are gone. The weakness I've felt for as long as I can remember is no longer in my bones.

"What did you do to me?" The words come so easy, without thought, that I gasp and clamp my hand over my mouth. My voice is strong again. I stare down at my body and jump up, confused. The body I've known, frail and thin, is gone. I have curves, my bones no longer sticking through my skin anywhere at all. I'm completely different.

"Welcome back, Alice," Jab grins. Someone shouts outside, but they don't try the office. Jab stands and steps up to me. I back up a few steps until I hit the desk with the back of my thighs. Jab slinks closer until he closes me in. I snarl like a caged animal, unsure of this new development, and for the first time, I feel the sharp teeth in my mouth, just like a vampire from the stories. What the hell? "So beautiful," he groans, his hand clamping around my hip. White hot desire crashes through me, adrenaline making my heart beat a frantic rhythm inside my chest.

"Who are you?" Jab isn't a doctor, that much is clear now. My brain isn't blocked anymore; my reasoning is sound now. No doctor would have been helping me this way.

"Well, I'm not a doctor," he admits, confirming my thoughts. He leans down and runs his lips against my collarbone. My breath stutters. "I'm a Jabberwocky."

"What's a Jabberwocky?" I ask, groaning when he nips at my collarbone. I'm torn between wanting to push him away, to attack him, or drag him closer. I've never felt like this, strong, in control, sexy. One of my hands threads into his hair, holding him to me as his lips drag up my neck.

"I'm a monster," he whispers against my skin. "Feared by many. Powerful beyond belief. But I'm only as powerful as my mate, and I want you as my Queen."

"I'm not powerful." He grinds his hardness against me in answer, and I groan.

"You're more powerful than any woman I've ever met, Alice." He draws back just enough to look into my eyes. They transform into the yellow orbs again, but I'm not afraid. It only makes me want to conquer him. "And you're mine."

I jerk his head back by his hair, surprised I have the strength to do so. "If I'm yours, then you are mine," I snarl, violence whispering in my veins. My new teeth ache in my gums, and I strike at his neck without thinking, forcing him to stumble back. I cling to him on instinct, his hands cupping my ass, a harsh sensual groan on his lips.

"Fuck." He moves backwards and collapses on the couch, my teeth still at his jugular as I pull more of his sweetness into my mouth. Power flows inside me, lust following rapidly behind. I'm suddenly wearing too many clothes. We both are.

As if he understands my thoughts—perhaps he does—he tears my shirt over my head, ripping me away from his neck. Blood drips down his skin, and when I pull his shirt apart, I watch as the red trails down his hard muscles. I lean forward and lick the blood away, up his pec, biting gently here and there.

"Is this the freedom you've been offering?" I ask. I trail a hand down his abs to tear open his slacks, freeing his steel. "You said you believed me."

"I do," he whispers, capturing my lips with his for a brief kiss. "We will return to Wonderland and slaughter them all. It's so easy now. Hatter, White and Cheshire have been chosen as the Sons. Kill Wonderland, and they all die."

A pang hits my chest, but I don't correct him. I won't slaughter all of them. Jab isn't my first love. There's someone I would like answers from first, but now isn't the time to bring that up. I'm still angry at the world, and killing them all sounds like the perfect punishment for their betrayal. I will make the Sons of Wonderland pay first. They're the ones who have wronged me.

Jab shoves my pants away from my body, his own kicked aside until we're skin against skin, until his hard flesh bumps against my body. I expect him to take control. They always do, using me until their own pleasure is reached, and then I'm left alone, but Jab never takes control. Not in the way I expect. He lifts me by my hips and slowly coaxes me down on his length, until he fills me up from the inside out, until I can't breathe for my emotions. I cling to his shoulders as I lift myself and slide him inside again. Again, and again, until a madness takes over, and I'm fucking him with wild abandon, my head thrown back in ecstasy.

I scream out in pleasure as waves crash down upon me. Only then does Jab take control, after I've taken from him first. He lifts me and throws me down on the couch, flipping me over onto my stomach. I don't have time to understand what he's doing before he enters me again from behind, slamming into me hard enough to bruise. I cry out in pleasure as sharp pinpricks touch my hips, a fierce growl from his throat.

Jab clenches a handful of my hair and jerks me backwards, my back bowing beneath his onslaught. He grips my neck in his hand and turns my head until his lips take mine in a furious kiss, so full of anger and dominance, cruelty and care. His lips leave mine and trail down to the skin between my shoulder and my neck, his tongue dancing across my skin.

"My Queen," he growls, animalistic, no evidence of the doctor from before. This is the monster he spoke of. The sound of it brings me to a violent climax. I scream in equal parts agony and ecstasy. His teeth sink into my skin as he slams inside me before finding his own release, pumping until we're both spent and collapse to the couch in exhaustion.

For the first time, I fall asleep in someone's arms, warm, sated, and safe. I've never felt safer than I do now.

Saints rarely are treated fairly. Sinners are even worse. If you're not normal in this world, it treats you as a demon, as trash. I will no longer allow that treatment. I will burn the world to the ground around me, as long as I have my Jabberwocky by my side.

I snuggle closer to Jab, his arms wrapped around me almost too tight. I don't complain, my eyes sliding closed as the thought crosses my mind. This place has labeled me a monster. Jab labeled himself a monster. Two monsters, so close that you can't tell where one ends and the other begins, hide in the office of an asylum.

But when is a monster not a monster anymore?

Such an easy answer.

A monster is no longer a monster when you love it.

IMMORTAL

When we wake up later, it's to a violent jiggling of the doorknob followed by someone slamming against it. I jerk upright and cover myself, my heart beating hard inside my chest.

I look down at Jab, his eyes open lazily as he smiles up at me.

"Should we be worried about that?" I point at the door as someone slams against it again.

"No." He nuzzles against my side. The door rattles as the force hits it once more.

"Open the door!" I don't recognize the voice shouting, but more join the exclamation.

"Are you sure?" I look down at Jab, his hair tousled from sleep and our earlier lovemaking.

"What do you say we escape today?" he asks, kissing my skin. "How would you like to make them all pay?"

I grin. "That sounds amazing."

Jab releases me and stands up, moving behind his desk and coming back out with a box. "Good. I have something for you to wear. Something you will wear as we storm Wonderland." He sets it down and reaches inside before pulling out a blue dress, so similar to the one I wore when I was a child that I crinkle my brow.

"Are you being serious?" It's a little different cut, the skirt a little shorter than I would have worn when I was eight, far shorter than my mother would have ever approved of. It's pale blue, cinched in at the waist, both innocent and sexy.

"Come now, Alice. Don't you want to look the part?"

Hesitantly, I stand and take the dress from him, stepping into the outfit and pulling it on. He motions for me to turn, so I do, letting him zip me up in the dress. He kisses me on the back of the neck, turning me to face him. "When we're in Wonderland, and you're the Queen, I'll dress you in the finest silks, the grandest jewels."

I smile just as someone slams against the door hard enough to shake the door frame. This time, the knife Jab presses into my hand isn't the small pocket one. The knife looks like one used in a kitchen, large and imposing. It could cause some real damage. I curl my fingers around the handle and hold it.

"Don't stab me with that one," he teases. "It would take a few minutes to heal, and I have a feeling the door won't hold much longer."

Sure enough, the office door slams open upon the next impact, and I'm moving faster than I ever have before. I dodge the orderly swinging a crowbar and slam the knife into his chest. He drops before he even knows what happened. The other people waiting outside the office watch me warily, Jab standing behind me naked. I glance at him and raise my brow at his nudity. Is it really the time to be standing there like that?

He grins and grabs a pair of slacks, different from the pair he was wearing before. He shrugs on a shirt just as I focus on the people in front of me. I fix my eyes on an orderly that's been here since I was a little girl. He's older now, slower. He'd never touched me in that way, but he raised his baton to me plenty. A sinister smile curls my lips.

They scatter as I charge, screams rending the air as I drive the knife home into his heart. They've called me a monster my whole life. Now, they will see exactly what kind of monster they created.

I don't hesitate to dive towards a nurse close by. Her screams cut off abruptly as I slit her throat, her hands clutching the gaping skin as she slides to the floor. I glance back towards Jab, a wicked grin on my face. He smiles.

"Go. You don't need me. You're plenty strong yourself. I'll be right behind you."

I sprint into the chaos around me, swinging the knife at anyone who draws too close, who thinks they can take me on. As I go, I slam the release lock for all the doors, letting the lunatics free, giving everyone the freedom I've wanted for years. Some of them don't immediately run out, thinking it's some sort of test or trap. The younger ones dart for the open doorways immediately, searching for an escape amid the screams and death.

"You will all pay for what you've done to me!" I snarl, swiping the knife across another neck. "You will all die."

There's a little girl crouched on the floor, fifteen at most, her arms wrapped around her legs as she rocks back and forth. The poor thing is terrified, confused. I wonder how long she's been here. I don't recognize her, but that doesn't mean anything. I haven't been allowed to mingle with other patients in years. She could have been admitted as young as I was.

I squat down beside her slowly, careful not to startle her. Bright-green eyes look up into mine. I see terror there, and fury. I see myself in her gaze.

"Are you angry?" I whisper gently. I was once this girl. I understand her.

"Y . . . yes."

I hold out the bloody knife to her. They hadn't even given her pants and a top like I'd had. The poor girl is in nothing but a hospital gown.

"Then do something about it."

The girl reaches forward, her hand shaking, and closes her fist around the handle of the knife. Her green eyes speak of thank you's and determination, and I know she will escape this place like I wasn't able to. I give her the tiniest smile. Coated in blood, I must look terrifying, but the little girl smiles back before standing up and racing in the direction I came from. It's not the way out, but I trust she'll find the exit.

I stand and continue my massacre, swiping newfound claws at those who dare to get too close. When an orderly holds out a needle to sedate me, I rip his throat out with my teeth, his blood giving me a small amount of power. Nothing like Jab's but something. I revel in the feeling of it.

I only make one other stop on my way out, in the storage room where they keep the items we come in with. I only have three things in my bag, still here after all these years. The dress I'd been wearing when I was admitted, a necklace my mother had given me for my sixth birthday, and the book Alex had given me. My copy of *the Princess and the Knave* is still in good condition after being sealed inside the bag. I tuck it away safely and leave the room.

As I make my way to the exit, my mind thinks on the girl I'd given the knife to again. Years ago, that was me. Desperate, hopeful, waiting for someone to save her. I would have killed for freedom, and now she will do the same. For a second, I worry about her safety, if I should go back in for her, but I dismiss the idea.

Besides, Jab is back that way. He would never hurt the child.

As I slam through the asylum, killing anyone who gets in my way, I finally make it to the front doors. When I push them open, and the sunlight hits my face for the first time in a long time, I close my eyes and breathe deeply.

A monster seeks nothing but freedom.

I'm free.

Chapter 13

IMMORTAL

Freedom isn't what I expected. I assumed the moment I walked through the doors of that asylum and into the sunshine, it would all be easier, that this was the moment I could truly start to live.

I was wrong.

My face is plastered across every paper, my name on every radio station. Everywhere I go, I see my face on a poster with the words WANTED bolded across the top. I'm still in a prison of someone else's making. I can't go into a restaurant and enjoy myself. I can't do anything. My name is forever linked to the Asylum Massacre, where I left the building and forty bodies behind.

The one bright spot in my world is Jab.

During the day, he leaves me alone to fend for myself, searching for White. He says he's looking for a way to lure White to open his rabbit hole into Wonderland. I have no reason not to trust him. At night, he comes back to me, curling into whatever bed we share. Then he's gone with the sunrise, a new stack of cash sitting on the nightstand for me.

That's been our system for three weeks, never deviating from it. We move towns every few days, making sure no one can recognize me. It's on day twenty-three when Jab comes home in the middle of the daytime, breaking the system we've followed. My first thought is that something is wrong, that we need to take off earlier than usual to avoid being found. I refuse to go back to a prison, and I won't. I'll kill anyone who thinks to try.

"What's happened?" I ask, standing from my place on the couch. I'd been reading my book for the hundredth time, memorizing it again after having been apart from the story for twenty-five years.

"I found him."

"Who?"

"The White Rabbit, of course."

Surprise fills me, but I'm not sure why. Jab has proven to me again and again that he's isn't a part of this world any more than I am. He has his own powers. It shouldn't be difficult to find the White Rabbit and convince him to take us to Wonderland.

"Well, where is he?" I ask, raising my brow.

"He's been frequenting a particular bar. I have a feeling his clock is telling him to be there, but he doesn't know why. I think he's waiting for you."

"Why on earth would he be waiting for me?" White had never once indicated that he was here to find me. He'd purposely left me in the asylum, no matter how hard I begged for help. He'd let them hurt me.

"I think Wonderland wants you home, Alice." Jab grins before picking up the blue dress again. He hadn't let me throw it out, but at least I had washed it after our escape. Now, it's as blue as it was before it had been covered in blood. "It's time to put on your dress."

"Do I really have to wear that?" I groan. I hate the dress. It reminds me too much of the gullible girl I'd been, wishing for the White Rabbit to take me away.

"We've discussed this. It's poetic."

"It's stupid."

Jab's lip curls, and I glare, but I ultimately grab the dress and humor him. If it wasn't for the Jabberwocky, I would still be stuck in that dirty room, wasting away, forgotten. Because he set me free, I can do something as simple as wear a childish blue dress. "Fine. When do we leave?"

"Right now. He's due there any moment."

"How do you know it's him?"

He raises one brow at me. "How do I know the man with rabbit ears on his head and silver eyes is really the White Rabbit?"

I smile as I pull on the blue dress. "Zip me up, please."

He does so without hesitation, pulling the closure up slowly, brushing his fingers the smallest amount against my skin. It's always a sensual action, something I love him doing. As per normal, he kisses me on the neck when he finishes and steps away.

"Are you ready?"

Am I? Am I ready to wreak havoc on Wonderland? Am I ready to make them all pay, to kill their world like they killed mine? They betrayed me over and over again, made a promise to a little girl they never intended to keep. They told me I would always be a part of their world and then forgot me. White came to look at me in my prison, in my hell, and still left me there.

They all deserved to die, so they could never do it again. No more little girls will fall victim to their world. The Sons of Wonderland must die.

I meet Jab's eyes, determination in mine. Am I ready?

"Yes. Let's go."

THE BAR THAT WHITE SUPPOSEDLY FREQUENTS IS A SHADY HOLE-IN-the-wall called The Three Sons. I don't know how much more appropriate that can be than it is. It's smoky and grimy, and I get plenty of stares as I walk inside in a short blue baby-doll dress. Some just raise their brows and return to their drink. Others catcall me.

Jab doesn't follow me inside. We both agreed that it was best to keep his existence a secret, to remain our secret weapon. So, I walk inside alone and take a seat at the bar.

"Can I get you something?" The bartender is a woman who's seen better days, her voice husky from too many cigarettes. She sets down a lit cig to take my order, the smoke adding to the atmosphere.

"Whatever doesn't taste like piss water," I reply to her question. I'm tasting a lot of things for the first time, but I figured out fairly quickly that I don't like beer.

She pours a glass of whiskey and slides it to me.

"It's not the greatest, but it's better than beer."

I salute her with the glass and take a sip, savoring the burn as it travels down my throat.

I feel him the moment he comes into the bar. I even feel him hesitate when his eyes find me. I don't turn and meet his eyes. I just continue to stare at the shelves lined with dusty bottles, sipping my whiskey from a cloudy glass.

Slowly, he comes forward and takes a seat next to me, gesturing for the bartender to give him a glass of Gin.

"Hello, White," I whisper.

All of the fear, the anger, the agony comes right back to me. I have so many questions, so many things I need to hear come from his mouth, but I can't ask. It's not the plan.

"Alice." There's an ache in his voice that I choose not to address. I don't know if he regrets his actions or if he wishes he wasn't here. "How are you here?"

"I escaped," I mumble. I leave out all the details because I can't speak without giving Jab away. White will never take me to Wonderland if he knows my plans. "I want to go home."

"Wonderland is not your home."

"You told me otherwise when I was a child," I remind him. "I'm here to beg you to let me back. This world," I motion around us, "is not my home. They don't accept me. I have nothing if Wonderland won't accept me, either."

Finally, I turn and meet White's eyes. I'm not prepared for the horrors in his gaze, the haunted look slamming into my own.

"What happened to your eyes, Alice?"

Jab and I had practiced my answer for this. I expected the question. "They did tests on me, stole everything. The eyes are a side effect of some of the tests." Once I had started taking power from Jab, my blue eyes had turned completely black, turning me even more into a monster. They flash back and forth, unpredictable when they'll be one color or the other.

"I'm sorry for the atrocities you've been subjected to."

I want to scream at him, that they were atrocities that he could have prevented. He had chance after chance to save me, and he didn't. But I don't want to bring up any of that, or else my anger will get the best of me. I need to conceal my powers for now.

"Just let me go back."

White shakes his head immediately. "I can't, Alice. You don't understand."

And my patience ends. My face morphs into a snarl. "Take me back, White!" He doesn't look alarmed. Why would he? Sons can't die, can't be killed by my hands, at least, that's what Jab told me. No, the way to kill a Son is to kill the world. I have to kill them all. "Give me a card." White owns the key to Wonderland, something I plan on taking as soon as I'm able. His cards serve to open the portals, but the key is what allows him through the doors. I need the card first. Jab can get us through the door if the key isn't on the table.

White's ear twitches at my anger, but his face remains motionless. I go with what I know he's not expecting: my new powers. I move faster than he expects and grab him around the throat. My hand is inside the pocket of his waistcoat before he can shove me away. My fingers close around a card just as he jerks from my grip and stumbles away.

"Have you gone mad, Alice?"

I grin. "It seems no matter what world I'm in, I'm labeled as mad. See you in Wonderland, White."

The bartender stands watching us, her hand under the counter on what I suspect is a gun. Bar fights are probably normal around here, but I'm willing to bet she never saw a fight quite like this.

"You're making a grave mistake," White warns as he backs away, always the rabbit, always running.

"No," I grin. "I'm fulfilling my destiny."

His eyes widen when I throw the card on the ground, uncaring who sees. White is pulled inside immediately, and I wait a moment for Jab to walk in the door. When he sees the swirling portal, he grins and grabs my hand.

"You first," he instructs. "That way he doesn't see me."

I kiss him on the lips and with a wild shout, I jump inside.

My entire life has been all about this moment. I've dreamed of returning to Wonderland, returning to the place where I felt like I belonged.

As I begin to fall in the swirling lights, I smile, true joy spreading through me for the first time in a long time.

It's time to go home and destroy it.

When I arrive, White scampers off without a second of hesitation, but I don't need him. I swipe the key and kick the table over, choosing the door I know will lead me to the Hatter's. Even if he can't die, I want to see him suffer for just a minute.

He's standing on his porch waiting for me, White at his side, obviously the message bringer. Hatter looks worried as he stares at the sight I must be. As I travelled through the forest, I took out anyone who got in my way, any creature. Now, my dress is once again coated in blood. The red dripping from my knife is fresh. Cheshire stands on the porch, a bored look on his face as usual, but the flick of his tail belies his unease. He knows more than Hatter seems to.

"What happened to you, Alice?" the Hatter asks.

"I grew up," I snarl, taking a step forward. There's only ten feet between us, and I itch to punish. "When you abandoned me to the woes of reality."

"You've lost your muchness." Hatter frowns even as Cheshire tenses. I watch as his claws slide out from his fingertips, but I only smile. He can't hurt me. He just doesn't know it yet.

"No," I reply, storming forward to close the distance. Hatter doesn't move, trusting me. That's his mistake. "I've gained power."

I thrust the knife into the Hatter's heart before he can react. I watch in satisfaction as shock crosses his face before he collapses to the ground.

"I'm home," I sing, a terrible grin crossing my face.

Chapter 14

IMMORTAL

I storm the castle, Jab staying with me but out of sight the entire time. I never need his assistance, and it's a great feeling. Power flows through my veins the likes of which I never imagined, and I will make this world mine before I kill it.

The old King and Queen had been easy targets, their trust making it possible for me to get close and take their heads. The sickened sound of the wet meat hitting the ground had been music to my ears. Now, their bodies pave the ground beneath my feet, as I stand in a dress stolen from the Queen's chambers. It's bright red, jewels glittering in the material, and I've never felt more like the Queen Jab has told me I am.

I'm covered in blood when Alex comes into the room, his sword raised. He's not as old as I am even though we were the same age when I left. Time in these worlds moves at odd bursts. Alex is beaten and bloody, one arm at an odd angle. I'm holding his mother's heart in my hand as I wait, expecting the Prince to come to the rescue at any moment. I bring it to my mouth and lick the blood, savoring the bitter yet sweet taste that's still not as satisfying as Jab's. The Prince flinches, and I feel terrible for doing it, but he betrayed me, too.

"Alice, you've become a monster."

It's like a slap to the face, the word coming from his mouth.

"I'm not the monster here," I whisper. "I was left in an asylum to rot. You all promised I was a part of Wonderland, but you abandoned me." I pull his book from the pocket of my dress and hold it aloft. "You said you loved me."

"We were eight, Alice. You've been gone for years and years. You never came back, so I moved on."

"Moved on?" My face twists into a grimace, and I drop the heart to the ground. Alex's eyes follow the organ, his jaw clenching. He won't let his fury get the better of him, a sign of his princely training.

"Silly Alice. Can't you see the truth?" Jab's voice comes from behind a pillar. He rounds it after his declaration, meeting my eyes. "This is his little kingdom, and you're not his Queen anymore."

"Who's this?" Alex asks, holding his sword higher.

"Alice," Jab coos. "Do it." I shake my head, and for the first time, a tear leaks from my eyes. I don't want to hurt Alex, even if he did move on and forget me. "Do it!"

"Do what?" Even after what he's seen, what he knows I did, Alex moves the slightest amount in front of me, protecting me against Jab, as if he's the real threat. It's the only evidence I need as to why I can't kill him.

"If you can't do it," Jab sneers, "then you're not the woman I thought you were."

My face hardens at his words, and I turn towards Alex again.

"Alice?" he whispers, meeting my eyes. When he sees whatever is in my eyes, he takes a step back, but he's still too close. "You're not my Alice."

I can't do it. I can't kill the Prince. With tears leaking down my face, I thrust my hand through his ribcage and swipe my other down his face. I push my power inside of him, corrupting him, taking control. If he can't be mine in heart, at least he can just be mine.

I rip my hand free, and where I touched him, roses grow in their place, a sign of our time together. I'll always remember painting the roses red.

"Oh, Alice," Jab sighs, staring at the Prince. "You should have just killed him."

"I couldn't." I wipe the tears from my face and compose myself. Alex stares at me waiting for his orders. "He's my Knave."

IMMORTAL

I step inside the dungeon, a wicked smile on my face. I've fallen into my role nicely; the hardest part over. Jab urges me to make them all pay, and I agree with him. They should all be punished for what they've done to me, what they've created, how they destroyed me. I used to be such a curious little girl, until I grew up and became what they will fear.

In front of me, the Hatter and the White Queen hang manacled to the wall. They were easy enough to capture. The White Queen's nature dictates that she never fights. And Hatter still thinks that I won't harm him, even after I stabbed him through the heart.

"Alice," he tries, jingling against his chains. I made sure they're enchanted enough to hold him, that they can hold any Son. Jab taught me how to do that, sharing far more secrets for the future.

There's a pleading note in the Hatter's voice, and it makes my anger flare up again. I turn on him, a snarl on my face.

"You were supposed to be my friend! You were supposed to be there for me! Where were you, Hatter? Where were you when I needed you?" The words I repeated to myself in the asylum, when I prayed for them to come for me, slip from my mouth without meaning to.

"We didn't know, Alice," he tries. Blood drips down his arms and bare chest with his movement. His hat and coat were stripped from him before he had been brought here. I couldn't have him pulling a fast one and escaping to the Here After. "Time moves differently here. It isn't linear. You could have left yesterday, or tomorrow, or a year before. There's no way to track it."

"I left twenty-five years ago," I snarl. "As soon as I left Wonderland and started spewing stories of talking flowers and rabbits and Hatters, I was thrown into the asylum. My own parents paid them to take me away for fear of embarrassment. They thought I was crazy! Do you know what they do to mad people in my world?"

"Please, Alice. We were friends. This isn't what you want to do."

I grin, stepping closer to him. I ignore his comment, continuing my story as if I never heard him speak.

"Electroshock treatments. Lobotomies. Did you know they cut into my brain? Said they would fix the part that suffered from insanity. Ask me if it worked. Ask me if I screamed, and screamed, and screamed." Rage drips from my words, fueling me. All the anger from my years in hell comes back like a hurricane, and I want to hurt and punish and make Hatter scream like I screamed. I want to make them feel what I felt.

"You're not my Alice," Hatter rasps. The enchantments on the manacles starts to take their toll, draining him of energy, turning him into an even easier target.

"This is exactly who I am, who I'm meant to be. The treatments didn't work. They just made me angry. Angry at the doctors for cutting into me. Angry with Wonderland for showing itself to me to begin with. Angry at you for abandoning me. Now, I want to see if you can die, Hatter."

I thrust my hand into his bare chest, my claws wrapping around his still beating heart. He screams out in agony, a tiny bit of blood trickling from the corner of his lips. Blood drips from where my hand is still buried in his chest. I squeeze, satisfied when the organ beats in answer.

"Alice," Hatter gurgles, his head slumping forward. "Alice." His voice lowers to a whisper, his body shutting down with the pain.

"No," I sneer, a laugh funneling up my throat as I rip his heart completely from his chest. I bring it to my lips, licking the blood, letting it drip down my chin and onto my chest. I smile even through the rage, even through the agony that this world has brought upon me. I crush his heart with a snarl. "I'm the Red Queen."

I will make sure to be the monster they made me. I will conquer this world, kill it, and move onto the next. Once upon a time, I'd been a naive little girl, but I grew up.

I'm the Queen of Hearts, and I will be the deadliest piece on the chessboard.

THE PRINCE & HIS HOPE

KENDRA MORENO

THE PRINCE AND HIS HOPE

Danica and Alexander only ever wanted to be together, even at the expense of tradition. Nothing could keep them apart, or so they thought.

Hope is for the living.

Prologue

A scream is the only thing we hear as we crouch behind a sofa. The scream abruptly cuts off, and a snarl takes its place. I clamp my hand over my mouth, barely holding in the giggles. We're going to be in so much trouble.

Alex wiggles his eyebrows at me when the maid starts sniffing for our scent. She'll find it alright, the scent of rotten Cracklebird Eggs. The maid is a hedgehog type creature, her nose sensitive. I feel bad sometimes about the tricks we pull on her, especially when she starts grunting, like she is now as she searches for us. The poor woman thought we were all bad as children. As teenagers, we'd only gotten better at pranking.

The maid comes across one of the rotten eggs and gags, backing away from the curtain we'd hidden it in.

"You children will be in so much trouble," she promises, before leaving the grand room. It's doubtful we will be. Alex is the prince, and Cheshire and I are only following his orders. That's the excuse we always use, anyway. Alex is a talker; he can talk his way out of anything with his parents. It works out great because Cheshire would rather growl than talk, and I shut down under the King's stern eyes. Win-win.

"Do you think she knows it's us?" I giggle, standing from our position. I crack my bones and stretch, my ears twitching in case the maid comes back. I like when she does, because then it's a chase.

Cheshire stares off into the hallway. "She definitely knows it's us.

Anyone with any sense would. Besides, she called us children. She knows."

"Who do we prank next?" I glance over at Alex, a grin on my face. "Should we try the guards?"

"We just pranked them yesterday, Dani." Alex shakes his head.

"But that's why they're the best targets. They won't be expecting it."

"Danica has a point." Cheshire grins at me, his ears already twitching. "Yesterday, they had to worry about their uniforms being wet. Today, maybe we should help dry them out."

I bounce on the balls of my feet, excitement coursing through my body. The boys always have the best prank ideas. Alex's are always harmless fun, like the rubber spider we dropped on the maid from above. Cheshire's can get out of hand and border on destructive, but it doesn't make them any less fun. I just have to keep a close eye on him. Together, we sort of balance each other out. I'm always in the middle just ready to have fun.

"We should avoid fire," Alex states, giving Cheshire a knowing look. "Last time, you almost burnt the whole castle down."

"It wasn't the whole castle. I had it under control."

"You burnt down the entire west wing, and the rest would have been taken with it if it wasn't for the White Queen coming to the rescue."

Cheshire rolls his eyes but relents. "Fine, no fire. Maybe just some very strong wind. I'll go search and see if I can find something that will generate that much energy. Meet me in the courtyard."

I watch as Cheshire Fades away, the process taking longer than it should. Both of us are still learning the skill, but Cheshire has always been better at it than me. I have to really concentrate on it in order to disappear completely, and I can't go nearly as far away as he can. It's frustrating, but I'm working on it.

"You think Chesh will go overboard?" Alex watches where Cheshire disappeared, worry between his brows.

I laugh. "Most definitely. We should keep a close eye on what he's searching for. If we're not careful, he'll find a Jabberwocky to flap its wings and destroy the castle in the process."

"Thank Wonder, Jabberwockies are extinct," Alex sighs, "but that doesn't mean he won't find something else to cause damage."

My tail twitches behind me as I study Alex, the firm set of his lips, his tense shoulders. The older we get, the less excited he gets about the pranks. I think his Prince training is starting to kick in, and he worries about people getting hurt now rather than pranking. He still laughs, still jumps in all the way when we prank, but he worries, and that's okay.

"It's going to be alright, Alex." I place my hand on his shoulder, and he looks down at the touch, his eyes taking in my fingers before looking into my eyes.

"How can you be certain?"

"I can't be. But Cheshire would never purposely hurt people."

"It's not on purpose that I'm worried about." Alex smiles, and I realize I still haven't moved my hand from his shoulder. I start to lift my fingers, but he grabs my own hand with his and keeps me from moving. "Don't. I like when you touch me."

The blush that rises to my cheeks is fast and bright, my tail twitching behind me in nervousness. Lately, the looks between Alex and I have been growing more frequent, but I assumed it was only me who had feelings I shouldn't. I really shouldn't be touching the future King, not with these emotions. He's meant for something more, and I'm just one of thousands in his kingdom. I'm perfectly ordinary.

"We shouldn't," I whisper, staring into his bright-blue eyes. I always assumed Alex and Alice would be an item. When she'd come to Wonderland, they'd been inseparable, but the years have gone on. Alice never returned, and Alex never speaks of her, and when he does, he never mentions any feelings. Perhaps, it was only Alice who loved Alex, and not the other way around. Still, Alice would be far better suited for a Prince than I would be. I have no noble blood, no true merit in the eyes of the King and Queen.

Alex grins, coming a little too close to be proper. His fingers gently cup my waist, drawing me in. "Now, Dani," he chides, his eyes twinkling, "when have we ever cared about what people think?"

He presses a fast kiss to my lips—it's over before I even realize what's happening—and then Alex lets me go and dances away, delight and laughter on his face. I watch him go, shocked, as I raise my fingers to my lips.

The Prince just kissed me, and I didn't stop him. The Prince just kissed me, and I want him to do it again.

What in Wonder have I gotten myself into?

"Is that the best you've got?" Alex goads, swinging his blade around to clash against my own.

I grin, throwing him backwards with all my weight before dancing out of the way. Alex may have brute strength, but I'm fast. He can't actually catch me if I don't want him to, but that isn't the point of these training sessions. Cheshire and I have plans to join the guard, to protect the monarchy. In a world that thrives on chaos, we want to keep the order. Cheshire enjoys the battles, but he doesn't want to be restrained. If he was a general, he'd have the freedom to choose. I can see why he wants the position.

Besides, Cheshire is one of the best warriors there is, and thanks to him, Alex and I are just as skilled.

"You talk too much," Cheshire comments, watching our session. He's always analyzing the best ways to move, which sides we need to work on more. "Focus on the blades and your feet."

"It's hard to focus when I'm fighting such a pretty woman," Alex comments and barely avoids my sword swiping across his armor.

Cheshire freezes, and his electric-blue eyes stare at Alex a little more closely. I realize immediately it was the wrong thing for Alex to say, and I prepare myself for the lecture. Instead, Cheshire holds up his hand, telling us to stop. Both Alex and I immediately back up. Alex is breathing a little hard, a side effect of trying, and failing, to keep up with my moves. My stamina from climbing trees and working with

Cheshire prevents me from suffering the safe effect. Overbearing brothers come in handy for something.

"My turn."

"No break?" Alex raises his brow, a smile on his face. I move off to the side, out of harm's way. I've been cut for standing too close before. I don't make the same mistake nowadays. Last time, Alex's blade sliced right across my bicep. I'd had to sit out for weeks while the wound healed, a far worse punishment than the actual cut.

"There are no breaks in battle. Or warnings." Cheshire swings his blade with his statement, and Alex barely has enough time to block the sword.

The sharp *ting* fills the courtyard as they stay balanced, there in the center, neither pushing to overpower each other. Their eyes lock, and I realize that this isn't just a training session.

"Cheshire?" I worry my bottom lip as they hover in the center.

"Again!" Cheshire Fades away and reappears behind Alex before he can react. His kicks Alex on the back of the knee, sending him to the floor with a clatter. Alex recovers quickly, a testament to his training, rolling on the floor and to his feet before Cheshire is on him. Alex swings his own blade in an attempt to catch Cheshire unaware, but my brother is nothing if not a professional. He's no longer in the same place, his own sword clash making Alex stumble back under the blow.

"Cheshire, stop," I try, taking a step forward.

"Stay back, Dani," Cheshire snarls, attacking Alex again.

Alex doesn't back down, and he doesn't ask him to stop. He won't. All of his training won't allow it. He's the Prince, and the Prince fights until his very last breath. Something bigger is going on between the two men, bigger than practice. Cheshire stares intensely into Alex's eyes, his gaze as sharp as the blades he swings. There's no hate there like his attacks speak of, but there's anger. Lots and lots of anger. And Cheshire is ruthless when he's pissed.

Alex grunts with the next blow, his arms shaking, his fatigue starting to show. Cheshire isn't even using his full strength, but he's using enough to hurt. Alex will be in pain tomorrow.

"That's enough!" I lift my own sword, preparing to join the fray. Alex is slowing down, leaving his side open. It's the weakness Cheshire has been trying to get Alex to overcome, but it doesn't come easily to him. Alex may be a Prince and a skilled warrior, but he's never been meant to be in actual battle; he's never quite mastered the art of showing no weakness.

"No, it's not," Cheshire growls, hitting harder, the clangs ringing around us. Alex dances like Cheshire taught him, his feet far slower than they should be.

Alex leaves his side open for a split second too long, and Cheshire kicks out his foot, tripping Alex and sending him to the stone so hard, I hear his teeth rattle. Alex tries to roll back to his feet, but Cheshire's blade is there to stop him, pointed right beneath his chin as if this is an actual battle. Alex is breathing hard, his heavy pants sawing from his chest, his neck tilted up to avoid the sharp edge. Cheshire's tail flicks back and forth behind him, the only sign of his tension.

"What are you doing?" I step forward, and Cheshire's eyes flick to me for the barest second before they're trained back on our friend.

"Teaching the Prince a lesson," Chesh replies. "Stay away from my sister."

"Cheshire!"

"She's a grown woman. She can make her own decisions." Alex meets Cheshire head on, unflinching beneath his hard gaze, always the Prince even as he's lying at the mercy of my brother.

"And when the Queen picks out your betrothed, what will you do then, hmm?"

"That's enough!" I shove Cheshire off Alex and glare at him. "You don't get to decide my fate, brother. Worry about your own."

"Your fate will be to suffer a broken heart if you let those affections I see so clearly in your eyes fester." Cheshire slides his sword away. "When he's forced to marry a Queen, you will be left alone and in pain, pining for a Prince who didn't care enough to leave you be."

"That's still my decision to make, Chesh. You cannot protect me. Besides, there's nothing to worry about. We're just friends."

I can feel the twitch behind me, the hurt I've just caused, but I don't turn. That would only prove to Cheshire that he's right, and I can't have him knowing, not if he's going to threaten Alex.

"Best that's all you are," Cheshire nods. He leans to the side to glare at Alex again. "Hands off my sister, Your Majesty."

"I don't follow your orders, Cheshire."

"Of course not. What Prince would listen to sound advice? Best not let the Queen find out."

Cheshire is gone before I can say another word, and my breath leaves me in a rush. When I turn to Alex, his face is solemn.

"Just friends?" He meets my eyes. "Is that all that we are?"

I shake my head. "We have to be more careful. He's right. If the Queen finds out, she will make sure we stay apart. And Cheshire cannot know. You saw how he reacted when he suspected. Imagine if he actually knew."

"We're not doing anything wrong."

I don't correct him, don't tell him that we're doing everything wrong. I am not royalty, not approved by the Queen. Alex will be crowned on his twenty-second birthday, and I will have to watch him bear the crown and take the hand of another woman. I already know our fates don't intertwine. They can't. I am nothing more than a creature of Wonderland.

A prince cannot marry a pauper.

No matter how much he may want to.

Chapter 9

Wonderland treats aging in an odd way. Sure, we grow older, and technically, I'm the ripe age of twenty, soon to be a year older if we go by the turnings of the clock, but we don't measure things in such ways, not unless you're someone important, like the Prince.

We live and we die, and that's it. There is no marking of time to claim we made it to a certain age. There is nothing but Wonderland, and then when we die, there's only the Here After.

Wonderland is a fickle world, determining fates as if it's her only duty. Sometimes, I imagine a woman sitting at a table, dressed completely at odds in mismatched clothing, garish to the eyes, really, as she chuckles over her decisions. We're just players on a chess board, moving in whatever way she sees fit. It's the reason everyone is preparing for her decisions now, because we haven't had any Sons for a long time. It's time for some of her creatures to rise as protectors. It's an event that spreads across the land, celebrations that will last for weeks once they are chosen. I'm looking forward to having time off from the Queen's guard.

Cheshire and I had been accepted into her guard easily, Cheshire rising much faster than I ever could. While I'm skilled enough to be deemed a lieutenant of my own squadron, Cheshire has risen to the General in such a short time, it made history. He leads the entire guard, as he should. He's the most skilled fighter in Wonderland, the perfect man to protect the crown.

We have a rare moment away from the castle, allowed to leave and prepare for the festival, but I have no obligations. Our parents had walked into the Here After years ago, leaving Cheshire and I alone. There's no one waiting at home for me to help with sweet breads, and this festival is an intimate one; I wouldn't be allowed to join other families in their preparations.

Now, I'm deep in the dark forest, sitting high in a tree, waiting for Cheshire to find me. My mind is awash with things it shouldn't be such as Princes with too tempting lips, with clever hands. I've had to stay away from Alex, the Queen watching too closely when our eyes meet, and it's killing me.

"Why are you in a tree?"

I smile when I hear Cheshire's voice, leaning over the edge of the branch to grin at him.

"Aren't we supposed to be living in the trees?"

"Sure, if we were feral creatures." Cheshire scales the tree much faster than even my swift feet allow, and I scowl when he takes a seat beside me. Everything is always so easy for my brother. "Don't be mad, Dani. You're younger than I am."

"Hardly." I roll my eyes. "We might as well be the same age."

"You'll always be my silly little sister." When he winks at me, I can't help the smile that curls my lips.

"And you'll always be my obnoxious big brother."

We fall into a silence heavy with things we want to say. Cheshire and I have always been close, best friends even before Alex joined our group, but lately, we've been keeping far too many secrets from each other. I want to tell him about Alex, to reassure him I know how stupid it is. I know Alex will never marry me, he can't, and I'll have to watch him love someone else after he's crowned. That knowledge doesn't keep my heart from speeding up when he smiles at me. It doesn't stop the stupid organ from beating out of my chest when he touches me.

Silly little sister, indeed. Cheshire sees right through me, but there hasn't been any more threats from him towards Alex since that time. As the General, he's supposed to keep his mouth shut, something that doesn't come naturally, but I'm certain it's for my feelings rather than any protocol. He knows I realize the idiocy I'm twisted in, and still he's there for me.

Cheshire has his own secrets, ones I can see just as clearly as he sees mine. Being promoted to General was supposed to make Cheshire happy; that was always the plan. It's the highest rank a Wonderland creature can hope to rise to without being chosen by the land herself. We should both be happy.

Instead, we're both miserable.

"Do you want to talk about it?" I whisper, staring up through the tree canopy to the small amounts of dark sunlight that manage to filter through.

"Do you?"

I sigh. Of course, I don't, but if Cheshire talks, I know I will spill everything. "Yes."

Cheshire balances on the branch as if we're not a hundred feet off the ground, his legs dangling over the side as if he's sitting on the edge of a lake. "I want to leave."

Surprised, I lean forward. "Leave where?"

"Wonderland. I want to leave Wonderland."

"But why?"

He takes a deep breath, before his electric eyes finally meet mine. "Dani, when I set my sights on becoming General, I thought it would come with freedom. I thought I could have some control over my life." He shakes his head. "I was naïve. There is no freedom here. If Wonderland isn't moving us around like chess pieces, then the Queen and King are giving me more rules, more laws to make."

"Shh." I glance around us. "You shouldn't be speaking of such things."

"I don't care. I've never cared. I only took the job because I knew you wanted to get higher ranking. I didn't want you to do it alone." I shake my head, already knowing where this is going, but Cheshire doesn't let me speak. "No matter how much rank you put on, what title you bear, it will never be good enough to be Queen, Dani. You have to know that."

I clench my jaw hard, so hard, it shoots pain through my head. Cheshire's eyes are sad when he looks at me, and I realize he's known all along. He's had to, and why wouldn't he? He's my best friend, my brother, after all.

"I do know that. I'm not stupid."

"Then why do you keep doing this to yourself? He'll be crowned in less than a year and married soon after to whatever woman the Queen approves of. A man who loves a woman would never do that to her." His eyes say it all, that he thinks Alex doesn't really love me at all. I can't argue that point because I don't really know. It doesn't matter, anyway.

"You wouldn't understand, Cheshire. You've never been in love. All you search for is freedom. There's freedom in accepting what you cannot change as well."

"That's the exact opposite of freedom."

I laugh, no humor in the sound. "One day, when a woman comes into your life and sweeps you off your feet, I can't wait to tell you 'I told you so.'" I meet his eyes. "And then, when you tell her that you want freedom more than her, I want you to look deep into her eyes and see what's she's feeling. If it doesn't hurt you to say it, you're not in love."

"No one could ever love me."

"I love you, even with all your attitude."

"You don't count. You have to love me. We're family."

"So, then trust me to know what I'm doing. I understand we aren't meant to be. But let me just pretend for a little while that we are. I just want to enjoy the time I'm able to."

Cheshire stares at me, studying me, looking for answers in my words.

"He's worth a broken heart?"

I stare up at the leaves above me again, a phantom wind shaking them. In the distance, some creature howls, but I don't worry. Nothing could ever sneak up on us.

"He's worth many things," I whisper, blinking back the tears that threaten to spill. "My broken heart will be nothing in the grand scheme of things."

"And still, you love him?"

I nod my head. "Still, I love him."

He sighs, his ears laying down on his head when he scrubs a hand through his hair.

"If you didn't care about him so much, I would have murdered him years ago. Damn the consequences." His tail twitches behind him. "But I realize there might not be only one broken heart when he's crowned King, and for that reason alone, I'll step back and keep your secret, even if I think he's being a self-centered asshole. Just, be careful, Dani. And when you need me, I'll be here."

I smile, my eyes wet with unshed emotion. We don't hug, though I have the urge to, but I reach forward and touch my hand to his, glad to have such a brother. I expect his hand to be warm, like the furnace he usually is, but it's ice-cold to the touch. I jerk my fingers away.

"Why are you so cold?"

"I don't know. My skin has been icy all day."

I touch my fingers to his skin again, the back of his hand so cold, it almost feels like it freezes my fingers. When we touch this time, tingles shoot up my arm, and I gasp.

"Do you feel that?" I've never felt this before, this overwhelming buzzing. Even as I say it, the buzzing gets more insistent, spreading across my entire body until I feel alive with it.

"What's happening?" Cheshire stares at his hand in confusion, the same buzzing obviously climbing up his arm. "What is this?"

Above us, a bright light flashes, nearly blinding in its intensity. Both of us shield our eyes to ease the pain it causes in the darkness, and when we lower our arms, there's a shape in the light, that of a woman. We can't see her features—they're too obscured by the light—but she's clearly powerful to harness the light around her.

"Cheshire and Danica. Brother and sister. Hard and gentle." Her voice sounds like hundreds speaking all at once, an echo that's not an echo. It's terrifying, and yet, I find myself leaning towards the voice, as if I know it deep in my soul. "Two sides of a coin in birth. Two sides of a coin in life."

"Who are you?" Cheshire asks, his claws sliding free in case she's a threat. "And what do you want with us?"

I can feel the woman smile even though I can't see her.

"Three Sons are chosen for Wonderland, but they are not alone.

Death, Time, and Justice are the Sons, but with them, come Memories and Hope."

"What the fuck does that mean?"

Mentally, I echo Cheshire's question. Why is this woman telling us about the Sons? Who is she?

In the distance, a howl rends the air, so full of sorrow, it makes my heart hurt.

"Justice and Hope are two sides of the same coin, my children. You both have been chosen."

"Chosen for what?" Cheshire asks, but I already know the answer. I can feel the power that begins to flow through me at her statement, gravity slipping away as I'm lifted into the air, her bright light licking at my skin. "Dani!" I gasp, my back bowing under the new power surging through me. "What the fuck are you doing with my sister?"

"Hope Bringer, you know your role," she continues as if Cheshire hadn't spoken. "Hands of Justice, you will know yours."

I hear Cheshire growl and fight as he's lifted into the air beside me. I can feel his horror from here, but I can't reach out to him, my own body still locked under the pouring of power. I want to tell him it's okay, that I'm here, but I can't. Oh, Wonder, I can't. His horror slams into me so hard, I whimper. I hear his groan of pain as power rushes into him, far more powerful than what's going into mine. I may be the Hope Bringer, but Cheshire will be a Son. Any choice he might have had before, it's gone. Wonderland will never let him leave now. Tears pour down my cheeks, sorrow for my brother taking precedence over any excitement I have.

Finally, after what feels like hours, she sets us back on the branch, both of us unsteady on our feet. I'm panting hard, my hand clenched against my chest where I feel like I'm going to explode with power, as if my body is bigger than the shell I have. Cheshire morphs in front of my eyes, fur sprouting along his skin, his anger palpable as his face twists into a savage scowl.

"Take. It. Back," he growls, enunciating each word.

"It is done." The light begins to fade before our eyes. Cheshire's answering roar of rage pierces my ears, and I wince.

"Take it the fuck back! I refuse! I refuse! I deny your power!"

Tinkling laughter reaches our ears, and I know, she's enjoying this far too much. Just like a game of chess, we're nothing more than pieces on a board. "Child," she speaks, those thousand voices rising, "there is no choice."

And then she's gone, and when I reach for Cheshire, he's gone, too.

Chapter 9

When the Sons are chosen, the festival begins, and everyone celebrates those that are picked to become so much more. The Sons and those chosen for other roles are forced to stand in front of the entire kingdom and announce their new positions. We should be honored. We should feel happy.

As I stand in front of the crowds, I feel far from happy, but there is a hope there. Hope Bringer is a far more distinguished title than Lieutenant. The Queen, however, hardly gives me a look as she addresses the crowd, even though she's watched me grow up within her walls.

"Wonderland has spoken. She has chosen those that she believes are necessary for our survival, and she has chosen well." Words. They're nothing more than flowery words. She doesn't believe a word of it. She's kind, and cares about her family and her people, but she doesn't believe we're necessary for Wonderland. This is a pageantry to her. Alex has mentioned her feelings before. She turns her eyes to us, seeing but not. I've been running through her castle since I could stand on my legs, and still, she hardly spares me a glance. She starts on the end, in front of The Hatter. We've known each other for years, but he keeps to himself in his house. Cheshire is friends with him, but I've never had the pleasure of a true conversation with the man. He comes from a long line of Sons. It's no wonder he was chosen as the next Protector.

"Hatter, you have been chosen as a Son, the Protector of the Here

After. May Wonderland have mercy on your soul." He nods in answer, his face solemn. He, too, understands this is not the honor we've been led to believe. This is not a choice.

She moves to the March Hare, his ears twitching far faster than normal. His jaw keeps clenching and unclenching, as if he's not sure what exactly is going on. I find myself pitying him.

"March, you have been chosen as the Keeper of Memories. May Wonderland have mercy on your soul."

White is another friend of Cheshire's, one he speaks of often. White works on strategy with Cheshire for the guard, his job to find the fastest way to win a war with the lowest amount of casualties. They were fast friends from the beginning, but the White Rabbit has stayed far away from me for whatever reason. "White, you have been chosen as a Son, the Time Keeper. May Wonderland have mercy on your soul."

Only Cheshire and I remain, and I know Cheshire wants to be anywhere but here, but both of us had felt the call. We have no choice, no freedom. Wonderland wants us to be here, and what she wants, must be done.

"Cheshire, you have been chosen as a Son, the Hands of Justice. May Wonderland have mercy on your soul."

Alex stands to the side of us, wearing his fancy clothing, the thread spun through with more gold than I can ever hope to own. His blue eyes crash into mine as the Queen steps in front of me, and I know I'm showing everything in my eyes. Hope and Fear swirl within me, and I want to smack myself for it. The Hope Bringer is not destined for the King. I'm one side of the coin, and Alex is not the other. Still, there's a small amount of Hope that the new title elevates me enough to be deemed worthy, as stupid as that sounds.

The Queen clears her throat, and I look into her eyes. It's frowned upon, but as a chosen one, she can no longer say anything. My rank is blessed by Wonderland. I no longer must bow, but that doesn't mean I can claim her son. There are rules, so many rules, always rules. I'm starting to understand my brother's aversion to them.

"Danica," she begins, staring deeply into my eyes, her disapproval so thick, I can taste it. Why? Why does she feel that way? "You have been chosen as the Hope Bringer. May Wonderland have mercy on your soul."

The crowd erupts in cheers, the festival officially beginning, a whole celebration for our loss of freedom. It might as well have been the same as a public hanging. Execution would be far easier.

As soon as Wonderland allows us, I move from my spot. I need to get away from this; I need to escape. Cheshire Fades away immediately, but my emotions are too extreme to focus. I can't Fade, so I settle for running, and running, and running.

Before I know it, I'm deep in the trees, the hissing flowers avoiding me now that I've been chosen. Tears start to flow down my cheeks without me realizing it, the proper dress I was put in for the ceremony ripping on the branches that don't move fast enough out of my way.

I finally reach a clearing and collapse, deep sobs wracking my body. I weep for Cheshire, for his loss of freedom, his dreams. I weep for the cruelty of Wonderland, for her games. I once told Cheshire that there's freedom in going with fate. I regret every word. There's no freedom in this. Perhaps, I should accept my role with humility, and thank the stars that I've been chosen, but all I see is endless loneliness, a brother who will never be happy, and the man I love marrying another.

All I see is the end, and still, I hope. That's the curse of the Hope Bringer, isn't it? To feel things so deeply, to be the only one who still hopes even in the face of such disaster.

Someone kneels in front of me, and I look up, surprised that I hadn't heard them approach. Alex watches me, concern in his eyes at the state I'm in. My dress is in shreds, dirty, my face blotchy and tear-streaked. I'm a mess, but he reaches forward to wipe my cheeks.

"You'll ruin your pants," I croak. His fancy outfit is white and gold, his knees already soaking in the dirt on the forest floor. He'll stain the material permanently, and it's something I can never afford to replace.

"Everything is going to be okay, Dani," he whispers.

"How can you say that?" I shove my hair back from my face, fighting the tears that still roll down my face. "Everything is far from okay."

"Being chosen as Hope Bringer is an honor."

I shake my head. "There is no honor in this role. And there was no choice. Wonderland made that clear. When she calls, I must go, no matter what. I'm nothing but a slave to the hope that flows through my body. I'm nothing but a vessel with a title that still means nothing when it comes to King."

"I don't want to become King," he sighs. "I understand having no choice far too well."

I clench my jaw, contrite. He's right. I've known for years that he doesn't want to become King, but there is no other heir.

"I'm sorry," I sniff.

"Don't be." He leans forward and pulls me into his arm. "I'm not looking forward to being told what to wear, who to speak to, who to love. I understand why you don't want the role, just as I understand why Cheshire is so angry. Neither of you want this life."

"But," I interject, "we've been called for greater purposes. I understand that." I try to gather my emotions. Pity parties aren't necessary here. What's done is done. There's no use crying about it.

"And that's why you're the perfect Hope Bringer," Alex says, his fingers tipping my chin up. "So perfect in every way."

My heart skips a beat in my chest as he looks deeply into my eyes, so much emotion shining there I can hardly stand it. I should pull away. I should end this. Our relationship has just been doomed completely, and still I clench my hands in the fancy jacket at his waist.

"I will never be considered eligible to be Queen," I remind him. "It's against the rules." That's the reason we should stop. It's the reason we should go our separate ways and be happy with the memories of stolen kisses and gentle touches.

"To hell with the rules." Alex's lips crash down on mine with a ferocity he's never shown, and I find myself responding to him even though I just told myself not to, even though I'm covered in dirt and my face is swollen with grief. I run my hands over his coat and around his neck. One of his hands threads through my wild hair, the other at my hip pulling me as close as possible. We don't break the kiss until neither of us can breathe. Both of us pant hard, as if we can't get enough air into our lungs, and the sound of the rapid rise and falls of our chests is the only thing we can hear.

"We should stop," I whisper even as my hand flicks the button free at the top of his elegant coat. Alex begins to slide the zipper down at my back, releasing the dress slowly from my chest.

"Do you love me?" he asks when the dress pools around my waist. I fumble with his buttons, but they don't come loose. Instead, I end up ripping the jacket open with my newly gifted strength, the shirt underneath going with it, revealing golden skin.

"Yes." There's no hesitation in my answer. I've loved Alex for years.

"I love you, too," he groans, his lips leaning down to capture the skin at the juncture of my neck and shoulder. "I love you so damn much. Nothing else matters. To hell with everyone. As long as I have you, I'm okay."

I don't tell him he's wrong, that we have no choice in the matter. If Wonderland doesn't deem us a match, then we will never be a match. We will never win this battle with her, but I don't speak. I shove his jacket frantically from his shoulders before he leans forward and lays us down on the dried leaves. My dress gets slipped off reverently, as if he's studying every detail. His fancy clothing is tossed to the side into the dirt, ruined beyond repair.

When he enters me, it feels different than any other time we've met. This time feels like a declaration of war, but I have a feeling Wonderland won't allow us to win. The Hope Bringer and the Red King are not destined for each other, and they're not a traditional match. But perhaps, there's no harm in fighting.

I moan when Alex slides inside of me, moving achingly slow, absorbing every detail. His weight comes down over me, covering me as we join together deep in the forest.

"I love you," he whispers, hooking my legs over his hips. He kisses my lips, my chest, my neck, anything he can reach, all while pumping inside me. "I love you."

I can't speak, can't tell him I love him, too. There's too much emotion, too much happening. I feel both suffocated and free, full of sorrow and happiness. My climax slowly begins to build, my emotions spilling over my eyelashes to run down the face. Alex only kisses the tears away, holding me gently as we make love, as we declare war on destiny.

When our climaxes crash into us, and the forest grows quiet with our declaration, our love hanging heavy in the air, I realize exactly what we've just done. There are rules for a reason. We will never be allowed to be together, not truly, but as if Wonderland knew exactly what she was doing when she chose me, the feeling fills my body.

Hope. There is always hope.

Chapter 4

I don't focus any more on the consequences. What's the point, really? It's already inevitable something bad could happen, that the Queen will never approve our match, that Wonderland herself will deny us the love. But I keep my hope close to my heart, and in between my Hope Bringer duties, I spend my time in Alex's arms.

Cheshire reluctantly fulfills his duties as the Hands of Justice. I know he's not happy, and we grow more distant the longer we're in our roles. Sadness unlike anything I've ever known fills me at the realization. My brother and I, we've had only each other for so long, have been best friends since we were children. To think I might lose him to Wonderland, to his fury at his fate, makes me wish I can reach out and bring him out of it.

But rage so deep isn't easily dismissed.

As Alex's coronation draws near, the impending heartbreak drawing closer and closer, our duties seem to come more frequently. Cheshire and I realized quickly that powers came with our duties. Strength was immediate. The first time I lifted five times the amount I normally could, I panicked so bad, I dropped the large tree on my foot. Cheshire's strength far outweighs mine, even though we should be perfectly balanced according to the laws of Wonderland. Our senses have grown drastically, Cheshire's hearing is insane. He heard me coming through the forest on silent feet long before I could even attempt to sneak up on him. It's a little unfair, that even after being chosen by Wonderland, Cheshire is still better than me at everything.

Being the Hope Bringer comes with more powers than just the strength and hearing, however. The night after we rose to our powers, I realized I gained a new ability. Dream Walkers are far and few in Wonderland, and those that contain the power are usually too weak to do more than peek in on dreams. I've been able to interact, to influence, while we're in a dream state, and recently, I've been able to manifest that power outside of my body in a protective bubble. The dome that spreads around me when I'm able to focus is golden in color, and impenetrable by outside forces. Alex has tried to get through, and he only succeeded when I grew too tired to maintain the bubble. It's a remarkable skill to have, and one I haven't told Cheshire about yet. I'm not sure I want to bring it up, to seal our fate even more. I'm scared of the powers, and I'm scared I'll walk inside Cheshire's dreams and see things that I never wanted to.

Along with the powers, we're expected to fulfill duties. Cheshire, as the Hands of Justice, punishes those beyond rehabilitation or reasoning. My job as the Hope Bringer, is the rehabilitation. When a creature of Wonderland commits a crime against her, we are called to their location. Being called is sort of like a tingling up and down our arms, so insistent that the longer we let it go, the less choice we have. If we try to ignore it, we're racked with intense pain. We'd tried at the beginning. I have no desire to repeat that torture. Cheshire still tries.

I sigh when the familiar tingling travels up my arm. It starts in my fingertips before spreading up my arm and into my chest. I leave the tree I'd been sitting in, contemplating everything that I have to worry about and follow the tugging until I arrive at the Royal Castle. It's full of bustling activity, preparations for the coronation no doubt. Alex is supposed to be somewhere listening to hours of lectures about his role as a King. I don't envy him.

The tingling brings me to the banquet hall, where the King and Queen host their dinner every night. For all their faults, they are a benevolent monarchy. Any creature or person of Wonderland can choose to join them for dinner any evening. There's never an excuse for someone to go hungry, not when they can simply walk into the castle doors and join in.

Today, it's empty save for the Queen on the dais, Alex beside her. He looks beat up, and I frown. He hadn't looked like that this morning. In front of them, kneeling on the floor, is a guard I know well. His wrists are shackled behind him, his face bruised. This man is one of my own, one I trained when I'd been a lieutenant. He's a good man from what I can remember, with a family at home. He'd always been honorable and never caused trouble while under my command.

"What's going on?" Cheshire's voice echoes around the stone walls as he appears beside me, his sharp eyes taking in the scene.

"I don't know." I'm hesitant to step forward, but I force my feet to move. Wonderland is demanding we take care of this situation, so we must.

"Alex?" I meet his eyes when we draw closer, tilting my head to the side in question.

"This man tried to kill me while I was walking through the courtyard." His voice is hard, harder than I've ever heard him use.

"Which would explain the call," Cheshire says, rolling his eyes. "Obviously, he didn't succeed."

Alex gives him a hard look, but Cheshire meets his eyes without flinching. His tail barely flicks behind him, my own completely still. I don't like that the appendage has a habit of belying my feelings. I'm working on keeping it from doing that. Cheshire doesn't care because he's always full of some emotion or the other. His tail could be moving because he's amused, angry, agitated, anything really. If it was still, I would be worried.

"I didn't try to kill him," the guard says, his voice shaking. He turns to meet my eyes. "Lieutenant, you know me. I have a family. I would never try to kill the Prince and forfeit my life."

"He's lying." I give Alex a sharp look when he speaks, but his face doesn't ease. Still, this is my jurisdiction. My job as the Hope Bringer is to reason, to decide if the man is guilty or not. No one else can take that job from me.

I kneel in front of the guard, staring into his brutalized face. One of his eyes is sealed shut with swelling, and I'm certain it's from the manhandling he, no doubt, suffered after the incident. Treason is not taken lightly. "Tell me what happened."

"I already told you," Alex interrupts.

I look over my shoulder at him, fury in my blood. Alex and I have never struggled with respect because he's always had a higher title than me, but as the Hope Bringer, this is my role, and I have the final say. He is the lower one right now, and I make sure to meet his eyes. "Hold your tongue, Prince." My power infuses the words, my voice sounding like an echo as it fills the room. Alex snaps his mouth shut and takes a small step back. I'm already turning away from him to look back at the guard, dismissing his condescension. Now isn't the time to discuss it. "Tell me."

"I was minding my own business, just fresh from training with Lieutenant Perry. He's the one who took over your squadron. I see the Prince walking toward me, and I step aside as per protocol. I stand at attention, but I accidentally elbowed one of the suits of armor. The axe fell just as he was walking by, nearly took off his face, but he's fast, luckily. He reacted instantly and started beating me. I tried to tell him it was an accident, that I would never attempt an assassination, but he wouldn't listen." A sob escapes his throat as he realizes exactly the kind of situation he's in. "I only tried to protect myself from him, landed a few blows in-between his hits when I tried to reason with his majesty. I never tried to kill the Prince, Hope Bringer. I swear it. I was only doing my job. I have a family. Please."

Cheshire stands back with his arms crossed, listening intently, waiting for my decision. I stand and face Alex.

"And what is your version of the story?"

I'm compelled to find out both sides before I give my judgement, even if I feel very strongly that the guard is not at fault.

"I was on my way to speak to some of the guards when this man purposely waits until I'm next to him, and he stuck out his elbow. Nearly took my head. When I turned towards him, he moved his hands as if he was going to pull another weapon to finish the job."

"I didn't. I swear it, Hope Bringer. I swear it. I was only trying to put my hands up in surrender. I was only trying to apologize. I had no weapons on me." His words grow increasingly more desperate, sobs wracking his body as he argues against the accusation. My chest settles with my knowledge, and I know where the fault lies.

"Innocent," I announce.

Cheshire relaxes.

"You're going to let him go after he almost killed me?" Alex scowls at me, but I meet his gaze with my chin tilted high.

"It was an accident that you overreacted to, Your Majesty. I've made my decision."

I lean down and break the manacles around his wrist, helping the guard to his feet.

"Thank you, Hope Bringer. Thank you." His words are almost indecipherable as he sways on his feet.

"Put some compound on that eye, soldier. It'll be nasty in the morning. Tell your wife I say hello."

He nods his head, mumbling more words of gratefulness as he stumbles from the room. Finally, I turn back to Alex. At some point, the Queen must have left, leaving us three to figure out our problems. I'm certain she only waited for my decision before she deemed her presence unnecessary.

"You let him go." Alex sounds entirely confused.

"As you should have before you beat him within an inch of his life. With a kingdom comes responsibility. You'll never earn respect as a King if you go around trying to punish innocent people."

I physically see him bristle, but I don't back down. We've been friends long enough, he should know I'll always tell him the truth, even if it isn't nice.

"Well, it's been fun, really, but I have things to do." Cheshire eyes us and Fades away, leaving Alex and I to stare at each other with unease. I watch my brother go sadly, wishing I could talk to him, tell him everything that I'm learning.

Alex sighs. "You're right. I should have let it go."

"Why didn't you?"

"I don't know. There were some other guards watching. I didn't want them to think me weak." He runs his hand through his hair. "I might have let my other feelings get to me and took them out on the guard."

"There is strength in admitting you're wrong. It's not a sign of weakness to have compassion." My mother used to tell me those words as a child. I think they sunk into me more than Cheshire.

Alex nods his head. "That is a lesson I will have to learn, unfortunately. It doesn't come easy to me. Walk with me?"

I nod my head hesitantly. It's been a long time since we've had a moment to ourselves. With the coronation drawing near, Alex has been busy with his duties, his lessons, and I suspect much of it has to do with his parents attempting to keep us apart. The Queen is far too perceptive not to know our feelings for each other; I'm certain she's doing it as a service, to make it easier when we have no other choice.

I've been kept busy with my duties as Hope Bringer that never seem to get easier. For the most part, it feels hopeless even though I'm constantly filled with hope. It's a blessing and a curse.

We walk in silence through the surprisingly empty castle halls, comfortable with each other's company even if there's something that's at the edges of our minds. There are so many things I want to say to Alex, that I love him, that I wish we were different people without titles, that I understand we will have to say goodbye before his coronation, but I don't speak first. I can't. There's too much that would slip out all at once.

"I'm sorry."

I peek at Alex from the corner of my eye, unsure where this is going. Which part is he apologizing for?

"For what?"

"Back there. In the banquet hall. I realize that I overstepped and spoke to you in a way I shouldn't have."

"You're used to being the only one with a title. I get it."

"That doesn't make it right." He sighs and comes to a stop. I follow suit and peer up at him. "Even had you not gained a title of your own, I should never have spoken that way to you. I respect you far too much for it, and I'm sorry."

I study him for a moment, searching his eyes, searching for the truth, but I don't have to look far. His shame is reflected in his gaze, and I give him a tiny smile.

"Apology accepted. I'm sorry I spoke to you in such a way as well."

He snorts. If his mother were here, she would have given him a disapproving look. Princes don't snort. "I deserved it. Besides," a grin spreads across his face, "It's sexy when you're being bossy."

I can't help the laugh that bubbles out, and it echoes around the stone room. Alex's callused hand slides into mine, and he's pulling me from the middle of the hallway into a doorway behind us. When we slip inside, it appears as nothing more than one of the dozens of spare rooms in the castle. Far too many of them stay empty; a waste, if you ask me.

We're shut inside the room, alone, cut off from the rest of the world. This chamber is used for nothing more than storage, a few crates stacked up against the walls, but nothing else decorates the walls. It's silent, and a little dusty, as if the maids don't clean here often.

"We should really head back. Don't you have more lessons to attend?"

"I'm so sick of hearing the same things over and over again," he groans. "Honestly, I've heard the history of Wonderland so often now that I can repeat it in my sleep. For example, did you know that White has been the key for years and years, far longer than anyone knows, but he was only chosen as a Son and the Time Keeper when you were chosen? Or that the Hatter was already a Son in all but name, because his father passed so long ago, and it was necessary for him to step into the duty. Wonderland waited until all three Sons were of age before she made it official."

"So, she was waiting on Cheshire?"

"And you." Alex tugs me closer to him. "You were worth the wait."

I laugh and wrap myself around him. We don't have long until we will be forced apart. The least we can do is enjoy the time we have.

"So, you thought to bring me to a broom closet and lecture me on the history of Wonderland?"

My hands slip beneath his tunic, searching for his warm skin. When I find it, the muscles jump beneath my fingers, tipped lightly with claws. Alex never complains; he seems to enjoy the feeling. Goosebumps rise on his flesh as I explore the planes of his stomach.

"There are other things I would like to do to you besides lecture."

A wicked smile tips his face, brighter than the thin gold circlet on his head. He's always required to wear the adornment around court. When he's King, he'll wear a larger one encrusted with jewels. I don't envy the weight that will always be on his head.

"Oh?" I raise my brow, teasing, as I grind my hips into his.

Today, I'm dressed in a flowing green dress, matching my stripes. Cheshire likes to tease that we both have an affinity for our own colors, and I can't deny it. I'm drawn to green just the same that Cheshire is drawn to his blue.

The dress makes for the perfect outfit when Alex pushes me back against the wall. My legs wrap around his waist, and the skirt slides up around my hips. His lips crash down on mine, desperate, as we take advantage of the stolen time we have. There's no telling how long before someone comes looking for the Prince, or before Wonderland calls me as the Hope Bringer. I'm barely unfastening his trousers before he's pushing my undergarments aside and pushing inside me. I gasp at the feeling, pressing my head against the wall when his lips find my neck, nipping along the sensitive flesh there.

"Alex," I groan, flexing my hips against his as he pumps inside of me, and we both climb higher. His hands grab at my ass, holding me up as he hits the sweet spot inside of me.

"Be my Queen," he groans against my neck, never slowing his pace, but his words surprise me, and I freeze.

"What?"

Sensing my unease, Alex slows his movements and comes to a stop, still nestled inside me. He draws back enough to meet my eyes. The love shining in his nearly kills me. My fingers clench at his shoulders.

"Be my Queen," he repeats, without hesitation.

"I can't." My words are no more than a whisper, moisture building in my eyes. How can he say that when he knows what our fates are to be? How can he ask me that right now in such an intimate position?

"Please, Dani. Just say yes."

"I'm the Hope Bringer." My voice is rough as I force the words out. "A Hope Bringer can't be the Queen."

"You can be both." His voice firm, he meets my eyes without flinching. "I've studied Wonderland for so long, all my life. She's nothing if not a supporter of love. Rules can be changed as long as two people love each other enough."

That damn hope blooms in my chest again, and I force it back.

"But your mother—"

"Can't decide for the soon-to-be King. Once I am crowned, I decide my destiny, and I'm choosing you, Danica. I'm choosing the Hope Bringer as my Queen."

The tears spill over my lashes with his words, seeking release. Happiness fills my body, a tiny smile curling my lips.

"Do you mean that?"

"Every word."

I bite my lip, uncertain but so full of hope I might burst. It can't be this easy, can it?

"I don't know what to say."

"Say yes," he chuckles, holding us still.

I look deep into his eyes, searching for the answers, knowing it won't so simple as that. We are two people who aren't supposed to end up together, but even as I think that thought, I can feel Wonderland's approval. Alex said she approves of love, so then how could she keep us apart when we're so determined to love one another? This feels right, and when a slight tingling begins in my chest, different from the call to duty, I grin and kiss Alex on the lips.

"Yes," I breathe out, and he begins to move inside me again.

This time, our coupling takes on a whole new meaning, and when we both reach our release, it feels as if nothing can come between us.

We're days away from the Coronation. We will have each other after all. We're taking on destiny, and we will win.

Happy tears flow freely down my face.

The day before the coronation, Cheshire and I decide to spend the day out in the trees. I haven't told him about Alex's and my plan, wanting it to be a surprise when it's announced in front of the whole kingdom. I'm not sure what he'll say, if he'll approve or hate us. I hope against everything that he'll be supportive, that he'll see how much we love each other and say, "Okay, I understand," but it can go either way when it comes to Cheshire. He could just as easily tell me all the things that can go wrong, all the problems we'll encounter, or that love is a lie. He could just as easily run.

Together, we move through the thick trees, practicing our stealth. While both of us were removed from our positions on the Queen's guard once we were chosen, we mutually agreed to keep up our skills. Extra strength and Dream Walker abilities can't allow me to grow complacent, no matter if they could give me the advantage. Everyone has weaknesses. Cheshire has one: his tendency to give into his emotions before he thinks things through. I have many: Alex, Cheshire, my compassion, and like my brother, emotions tend to get the better of me. We're working on making sure we don't have those weaknesses, but I doubt it'll ever be solved. We're just hardwired that way. My mom would say it's in our natures.

With that thought, as if my body lights up under electricity, the telltale tingles start in my finger tips and spreads far quicker up my arm than usual. I frown and flex my fist, trying to shake the feeling away. It never works, but that doesn't stop me from trying.

"Do you feel that?" Cheshire asks, hardly loud enough to hear. I see his forearm twitch under the same tingling sensation I have, the call catching both of us.

"Yes," I breathe, turning my face up to sense the air. "Something big is happening."

Cheshire stands taller, his ears twisting as he takes in the world around us. Mine do the same, listening to the sounds of the forests. Creatures caw around us, a discomfort felt throughout the land. Something runs through the underbrush behind us, something small. Far, far in the distance, a howl pierces the air, such sadness in the sound that I automatically clench my hand against my heart.

"We're being called," I whisper pointlessly. It's obvious something is wrong, and Wonderland needs the Hands of Justice and the Hope Bringer.

It almost feels different than all the other times we've been called, a sense of dread filling my body to the point of shivering. It makes me want to run, but that isn't my role. No, I must face whatever this is. At least I have Cheshire. His tail sways back and forth, my first sign that I'm not the only one that feels the difference.

"I don't think this is a normal calling." His whisper is so light, I barely catch it.

"Do you think it has to do with Alice's return?" There had been a few mumbles that the little girl from years ago had returned, but anything that reached our ears immediately fizzled out, as if someone willed it to stay secret. I wasn't worried before. Alex and I have had years to build our relationship, and we're going to be married soon. I expect a fight with the Queen at some point—the King and the Hope Bringer just aren't supposed to be together—but we're going to tackle that when it comes time. Perhaps, I should have been more worried.

Cheshire doesn't answer me, but he doesn't need to. As soon as the words leave my mouth, I know without a doubt that this calling deals with Alice somehow. Wonderland has a way of communicating through us, and she practically confirms the idea with a sharp stab of pain behind my ear. Suddenly, the whispers of Alice coming back full of hatred seem more real. Cheshire hadn't spoken to me about it when the whispers first began. I have a feeling he knows what Alice is, and that she's already done something wrong; that the little girl full of curiosity is no longer inside her. I hope that isn't the case. I hope I'm wrong, that the whispers were nothing more than nonsense.

The sharp stab of pain comes again.

Cheshire draws his sword, and I follow suit, pulling the strong blade from my back. Together, we Fade, Wonderland automatically pulling us in the direction we need to go. Slowly, we reappear in the castle gardens, and the scene that unfolds in front of us nearly brings me to my knees.

"How sweet of you to join me," Alice purrs, her new pitch-black eyes zeroing in on us. We both tense, and I force myself to raise my chin and face off against the monster in front of me. This can't be Alice, not this woman dressed in blood.

Cheshire is always meant to punish, but he typically waits until I attempt my powers. Today, he doesn't seem too concerned with waiting for me to give my verdict. It's obvious that Alice is no longer that little girl that came so long ago.

As a child, she used to be petite, so full of curiosity and life. Now, she stands before us older, a woman older than me, as if her world had moved faster than ours. Her skin is pale, her hair lighter than I remember. By far, the most noticeable difference is her eyes. They used to be a beautiful blue. Now, they're so black that they seem to absorb all light.

"Alice, what have you become?" I ask. My voice is strong, but I can't help the tiny twinge of sadness that leaks through. I mourn the loss of Alice, the girl that Alex used to call friend.

"I've become exactly who I'm meant to be," she replies, a smile curling her lips. Even her voice has changed, although it's still tinkling and girlish. Around us, bodies cover the ground, some very obviously my brethren from the guard, others so mutilated that it's hard to tell who they are. Their blood coats Alice's dress and body. Their blood paints the ground and drips from her lips.

"Where are the King and Queen?" Cheshire asks, his sword resting on his shoulder as if he could care less what's going on. I know different. He's coiled tension and can strike at any moment.

"Where's Alexander?" I add, my voice automatically coming out a hiss I can't hide. I'm not supposed to be angry, but I know she's done something horrible. We wouldn't have been called had that not been the case.

Her smile grows wider, and I see pointed teeth peek from the edge of her lips.

"The Prince is alive." Those eyes meet mine, and her gaze feels like spiders crawling across my skin. Her words don't put me at ease. "Although, I'm afraid he's rather lost himself. The King and Queen, well, they lost their heads."

"Where's Alex?" I ask again because she didn't truly answer my question. I can feel Cheshire glancing at me from the corner of his eye, but I ignore him. He won't understand. We've been trained to act first, to hide our emotions, to find all the information. I'm going against all our training, but still he prepares to fight by my side and follows my lead.

Alice keeps her eyes on me as she turns her head and calls over her shoulder, "Knave!"

'Knave?' Who is the Knave? And why does the name fill me such dread that my legs begin to shake.

Cheshire and I both hear the footsteps at the same time. We tense, prepared for whatever is coming, but nothing could have truly readied me. The man that steps out from behind Alice is dressed in the Prince's armor, though it's dented and dirty. One crystal-clear blue eye stares at me without emotion, and I gasp, involuntarily taking a step forward that Cheshire stops with his hand.

Alex looks all wrong, a sign of brutality that Wonderland hadn't called us for. Why had she waited? Half of the Prince's face is ripped away, including one eye. Red roses bloom in the mottled flesh, the flower reminding me of a memory from when we were children. Where Alex's heart should be, a similar wound appears, a gaping hole that should not be there. Alice runs a finger down the side of Alex's mutilated face, a touch he doesn't react to, as if he can't feel it at all.

Those blood-red roses stand out against my lover's pale skin, the same red as Alice's dress.

"What have you done to him?" I snarl, my sword raised.

She giggles, the sound so full of madness that it only intensifies my anger. It's the exact same giggle she'd had as a child, the same mocking sound I've always detested. It makes her feel like more of a threat, and Cheshire bends his knees in preparation, sensing the complete wrongness of the situation. Alex hardly spares us a glance, as if he doesn't recognize his best friends. That hurts the most.

"I don't think it's Alex anymore," Cheshire whispers, but I can't listen to those words. My face morphs into the absolute fury that fills me. That's the man I'm going to claim as mine tomorrow. That's the love of my life.

"What have you done to him?" I scream, my fingers turning white around my sword pommel.

"I've given him purpose," Alice finally answers, studying her nails. "And I'm tiring of this already. Knave, get rid of them."

Alex moves towards us without hesitation, his own sword pulling free of the sheath and prepared for battle. He wouldn't? Surely, Alex is still in there beneath Alice's spell.

My lover, my Alex attacks Cheshire first, his sword coming down so fast that Cheshire barely has time to block the killing blow that was aimed for his neck. I watch in horror as Alex swings his sword at my brother, at his childhood friend. There's no resistance at all in his eyes.

"You take him," Cheshire growls at me, shoving the Prince away. Alex hardly reacts besides a small stumble. "I'll take Alice."

I can see the look in Cheshire's eyes. Wonderland is calling for blood, his urge for punishment filling his body. Cheshire storms up to Alice, who barely bats an eye. She doesn't even flinch.

Alex turns towards me, the only other target around, and storms closer.

"Wake up, Alex," I say, dodging the sword he swings at me. I don't raise my own, determined to get through to him. "Wake up!"

I chance a quick look towards Cheshire who hesitates over Alice, very obviously not punishing her. What's going on? I dodge another swing.

I spin and roll away, and Alex follows, his movements so much smoother than they'd been before whatever Alice has done. He'd never been the best fighter, so how is he keeping up with my movements now? This is wrong. This is all wrong. I narrowly miss another swing and stumble backwards. He keeps coming, keeps advancing, and he never hesitates.

"Wake up! Alex, wake up!" I cry, agony in my voice. I can't raise my sword against him. I can't kill the man I've given my heart to, no matter what Alice has done to him.

"What are you doing?" Cheshire snarls at me, but I ignore him. I won't kill him. I can't.

"Knave," Alice calls, and Alex turns his blue eye to her, waiting for her command. "End her."

"No," Cheshire growls, jumping from the dais and running towards me, but I know he will never reach us in time. He can't, no matter how fast he is.

Everything slows around me, as if Wonderland is determined to draw this moment out as long as possible. A flash of panic crosses Alex's eye, but it's gone so fast, I don't know if I truly saw it. He's in there, somewhere, and I won't raise my weapon. Slowly, Alex lifts his own sword, and I watch, realizing exactly what this is.

"Protect yourself!" Cheshire snarls. "Move! Danica, move!"

We were never meant to be, Alex and I, but I'm glad that for a moment we were. Destinies are funny things, our fate already decided for us by a being we have no true knowledge of. I can feel the certainty in my bones, that this moment has been preordained since before I was born, that my life was never my own, that I was never meant to be the Hope Bringer for long.

I was never going to be allowed to marry the King.

Tears slip over my lashes as I meet Alex's single blue eye, and my grip loosens on my sword. It's useless because everything has already been decided. Wonderland, in her cruel way, has decided that I must die at the hands of the man I love, and I have to believe that it's for some greater cause. Still, I try one more time.

"Alex, wake up. You have to wake up. Please." I clench my hand into a fist and lower my voice. "Alex, I love you. Please, just know that

I love you." Recognition flashes in Alex's eye for a moment, and hope fills my body.

It's only another cruel trick. The Hope Bringer must hope, even when it's futile.

"Danica!" Cheshire screams, still too far away, still moving in slow motion as the Prince thrusts the royal sword towards my sternum. "Move!"

Alice's laughter fills the air, taunting, and I hope that Cheshire kills the bitch for what she's done.

I don't feel the sword slice through my body, but I gasp at the coldness that explodes outward around it. Even though I saw it coming, I'm still shocked when I look down at the sword protruding from me, Alex's hand still wrapped around the hilt flush with my skin. The cold gets so intense that I can hardly stand it, and my lip trembles when I look up again at the man standing over me, against me, the one I gave my heart to. His clear eye meets mine, and there's sadness there; there's horror, that's replaced with indifference far too quickly, my Alex losing the battle to Alice's influence.

"No!" Cheshire screams, his arms catching me just as my sword drops from my fingers, and I collapse. Alex backs away, leaving me in my brother's arms. "What's wrong with you?" Cheshire shouts at Alex, his anger so potent that I can feel it through the overwhelming chill wracking my body. Alex stumbles back another step at his outburst, a single tear running down his face. It's the only sign I need, that he's still in there, that there's a chance someone can save him. The emotion is wiped clean from his face just as quickly, and the man I love backs away, nothing more than a dog for the Queen to command.

There's a tickle at the corner of my lips, and I know it for the bad sign it is. I've seen what happens when a person is killed with a sword. It isn't pretty. My body starts to shut down, and I mourn the loss of so many things. I will never get to marry Alex, to openly claim him as my own, as he would me. I won't be there to see the crown placed on his head or fight his mother for the right to marry him in the first place. I won't be there beside Cheshire to offer hope, and I know he'll blame himself, and that he'll give in to his emotions.

"Wake up, Alex," I breathe, my voice rattling in my chest. "Alex, wake up." It's hard to focus, my eyes staring unseeing into the dark sky even as Cheshire shakes beneath me.

Don't cry, brother, I want to say. I want to say so many things, but it's getting harder and harder to breath.

"Danica," Cheshire grunts, and something wet drips on my face. My own eyes leak tears from the corner of my eyes, agonized over leaving Cheshire in this madness, leaving him when he needs me most. "I'll kill you, if it's the last thing I do, I'll rip your head clean from your body." Cheshire must be talking to Alice, I think, and it's confirmed when her laughter reaches my ears. It's muted, as if I'm in a tunnel, but still, I hear it.

"Good luck, Grimalkin. Come along, Knave." I can't hear what else she says, my body shutting down against my will.

The only thing I'm aware of after that is shaking beneath me, Cheshire fighting his emotions, attempting to stop the flow of blood from my chest. It's a comfort to have him here with me in these final moments, and I wish I can tell him that I love him, that I'm sorry for all the pain this is causing. I wish I could explain everything.

My heart gives a harsh throb inside my chest, and I know it's the time. This is it. I will be led into the Here After by the Hatter, doomed to watch whatever horror that will unfold while I'm gone. The only thing I can do, before my heart gives out completely, is meet Cheshire's glowing eyes.

"Cheshire . . .," I breathe, barely forcing the words out, before everything darkens around me, and I'm ripped away from my body.

Brother, do not mourn for me, for I am merely the first step in your fate.

Lover, do not give up, for I am waiting for you on the other side.

Alice, you do not know what destruction you have unleashed, or what you have brought upon yourself.

I am the Hope Bringer that was brave enough to love the Future King. Hope is never gone, and though I may be, I will wait for punishment to be brought down on your head.

My Prince, we were never meant to be, never meant to love or to live, but I'm thankful that, for a moment, we were together.

For a moment, we were happy.

THE PRINCE & HIS HOPE

"Danica, wake up . . ."
I'm sorry, brother . . .

THE FLAMINGO AND THE DODO BIRD

KENDRA MORENO

THE FLAMINGO AND THE DODO BIRD

Their story was one that was revered around Wonderland. Follow the tale of how they met, and how two creatures completely at odds fell in love.

Chapter 11

DODO

"Have you heard the latest news?"

I have to physically fight myself to keep from rolling my eyes at my mother. The old bird loves a good rumor, no matter whose expense it's at. My mother is the resident rumor mill in our section of the forest, and she always seems to know exactly what's going on. Sometimes, I find myself curious how she finds the information, wondering what she's traded for it, but I dismiss it quickly. The moment I try to understand my mother is the moment I become her. I have no desire to turn into the Keeper of Secrets.

"No, mother, and I do not wish to." I don't even look up from the book I'm reading to discourage further discussion. As usual, it doesn't work.

"It's about that Flamingo lad. You know the rumors about his parentage, don't you?"

I do, but I don't say so. To speak of it might bring Wonderland down on my head. Some things were best left to be forgotten. My mother, however, takes my silence as waiting for her to continue. I almost groan when she starts to speak again.

"The poor dear had the loveliest Flamingo for a mother but somehow, the gentle thing took a liking to a Jabberwocky. Nasty creatures if you ask me. I remember the uproar when they became an item, before the Jabberwockies were wiped from the land. It was absolute blasphemy when they had a child together."

"Why are you telling me all of this, mother?" I can't help the curiosity at the mention of the Flamingo. Even though I try not to, I hear the rumors. Most of them come from my friends that talk of how beautiful he is, like a warrior dressed in the colors of his mother. His birth may have been blasphemy, but from the rumors, none of that had touched his appearance. I've been curious but have, so far, not encountered him. That's probably because I don't frequent the same parties as my friends. No, I prefer the solitude of books to the uproarious Wonderland gatherings. My mother, however, attends every single one. The Hatter's tea loosens lips, after all.

"Because he's, apparently, making a name for himself, and not a good one. Some say he's developed the brutality of his father and his mother's inner turmoil."

"Which would make him a walking juxtaposition."

"Exactly. He's brutal, but only when necessary. I've heard he never lifts his fist for the sake of doing so. It seems there are many who judge him for his lineage, and those are the ones who he gets in altercations with."

"Can you blame him? The creatures of Wonderland can be cruel."

"I never said I blame him," my mother chides. She collects rumors, but she never twists them. She never likes anyone putting words into her mouth. "I was simply stating what seems to be going on around him."

I nod my head at her and return my gaze to the book in my lap, but I'm no longer reading the words, even after my mother leaves me in peace. Perhaps, I should attend one of the parties, after all. I hear the Flamingo likes to frequent such things, even if he always leaves with a new bruise or split lip.

He sounds like a creature I should steer clear of, and yet, I find myself lingering on the circumstances that brought him into this world.

What would a man be with the brutality of a Jabberwocky, and the gentleness of a Flamingo?

Dangerous. That man would be dangerous.

Chapter

FLAMINGO

"What the fuck did you just say to me?" I growl. The bulky creature in front of me snorts at my question, his tusks standing proud and intricate in front of his face. His kind carves details into their tusks when they achieve a life event. This man has many carvings, but none of a warrior. Why he thinks he can pick a fight with me, I don't understand, but I won't allow for such things to be said about my mother.

"I said, your mother was a fucking idiot creating an abomination like you." He's completely confident in his words, even as his friends take a step back. Their eyes dart between the tattoos covering my skin and their friend still standing tall and proud on one side of the bonfire.

Tonight was supposed to be fun, relaxing even. Come out to the Dancing of the Stars, watch the celestial beings get brighter and put on a show in the sky, maybe go home with a lovely creature at the end of the night. Instead, I've barely joined the party, can't even take a drink of the Hatter's tea, and this fucking asshole is making comments about my mother, a woman he's never met. He doesn't know me, nor my parents, so why do so many think that gives them a right to judge at all?

"You can call me an abomination all you want," I say, grinning. "I'll still go home with a pretty little number that you wish you could get."

But, if you ever mention my mother again, I'll rip the tongue from your throat."

His friends take another step back, panic in their eyes. So, they've heard the rumors then? Unfortunately for their friend, he didn't seem to get the memo. He takes a step forward, his oddly lined eyes meeting mine.

"I'm glad the bitch and your monster of a father are dead. I'd kill them myself if I could. Hell, I'll gladly kill you."

Around us, creatures party, laugh, joke as if nothing is happening, but those close enough can sense the growing tension. My powers have gone unchecked for so long, growing more difficult to control each day, but I try my best to keep the powers from snaking out and stroking down the arms of the creatures around us. Now isn't the time to transform into my other form. It would be a real mood killer. But I can't let his comment go unchecked. More and more creatures have come forward and made similar remarks, and I've made them all pay. I don't care if it's useless, if their opinions never change, if I prove them right. All I care about is that they don't say them to me. My mother was a fucking saint who tamed a monster. There was nothing wrong with her even if I'm everything wrong born from their match.

"You're gonna regret saying that, Swine."

I don't have to attack the warthog-like man. He lunges towards me first, as if he can catch me off guard. He's a fucking idiot. I may be wearing the colors of my mother, but I am far from her cordial nature. I'm already moving to the side before the man's fist can swing where my face used to be. He doesn't play around, going right for my jaw. Pity he's so slow.

I don't waste time. I throw my own fist towards his abdomen, knocking the air from his lungs. The action leaves my face open, and that's my mistake. I expect his friends to stay out of it. Instead, they jump in when I'm not looking, thinking they have a better chance with numbers, and attack. One of their fists catches me on the mouth, splitting my lip until I taste blood. It does nothing but piss me off; it certainly doesn't actually harm me. Only cowards try to overtake a man and protect their stupidity with numbers.

It devolves into a mess of fists and leather jackets. Their hits are easy enough to shake off, their strength far less than mine, but I get annoyed with the situation quickly. Why the fuck am I even doing this anymore? Mother would be so upset with me for fighting these men for her honor when she's gone. *People will think what they want, Flam. Let them. You cannot change everyone's minds. The only one that matters is what you think of yourself.* Her words flicker through my mind, and I pause mid-swing, which is exactly the wrong thing to do. The three idiots think I'm tiring and attack all at once, knocking me from my feet and raining down punches that barely hurt. I sigh. Is this really all they've got? It's sad, so very sad.

"Enough," I growl, shoving them all away as if they weigh no more than a feather. "I tire of this game."

They look at me, confused, as I wipe the blood from my chin. Fucking warthogs can't even make me bleed correctly.

"I'm gonna kick your ass," lead dumbass snorts, taking a step towards me.

I pull myself to my feet and dust off my leather jacket, making sure it isn't torn from the small scuffle.

"Run along before I really get angry." I meet his eyes, knowing my own glow with my father's powers of influence. It doesn't work on everyone, but it always does on weaker minds. Lead dumbass is definitely affected by it. He immediately spins on his heel and walks away, as if he didn't just start a fight with one of the most dangerous creatures in Wonderland. Not by choice, though. No, I'm not dangerous by choice.

My powers won't stop growing. Pretty soon, I'll have to go ask the King and Queen for help, or Wonderland will decide my fate for me. I don't want to disappoint my mother, even if she's no longer here to be disappointed.

The creatures who had been watching the fight all conveniently look away when I glance towards them, pretending as if nothing happened, pretending as if I'm not a monster in their midst. It's easy to ignore the danger with a good cup of tea in your hands.

But not everyone looks away from me, and the feeling of being watched tingles down my spine. Who dares to stare at the Flamingo?

I turn, searching for the culprit, and find only a single person. I think my heart stops when her eyes meet mine, when her lips part on a breath as she takes me in. For once, I puff up at the attention, and the urge to slide my leather jacket from my shoulders to give her a real show hits me strong. Normally, I would ignore the thought, not that I've had it that often. My jacket is one of my pride and joys; it's not meant to be thrown around. That doesn't stop me from slowly sliding it from my arms, revealing corded muscles, before I drape it over my shoulder. A satisfied hum fills my throat when her eyes follow the movement, taking me all in. Who is this creature that dares to tempt the Flamingo?

She's far enough away that I can't see the color of her eyes, but the color of the feathers threaded through her hair stand out in sharp relief. Every color imaginable flashes in the light of the bright stars and the bonfire. Beautiful. She's the most beautiful creature I've ever seen.

I take a step towards her, expecting her to run, but she meets my eyes, unflinching. Her chin tips up when I take another, her graceful fingers closed around a book. Slowly, I make my way through the already drunken crowd, expecting her to turn and run at any moment. Most would with the intensity in my eyes. I can feel that they're glowing pink in the darkness. Creatures in my way hurry to move from my path.

I give her plenty of time to change her mind, waiting for her to turn away, but she never does. Her eyes are so full of curiosity; I wonder what she's curious about. I wonder if I can bring more emotions to her eyes other than that.

I stop a few feet in front of her and look into her eyes. We're nearly the same height, her long legs hidden beneath a pale-pink dress. How appropriate that she wears a version of my color.

"I think I've died and gone to the Here After," I say, studying her face. "How else could someone so beautiful be standing in front of me?"

When she snorts and laughs, I nearly purr with pleasure. I want her to laugh again. She shakes her head at the look on my face, her eyes scanning my body.

"You still have blood on your knuckles, and you dare to come up and proposition me?" Her voice is soft, tinkling, and strong. She doesn't back down from me one bit. I like it entirely too much.

I glance down at my knuckles and see the blood she speaks of. It's of no consequence. I really don't care about the warthogs. I take another step forward.

"It's not a proposition," I whisper, a grin on my face. The corner of her lip curls the tiniest amount. "When I proposition you, you'll know it, little bird."

"Is that how you've gotten other women before?" Her words catch me off-guard but don't really surprise me when I think about it. Of course, she's different. Of course, she can't be won with pretty words.

"Yes," I answer honestly, "but it seems I've made a mistake. You're far too special for such lines. Would you like me to try again?"

A full smile spreads across her lips then, and she tilts her head to study me. "If you think you can do better, sure. Let's hear it."

I step closer, and she gasps when our bodies come within centimeters of each other. I lean down, closing the slight distance between us, to whisper into her ear.

"I came here tonight to watch the stars dance, and instead, I find that their beauty is far lacking compared to yours. I long to stroke my finger down your thighs and see if I can make you shine far more brightly than they do on this night." I don't touch her, not without her permission, but I get as close as possible. She doesn't push me away, and I revel in the skipping of her breath at my words. She's not nearly as unaffected as she plays, and I long to have her let go completely with me.

"That's a good line," she whispers, pulling back enough to meet my eyes.

I smile devilishly, tempted to steal a kiss, but I refrain. That would be far too quick. "I can do one better." I wink at her. "I'm gonna call you my wife one day."

She laughs, the sound so deep and full of mirth that I find my own smile spreading. If she was beautiful when she smiles, she's perfect when she laughs. Determination fills me. I want her, but more than that, I want her heart.

"The Flamingo is charming," she says once she calms her laughter.

"Who would have thought you could be such after you barely stopped yourself from beating those three creatures into the dirt?" There's no judgement in her eyes. In fact, there only seems to be understanding, and it's the first time I've ever encountered such emotions towards me. Oh yes, she's very different. "Alas, I think you'll have to keep dreaming on the wife dreams." She winks at me, and it's far more awkward than mine, as if she's never done it before. It only endears her to me more. "Keep working on your lines, Flock Boy."

She turns and starts to walk away, leaving me there in the midst of drunken creatures.

"I didn't catch your name!" I shout, loud enough to be heard over the party. She merely turns and looks at me over her shoulder. A smile curls her lips, but she doesn't answer me, a teasing glint in her eye. It's not an issue. Someone is bound to know who she is. She cuts through the crowd like she owns the place and disappears into the forest.

I stand there for a long time after, staring at the space she left, wishing I could chase after her, but knowing I shouldn't. A Flamingo doesn't just chase down a woman he likes against her wishes. That's what a Jabberwocky would do. I'm just as much my mother's son as I am my father's, so I leave the party, ignoring the judging eyes and the harsh comments, and prepare to enter the long hunt.

I hear her name from a passing creature, the Dodo bird, the daughter of the Mockingbird.

That night, for the first time in a while, I don't have nightmares brought on by my powers.

No, I dream of iridescent feathers of every color imaginable.

DODO

My mother drags me along with her to her meetings, even though I told her I have things to do. Her answer is always a quick "your books can wait" before she drags me from my cottage and to the castle.

The Queen has a penchant for secrets, a fact I was surprised to learn. As much as her majesty likes to hoard them herself, apparently, she always likes to trade secrets with mother, too. Honestly, these meetings are always so tiresome, and I despise them. The only reason mother brings me is because she hopes that some noble man will see me standing there and propose. Unfortunately for her, I keep my attention off the men who throw me any sort of glance and instead wander away from the Queen's hushed excitement about some new secret. I have no desire to stick around, so under my mother's disapproving gaze, I walk casually in the direction of the hedge maze. I won't be going inside of it–I've spent too often between the hedges that I've memorized which ways to go–but I do take up my position on the edge of a large fountain. The statue in the center is a depiction of the King and Queen, their regal looks forever set in stone. They hold a heart in their hands that water flows from, lending the area a soothing ambience. I grin as I sneak the book from my skirt that my mother had tried to get me to leave behind. She didn't think to look for pockets in my dress. She should know better.

I open the pages and dive into a different world, the waters trickling behind me relaxing me so much, the world fades away.

"What are you reading?" I startle so violently that I drop the book and slide from the concrete seat. I would have slammed my tailbone into the ground if it isn't for the strong arms that wrap around me, saving me from the pain. "Whoa, I didn't mean to scare you."

I look up into the eyes of the man holding me up and take a deep breath. The Flamingo smiles, his bright-pink eyes glowing with mirth at my predicament.

"What are you doing here?" I ask, gently prying his arms from around my waist and settling on the stone bench again. I glance over his shoulder towards my mother and the Queen. The former glances over at us in curiosity, her eyes taking in every detail. I clear my throat and rearrange my skirt around me. "Nevermind. That was rude of me to ask."

"I don't mind," he replies, taking a seat beside me. He's close but not so close as to be improper. Does he realize my mother and the Queen are watching us? "I had an audience with the King and Queen. When I came outside, preparing to leave, I saw the loveliest creature sitting all alone and thought I should give her some company."

I raise my brow. "I wasn't alone." I hold my book up. "I have a whole host of people to keep me company."

"Would you like me to leave?" His eyes linger on the book for a moment before meeting mine. I can tell, if I say yes, he'll get up without protest.

I shake my head. "You don't have to leave." I set my novel aside and turn so that I can speak to him without craning my neck. He watches my movements, pleased with my decision. He turns slightly so that our knees are almost touching. Perhaps, I should move away? "What can I help you with Flamingo?"

"Flam," he corrects. "And I'm just here for the pleasure of your company, Doe."

"You did your research." I should be concerned about that, but I can't help the pleasure that fills me knowing I made enough of an impression that he searched for my name.

"Does that concern you?"

"It was easy enough to find out, I'm sure. There's no need to be concerned." I can see my words affect him in some way, as if he expected me to be upset, but I don't know why. Do people really get frightened if the Flamingo knows their name? He doesn't seem like he goes looking for fights. They seem to find him instead. "Tell me something, Flam," I start, staring deeply into his fuchsia-colored eyes. They're really a gorgeous color. "Why did you bother to find out my name in the first place?"

A grin full of mischief pulls at his lips, and it lights up his face in ways I never expected. I feel my heart skip a beat in answer, and I clench my hands tightly in my skirts. Dangerous, indeed.

"I told you that I'm going to marry you."

"I'm certain you say that to all your lovers."

Flam reaches forward, forgoing what is proper, and untangles my hand from my skirts. He smooths my fingers out, rubbing the tension away gently, before he raises my hand to his lips and presses a lingering kiss against my skin. It should have been innocent enough, but when his lips make contact, my thighs clench tight, and I can't help but imagine his mouth in other places.

"I didn't believe I would ever get married. Most are only curious before they run. I'm too much of a monster."

"I don't think you're a monster, at all," I whisper, hyper aware of his fingers still holding mine.

"The thing is, I'm exactly what they think I am." I open my mouth to argue, but he shakes his head. "I've come to terms with who I am, and before now, I thought I was content to live life alone." His thumb strokes gently against the back of my hand. "I'm not ashamed to say I'm smitten."

"You don't even know me." I wrinkle my brow. "I could be some sort of creature that kills you in your sleep."

Flam laughs, a full-bellied booming laugh that makes him so beautiful, I'm tempted to move closer. There's something about the Flamingo that draws me to him, that makes me want to continue making him laugh.

"You know what?" he says when he calms his mirth. "I'm perfectly willing to take that risk."

"I could kill you if I wanted." I smile, raising my brow at him.

"I have no doubt about that." And then he completely catches me off guard when he leans forward and presses a kiss against my cheek. It's fast, too fast to react to, but it still sends a tingle through my body. "Meet me at the Queen's Garden Party," he whispers in my ear.

"And if I say no?" I breathe, drawing back enough to meet his eyes.

"Don't say no."

My eyes drop to his full lips for a moment before looking back up into his eyes. I consider saying no, anyway. I don't particularly like the garden parties because my mother takes the opportunity to pair me with every eligible man willing to dance. But something inside of me urges me to say yes. Perhaps, it's just curiosity, but I have a feeling it's something more. The Flamingo is intriguing, and my mother would never approve, but I can't help but want him, anyway.

"Yes," I whisper just as my mother bids the Queen goodbye and starts to cross the garden towards us. "Now go, before the Mockingbird tries to wrangle secrets from your lips."

Those lips curl up in answer, and he places them against my hand again. "I'll meet you there." His eyes flick over to my mother drawing closer. "Wear something pink." And then he releases me and stands, leaving just in time for my mother to arrive, a frown on her face.

"You looked very cozy with the Flamingo, dear." I don't answer, just clench my book in my lap. Her eyes go right to it. "And I see you managed to sneak that with you as well."

"I find him fascinating," I comment, watching the pink leather of his jacket as he slips into the woods. He turns back once, catching my stare, grinning at me as if we share a secret. He winks and disappears into the trees, gone faster than I can follow.

"As long as it's only fascination. You need a proper husband."

"Who are we to decide if he's proper or not?" I comment, but mother is already going on about something else, talking about things she learned from the Queen.

"We've been invited to be guests of honor for the Queen's Garden

Party," she continues. "We need to have a dress made for you. Something lovely. Which color do you prefer this time?"

I think on Flam's words, how he wants me to wear his colors, but I'm nothing if not difficult, and I don't take orders from anyone, even a handsome Flamingo. "Black," I respond. "I want my dress to be black."

After all, the Flamingo has more than one color to his name.

Chapter 4

FLAMINGO

I feel out of place at the Queen's Garden Party even though I'm surrounded by creatures far more outrageous-looking than I am, but I don't let my discomfort show as I lean against a stone pillar, watching the creatures arrive. I'm nervous, and it's something I'm not really used to. I've never been nervous for a woman before, or really at all, but there's something about the Dodo bird that calls to some primal beast in me. I'm barely able to contain myself when she's around, and I'm not certain if that's a good thing to encourage or not, but I don't really care.

There's a break in the crowd as the trumpet sounds, alerting everyone that someone new has arrived. I try not to look too eager as I watch carefully. The Mockingbird enters first, her lithe form wrapped in a purple dress. She smiles pleasantly at everyone she passes, no doubt excited about the secrets she'll learn tonight. They say if you have a secret to keep, never speak it out loud, or the Mockingbird will know. She has her ways. If she wasn't such an iron lock when it came to those secrets, she would be considered a threat, but she only tells the secrets that are trivial or that are a threat to Wonderland. I can't help but respect her for that.

Doe follows slowly behind her, a nice enough smile on her face as she greets the people around her; it's nice but fake. The Dodo bird doesn't seem to have much patience for such events as these. I glance down her body and realize with a start that she's not wearing pink at all. No, she wears the color of my father instead, of the other side of me. I stiffen at the sight of the black dress, frowning when I realize I like her just as much in the color as much as I do pink.

When her eyes lock on me, I smooth my expression out and let a tiny smile curl my lips. She says something to her mother, and makes her way in my direction. My eyes fall to the slit in the black material, a good portion of her leg is revealed with each stride. My body hums to life. She doesn't wear any ornamentation around her slender neck, no earrings on her ears. No, the Dodo bird is plenty radiant with the rainbow feathers threaded throughout her hair.

She stops a few feet before me and smiles. "Hello, Flam," she whispers. I shouldn't be able to hear her, not with the bustle of the party around us, but her words vibrate through me just the same.

"You're wearing black." My eyes trail her body, taking in the shape of her waist where the dress curves inward. The skirt touches the grass, the whole outfit fitting the dress code easily. She shifts a little bit on her feet and a tempting bit of skin appears between the slit again. My hand twitches at my side.

"I'm wearing black," she repeats, a twinkle in her eyes. "After all, pink isn't your only color."

"It's the only color I claim." I've long rebuked anything representing my father. My mother fell in love with the brute, and he loved her completely, but he wasn't as gentle with his son or anyone else. No, it was best that he died in the extermination. I just wish my mother hadn't followed him into the Here After.

"I'm also not a pushover," she says, interrupting my thoughts. "You can request I wear a color, sure, but I am my own person, and I'll wear whatever I want. Besides," she grins, "I think you rather like this dress on me."

Bold, so bold, the Dodo bird is, and yet, she shies away from other people. She's a walking contradiction, a puzzle I want to figure out.

I reach forward slowly, waiting for her to slap my hand away or back up. She doesn't, meeting my gaze boldly, so I continue forward and wrap my fingers around her hip. I tug her towards me, perhaps a little too rough, and she trips the smallest amount, falling against my chest. I'm required to wear a shirt for the Queen's party—everyone is—and I'm damning that fact when I can't feel her against my skin. We're surrounded by people, many of their eyes on us as we stand far too close to be proper in their eyes, but that doesn't stop me from dropping my other hand out of sight and finding the opening in the dress. I lean down and touch my lips to the shell of her hair, smiling when I feel her breath shake.

"I never said I don't like the dress," I whisper roughly, my fingers gently trailing along the skin of her upper thigh slowly, always giving her a chance to move away. "Such a risqué choice, little bird. Did you have plans of seduction tonight?"

Her nails pierce through my shirt and draw the smallest amount of blood on my chest. The feeling makes me growl softly, wishing that we weren't at this party, that we weren't being watched by the Mockingbird and the Queen.

"Perhaps, I did," she responds, her words so low, I barely catch them. She leans away then, looking up into my eyes. She doesn't seem to know how many people are watching us; that, or she doesn't care. "Would you like to dance with me?"

I raise my brow. "What makes you think that the Flamingo dances?"

"I've heard you're a beautiful dancer," she chuckles, smoothing her hand against the tiny pinpricks of red on my shirt, a little distressed about the stain. I clamp my hand over hers, right over the marks.

"I don't mind wearing your marks," I tell her, my voice not so soft this time. Someone near us, a lizard creature, gasps and stares at us with wide eyes before scurrying off.

"Now, look what you did," she chides, a smile pulling at her lips. "You've devastated that poor woman's sensibilities."

"Then let her be devastated." I don't wait for Doe to move to the dance floor. I simply spin her where we stand, before I dip her low enough that her leg automatically curls around my hip to steady herself. Her dress falls away, revealing her bare skin, and I run my hand along the smoothness there before hooking my fingers behind her knee. Her lashes drop a little as she meets my eyes.

"Please keep in mind my mother is in attendance, pretty bird."

She's teasing me, and damn it all to Wonder, it stirs my body in ways I never expected. I growl and stand her on her feet again before leading her towards the dance floor. "I'm not pretty." I clamp my hand around her waist like expected before seamlessly moving us among the other waltzing couples. She was correct about me being able to dance. My mother made sure to teach me everything I would need to know to be a gentleman. Too bad my lineage was the only thing she couldn't change.

"I think you're beautiful." Doe grins up at me, following my lead like the good girl she is. I have a feeling she's not quite so good as her mother wants her to be. "There's no reason to be ashamed."

"Handsome, maybe. Sensual, definitely. I think most people would argue your comment."

"Only because they're idiots." My eyes snap to hers from where I'd glanced towards her mother. I can feel the Mockingbird's eyes on us with every step. "Those who think you anything less than glorious only fear the unknown. Fear does no one any good."

I pull her closer to me, ignoring the etiquette. "Are you not afraid of me, little bird?"

She shakes her head, squeezing my hand in answer. "What have I to be afraid of," she pauses, a smile curling her lips, "pretty bird?"

"You've heard of my exploits, I've no doubt." I glance up again. This time, it feels as if every eye is upon us. I try my best not to tense at their gazes, but it's difficult with so many. They range in different emotions—curiosity, confusion, and anger. It seems some of them don't think I should be dancing with the Dodo bird.

"I've heard many things about you, Flam." She shrugs. "That has nothing to do with fear. I don't fear you because you've given me nothing to fear. Would you hurt me?"

"Not intentionally." My powers have gotten stronger, almost too difficult to control at times. Sometimes, I go too far in the fights. Sometimes, I regret that I can't be more like my mother and turn the other way.

"Exactly." She releases my shoulder, and her fingers gently cup my cheek, turning my gaze back to hers. "I do not fear death, Flam. I only fear not living."

My nostrils flare. There's too much in her eyes, too much understanding, and I can see how my father fell in love with my mother. It felt good for someone to look at me that way, to not judge me based on things I can't control. If my mother looked at him the same, I know how she tamed the beast.

"He's an abomination," someone behind us whispers, not quiet enough for my sensitive ears to miss. "Should have been put down as a babe."

I growl, preparing to turn, but Doe clamps both hands around my face, keeping me focused on her and nothing else. My hands clench hard at her waist as I try to control the anger in my blood, but she doesn't even flinch.

"I heard he acts just like his father. Nothing but a leech."

My body hums, eager for my power to release, but Doe keeps my eyes trained on her, her fingers strong on my face.

"No one can make you feel unworthy except for you," she whispers, keeping the words just between us. "You are perfect the way you are, Flam. Their words mean nothing."

So, she heard it, too. I take a deep breath and nod my head, focused on her bottomless dark eyes. She keeps me grounded, and I find my anger slowly shrink. I realize we're not dancing anymore, and I start to swing us side to side, ignoring the other couples still waltzing around us.

"Girl is stupid if you ask me. The Dodo Bird must be nothing more than a harlot for hanging out with the abomination. No desirable man will have her when she associates with that lowlife." The voice is definitely female, and the offending woman is standing right behind me.

I snarl, and Doe's fingers clench hard around my face. My hands raise up to her wrists, grabbing gently, prepared to move her before I turn. "It's okay," she says. "Flam, it's okay. I've never cared what people thought of me."

"They'll keep your name out of their mouths," I bite. I'm careful not to hurt her as I move her wrists and spin on my feet, meeting the eyes of a woman with small goat horns curling elegantly around her curls. She stares at me for a moment, her eyes widening when she realizes I was able to hear her. I can't help the roar that comes out of my mouth, the sound so un-flamingo-like that it startles everyone around us. The music stops, the party guests turn and stare, as the goat woman scrambles backwards, away from me as the ground shakes. Silence fills the garden, and shame floods me. Their eyes tell me the words that always pass their lips—abomination, heathen, lowlife. If I continue to pursue the Dodo bird, she'll be subjected to the same looks.

Doe laughs, the sound so full of mirth, that I turn to her in confusion. And then the rest of the guests join in, happy to let the tension pass. The music starts back up again, and everyone returns to their tea.

"Are you laughing at me?" I ask, my chest rising and falling rapidly with anger at the goat woman.

Doe grins at me, wrapping the fingers of one hand through mine and threading her others into the hair at the base of my neck. My free hand falls to her waist automatically as we begin to move again. "Would you punish me if I said yes?" she asks. Her nails curl at the base of my skull, tugging gently. She leans forward, close, so no one else can hear her next words. "Would you kiss me if I said the sound of your roar made me tingle?"

I stop moving completely and look down at her, tilting my head. My eyes flick to the maze just to the right of us, and I'm dragging her that way so suddenly that she trips. I don't wait for her to get her footing again; I scoop her off the ground and move swiftly into the hedges, taking turn after turn until the sounds of the garden party fade away. When I step into a small sitting area, I stop and set her on her feet.

She laughs, but I don't let her say anything. I jerk the Dodo bird against my chest hard and claim her lips in hunger. She mews against my mouth in surprise but doesn't back down. No, the Dodo bird tries to dominate me much the same I try to dominate her. I twist my fingers into her hair, careful not to pull her feathers as I angle her mouth for better access. My other hand falls to her ass as she hooks her leg around my waist. *I should slow*, I think, *romance her more*, but my body hums with pleasure at her taste of ripe blackberries and something tangy. Need slams through my body.

I break the kiss to trail down her neck, nipping against her skin. "I don't think your mother approves of us talking to each other."

"I don't care," Doe groans. "Wonder, I don't care." She moans when I latch onto the joining of her neck and throat and suck gently against her skin.

"I'm sorry I lost my temper."

"It's okay," she chuckles, grinding her hips against mine. "Who would have thought the Flamingo could roar?"

I freeze, my jaw clenching against her skin before I pull away and look into her eyes. She looks at me with those dark hooded eyes, her lips parted on a sigh. Gently, I uncurl her leg from around my hip and set her on her feet. She stumbles, and I steady her to keep her from falling. And then I back away.

"Flam?" She frowns, reaching towards me, but I avoid her fingers. "Where are you going?"

Sadness fills me, shame taking over, and I take another step back. Here's this glorious creature, drunk on my words, and she doesn't even understand that she's let a monster kiss against her flesh. A single twist of my wrist, a small shred of my control slips, and she will die. She jokes as if she doesn't understand the beast I truly am.

"You know why I can roar, little bird," I whisper, sliding my mask into place. I should stay away, no matter how badly my heart beats at that thought, how badly I want her to keep looking at me in wonder. "I have to go."

Her eyes open completely at my words, the desire gone from her eyes. I immediately want to chase away the hurt she tries, and fails, to hide. "What?"

"I have to go," I repeat, my voice hard. "You're too beautiful to clip your wings."

And then I turn and flee to the trees, trying my hardest to ignore her cry, her reaching fingers, the confusion in her voice. I try to tell myself that it's for the best. . . .

But I fail at that, too.

Chapter 5

DODO

Five days later, I turn the page on my book but I'm not really reading the words. I haven't been able to sink into a good book since the Queen's Garden Party, my mind stuck on the image of the Flamingo backing away from me in shame. I'd tried to go after him, but he was far too clever, disappearing much faster than I can run, and I'm the fastest in Wonderland.

Sighing, I drop the book on a table and stand, stretching my body out. Perhaps a bit of painting will keep my mind from fuchsia-colored eyes and tattooed skin.

The sky today is clear, not bright—Wonderland is never sunny like other worlds—but still plenty of light to see by. While the stars might not be out, like at night, some light source keeps our world from being pitch black.

I set up my easel and canvas away from my cottage, beneath the shade of a tree, and dip my brush into paint. I start with long strokes, blending colors together, losing my mind in the process of art. My mother thinks that it's a great skill to have to obtain a husband. She doesn't realize that it's for my benefit more than anyone else's. My whole cottage is decorated with paintings of various creatures in Wonderland, and I like it that way. Every now and then, I'll paint over one of the murals and create a new one depending on my mood.

I drop my brush in a cup full of water and stare at the image on my canvas, of a tattooed man with bright-pink eyes. Even in my escape, I can't escape the image. I rub my head. Five days, and Flam hasn't come to find me. Five days, and I haven't thought of anything but him and his kiss. All of Wonderland talks about us, about how they think I'm taming the Flamingo. They're wrong.

The Flamingo isn't meant to be tamed.

I don't want to tame him. I want him to stay just as he is, brooding, perhaps a bit brutal, caring, intriguing. There will be no caging the Flamingo, and I don't want to be his cage. I want to be his wings.

But the asshole hasn't come back, so I can tell him that.

Huffing in annoyance, I grab the canvas from the easel and move to my porch, dropping it with the dozen or so other artworks of the same man. Yes, every time I've tried to paint, it's the same process: decide I'm going to paint a nice landscape and end up with the Flamingo. It's frustrating.

I'm walking through the high grass to retrieve my paints and easel when a large shadow passes over me. My face turns up, curious as to what creature is so large, and that's when I see him. My breath rushes from my body, and I clutch for the small gate of my cottage to steady myself.

I've seen images of Jabberwockies in books, rough sketches of what they looked like when shifted. The only Jabberwocky I've ever seen in person was Flam's father, but he was always in his human form. Flam has the structure of a Jabberwocky, the long serpentine body, the great weathered wings, the harsh black spikes running down his back; he even has a gentle mane around his head like all Jabberwockies have. There's one major difference between a pure Jabberwocky and the Flamingo. Instead of the black scales I expected, he's covered in bright-pink feathers, beautiful and yet a little ridiculous. He's no less intimidating, however, as he swirls in the air, his eyes looking down to where I stand watching him.

I'm not afraid of him, though I feel as if he's hoping I will be. I don't run into my cottage and hide. I watch him with barely contained wonder and awe.

Flam dives suddenly for my clearing, his large body growing larger and larger, and he drops to the ground like a torpedo. I gasp, expecting him to crash to the dirt, but he rights himself at the last moment and lands gently on clawed feet. A massive gust of wind from his wings hits me in the face along with the scent of citrus fruits and night.

"Hello, Flam," I say, tipping my chin up. I'm still upset with him for leaving me at the party, so I keep my voice neutral.

His great mane moves as he shakes his head. *Doe.* The word appears in my mind, his voice penetrating the walls of my consciousness to speak.

Flam throws his head back, and I hear the distinct sound of bones popping as his body shifts before my eyes. It's a similar process when I shift, the pain great but comfortable. I can't imagine what such a large form feels like as he transforms back to his human body, a very naked human body. My eyes trail down his body, taking in the tattoos that cover every inch of his skin. His muscles are tense as he stands in the clearing outside my cottage, waiting for my reaction. When I meet his eyes, his jaw is clenched hard, his gaze intense.

"What are you doing at my home, Flamingo?" I hide how enthralled I am with him, how much I want to rush forward and throw my arms around him. He has some explaining to do first.

He raises a brow at me, his eyes finding the stack of paintings against my wall, and I curse myself that I didn't turn them backwards when I set them there. "I couldn't stay away." His voice is rough, as if he hasn't talked for a while.

"It's been five days."

"I know."

"Five days," I repeat, my voice harsh. "You left me without explanation, and then didn't come back for five days."

"I know," he growls. "And I would have stayed away longer if I could help it."

I sniff and cross my arms. "Then you can just turn right back around and disappear, pretty bird. I don't have time for someone who doesn't know what they want."

"That's the problem." Flam takes a step closer, but I don't react. "I know exactly what I want, but that doesn't mean I should have it."

"And why is that?" I glare at him. "Because of who your father was? Because everyone thinks you're some sort of brutal beast? Because you hurt yourself with those thoughts far more than anyone else can? That's shit, Flam." I sigh and drop my arms, rubbing my temple instead. "No one can decide your fate except for you, and right now, the only one standing between us is you, not your father."

Flam's jaw clenches hard before a husky chuckle slips from his lips. "Leave it to the Dodo bird to tell me who I am. You don't know me, little bird. I'm not some pet."

"And who told you I wanted a pet?" I step forward. "Who told you that I am a cage? Or that you would clip my wings?" When he doesn't answer, I storm forward until we're toe to toe, until I can glare up into his face. All my anger comes tumbling out, sharp as a whip, as I stab him in the chest with my finger. "You're making up false versions of what us being together could mean, Flam, and I won't have it."

"I'm only trying to protect you," he snarls, wrapping strong fingers around my wrist when I try to stab him with my nail again. "You could die!"

"Then that is my decision, my risk to take. I don't need your protection. I want your heart, you ignorant asshole, not some false sense of safety."

Those words hang in the air between us, and his face softens marginally. "Are you sure I have a heart, little bird?" he whispers, his fingers soft around my wrist. "Are you sure I'm worth the risk?"

I scoff, ignoring the tingles shooting down my arm and into my core as his thumb gently rubs against my skin. "Are those really the questions you need to ask?" I shake my head. "I wouldn't be here if either of my answers were no."

Flam's other hand gently cups my hip, and the one round my wrist releases it and slides down to grab my waist. "If I let myself claim you," he whispers, "it won't be possible for me to stay away when I become too much, when I scare you. It's not in my nature. You'll have to put me down."

I shake my head at him. "There's no reason to worry, Flam. I'm not afraid of you."

"Even though being with me means a lifetime of being spoken about behind your back, of being shunned, or dealing with my beast?"

"First, let people speak. I don't care what they think. Second, if I'm invited to less parties, then that's a win in my book. And finally, there's nothing to deal with. Just let go, Flam. There's nothing holding you back but your own mind."

"You'll put me down if I lose control?" he asks, his voice rough.

"I won't—"

"You have to promise," he growls, and then realizes what he said. "Please?"

"I won't promise that." I narrow my eyes. "There's no need for such a promise."

"You're so fucking stubborn," he snarls, his hands clenching hard at my sides, but I don't back down. "I'm a fucking monster, and I'm trying to protect you!" I roll my eyes which only seems to set him off more. He yanks me hard against him, and I feel his hardness against my stomach. My eyes widen, and I look down, but we're pressed too closely to see anything. "You seriously rolled your eyes at me?"

"Stop being an idiot, and I wouldn't have to do so." I keep my voice calm, but I can't help the quiver that threads through my words. It isn't from fear, no, far from it. Arousal courses through my body as I curl my hands around Flam's strong shoulders.

"You're infuriating!"

"Everyone says that, yes."

Words don't even penetrate his next snarl. He just dips his head and latches his teeth around the sensitive muscle of my shoulder, the bite painful for a split second before it transforms to pleasure. My legs turn to jelly on a gasp, and my core grows damp. He clamps down a little harder, and I cry out, ready to melt into a puddle.

When he releases my shoulder, I know there will be a mark there, one he purposely leaves behind. He kisses the spot gently, his tongue dancing against my skin. "Aren't you going to invite me into your home?" he asks, his voice thick with arousal.

"Why would I do that?" I groan, my eyes sliding closed as his lips continue to trail along my shoulder.

"Because you want to."

The urge to tease overtakes me, and I lean back a little from him.

"You mean, I should invite the big bad pretty bird into my house?" I grin at him. "Everyone will say how brutal the Flamingo is, how much of a harlot I am." I mock gasp. "What would my mother say?"

"Keep teasing, Doe," he growls, "and I'll make sure you won't be able to after I'm done with you." I laugh, amused, but Flam doesn't seem to be in a joking mood. A wicked smile curls his lips as he threads his fingers through my hair and wrenches my head back, exposing my neck to him. Fire dances in his eyes as his other hand keeps my body tightly pressed against his. "Do you think I'm brutal, little bird?"

I wiggle against him, so turned on I can't quite figure out what to do with myself, so I wrap my own claws around his neck, curling them against the corded muscle there. "Yes," I breathe.

Mischief curls his lips, so wicked I can hardly bear it. "Good," he growls, and then he claims my lips with his.

FLAMINGO

My thoughts are scattered and yet arrowed as I roughly take Doe's lips, as I imagine taking her soul within mine. Here's this woman offering herself up on a silver platter, and fuck it all, I want her! No matter my insecurities, or my fears, both of my warring sides want to possess her in ways I've never wanted to before. My mind dances on the paintings she has stacked against her home, of the dozens of images of me in different settings, different poses. I almost purr at the thought that I've been in her mind as much as she's been in mine. Some logical side of myself says that's not a good thing, that I should walk away now and leave her alone, but I'm already in too deep. There's no going back, and even though she wouldn't make the promise to put me down if I become too much, I'll make sure there's something in place should it come to that. I may be a beast, but I don't want to be a killer.

I back Doe against the nearest tree, her easel and paints she had set up there scattering as I push them away. Doe breaks the kiss.

"Those were good supplies, you—"

I don't let her finish her sentence. I claim her mouth again quickly before breaking it to kiss her neck. "I'll get you new ones," I growl, pressing her back hard against the bark of the tree. She's wearing a dress today in pale blue, a color that brings out the blue in her feathers, and I hum in pleasure when I find a break in the skirts. It's not as high as the one she'd been wearing at the Queen's Tea Party but it's enough. I drop to my knees before her, hiking her leg over my shoulder, before she knows what's happening.

"What are you doing?" she asks in surprise, grabbing hold of my other shoulder to steady herself. I don't answer her. I take her completely off of her feet, draping her other leg around my shoulder so that it's only me and the tree holding her aloft. She lets out a startled squeak that turns into a long moan when I place my mouth against her core and suck. She bucks against my face, and I dart my tongue out to stroke. I might be half flamingo, but I still have the tongue of a Jabberwocky. "Oh!" she cries, her claws digging into my scalp, painful but perfect. I have the urge to make her as brutal as I am.

"Is this what you want?" I groan against her core. "To see me on my knees before you?"

She clamps her thighs around my head in answer. "Don't start," she snarls, and shoves my face in harder against her. She's strong, but not as strong as I am. I resist, keeping my lips away from her core. I laugh.

"You said I was brutal, little bird. You teased me," I slip my finger into her core, and she moans, but I don't replace my lips, "and yet, you don't want to be teased."

"You're right," she moans. "I'm sorry I teased you."

"You're not." I press my lips against her inner thigh, lingering there. "You're just trying to get me to eat you again."

"Wonder, if you don't stop talking, I can promise I will eat you whole," she growls, shoving me back away from her. I let her push me, careful to make sure she doesn't hurt herself as we both tumble backwards into the high grass. I land with her on top of me, my cock standing straight up in anticipation. "You want to tease, pretty bird?" she purrs, licking a path up my chest that makes my brain short-circuit. "I've read that Jabberwockies like to chase their mates," she whispers.

I don't have a chance to comment, or deny, or tell her anything. She's gone from my chest before I can blink, and I barely catch the skirt of her dress disappearing into the trees. Everything inside of me awakens, and a roar bellows from my throat. I'm on my feet before I realize it, chasing after the Dodo bird.

In all my years, I've never had the pleasure of a chase, most women far too apprehensive to do more than a quick fuck out of curiosity before they leave. My chest rumbles as I dart into the woods, following the sound of Doe's steps.

"That wasn't wise, little bird," I call as I run, knowing she can hear me. "When I catch you, you'll pay for that."

Laughter reaches my ears, and I change directions, following the sound. "You mean if you catch me," she answers in a breathy pant. "I'm the fastest in Wonderland, pretty bird."

I growl. Such a naughty little bird.

DODO

I sprint through the forest on strong legs, the thrill of the chase lighting me up in ways I'd never planned for. I had read the small line in a book long ago, that Jabberwockies like to chase, but I had been taking a chance running from Flam. He's only half Jabberwocky; he could have easily lost that trait to his flamingo side, but the sound of him growling behind me lets me know exactly what he thinks about it.

The Flamingo is excited.

I'm much faster in my dodo form, but that isn't the game we're playing. I want to be caught eventually, not actually run from him.

I circle around my cottage, keeping us close but not risking being caught too soon.

"Little bird," he teases. "You can't evade me for long."

I chuckle, darting around a tree. I debate scaling one of the things and letting him pass me, but I'm not certain if he would fall for that trick.

"Pretty bird," I coo. "You can't catch me."

He snarls in answer, and I hear him pick up speed. Oops, probably shouldn't have challenged .

"When I catch you," he pants, "all of Wonderland will hear you scream out my name." I stumble over a root but catch myself, sprinting as fast as possible. My dress catches on thorns, shredding the skirt, but

I don't care. "You'll beg me to take you, to claim you, to possess your body, and when you think you can go no more, I'll take you again, until I'm a brand on your soul."

"That's a pretty big promise." I swerve around another tree, hearing him get closer. He's apparently faster than me in human form, something I didn't account for. Maybe I should find somewhere to hide, after all. I head in the direction of my cottage. I hear the exact moment Flam changes, too, heading for me.

I dart out of the tree line right into my clearing with barely enough time to duck behind the giant tree I'd been painting under, the trunk wide enough to conceal me. I hear Flam come out a second later and pause. I take slow, silent breaths, trying to calm my racing heart.

"Little bird," he calls, taking slow steps into the clearing. "Where are you hiding?"

As he moves further into the clearing, I slowly shift around the trunk, keeping myself hidden. Flam pauses. I wait for a minute without hearing him move before I wrinkle my brow in confusion. I close my eyes, searching wide with my senses, listening. Nothing, I hear nothing. Did he leave? I open my eyes, ready to step out of my hiding spot, and gasp.

Flam stands in front of me, his chest heaving up and down, a wicked smile on his face. "Caught you."

"Not yet!" I laugh, darting to the side, but he's too close, and I don't really want to keep running, anyway.

Flam loops an arm around my hips and scoops me up, his chest pressed into my back. "Ah, ah, ah," he chides, his fingers closing around my breast and squeezing. "I have plans for you." His fingers find the edge of my dress, and he shreds it from my body with claws that never nick my skin. The material pools at my feet until we're both nude, standing flesh to flesh. "You want my beast?" he whispers in my ear, his fingers clenching my breast again while the other dives between my legs and strokes me. I gasp, grinding back against his hardness.

"I want you however you are," I moan. My legs fall out from underneath me as he takes me down to the grass, my breath leaving me on a laugh. I stop laughing, however, when he slides his cock between my folds, rubbing there. But he pauses, and I groan in frustration. "Stop hesitating," I growl, twisting to look at him over my shoulder. The indecisiveness I saw on his face disappears, and his brutality takes over, the challenge met.

Flam slams home inside my core, hard enough that I cry out. He doesn't give me time to adjust before he repeats the motion, pulling out and slamming in again. "Fuck!" he snarls, before he loses all control, and I feel his powers dance out and kiss my skin as he fucks me harder. I scream in pleasure, gripping the grass beneath my fingers, the pace punishing and perfect. Something smells like it's burning, but I can't think clearly enough to focus on it as the Flamingo claims me completely.

Phantom fingers circle my breasts, ramping my pleasure higher, as his powers spread and feed off of his arousal.

"Yes!" I scream, "Flam!"

"Louder!" he snarls, "scream it louder. Tell everyone who claims you." He spears me so hard I nearly choke at the pleasure-pain, my body tightening hard in answer. "Scream for all of Wonderland to hear."

My orgasm hits me with his words, and I scream his name so loud that my voice cracks. An answering roar spills from his lips as his fingers clamp around my hips in a bruising grasp, his rhythm stuttering as he pumps his seed into my body.

We both collapse into the grass, panting hard, my hair a wild tumble around me. Flam stays nestled inside me as we lay there, trying to regain some of our senses.

That's until the smell of smoke and fire reaches my senses completely.

I sit up with a start to see that we're laying in a ring of pink flames, the grass it sits on black and charred. My favorite tree is safe at least, and the flames don't touch us.

"Umm, Flam?" I ask, staring in wonder at the sight. The flames die before my eyes when he clamps his hand around my waist and nuzzles into my side.

"I'm sorry. I lost control."

"It's okay," I grin, leaning down to place a kiss against his skin. "I like when you lose control."

Flam pulls me down and climbs on top of me, his fuchsia eyes bright with the flames that had surrounded us. "It doesn't scare you?" His eyes drop to my breasts, and he leans down to capture one between his lips.

"I'm not afraid of you," I groan, wrapping my legs around his hips.

"Good."

Our next coupling is slow and languid, and when the Flamingo brings us to a rising crescendo before carrying me inside my cottage, I give him my heart on a silver platter.

The beautiful thing is, he gives me his, too.

FLAMINGO

"Care to accompany me to the Heathen Festival, little bird?"

Doe groans, covering her face with the book she'd been reading. We're relaxing out in her clearing, she's happy with a book, and I'm happy to watch her in comfort. We seem to work well together, and it has calmed my insecurities a little.

"Another party?" Her voice is muffled by the book she holds over her lips, and I reach up and pull it away. Her dark eyes meet mine, and although she had sounded annoyed, there's a smile on her lips.

"This one, though, is celebrated for the creatures like me," I remind her.

The Heathen Festival is celebrated every year like clockwork, and while there have been many who oppose the celebration, the King and Queen have been adamant on their stance. Wonderland is not only for the normal and the safe; there are monsters here who just want to fit in and celebrate without judgement. And so, the Heathen Festival is a grotesque masquerade, horrifying masks covering every face that chooses to attend. It's always fun to go just to see the elaborate masks people dream up. There are always a handful of those who wear Jabberwocky masks. The night is spent full of debauchery, wild drinking, and a gathering of howls and a chase at the end of the night.

"I don't have a mask." Doe runs her fingers down my jaw, and I know she'll attend with me, no matter what. She's held true to her word, that she's never afraid, never worried that I'll snap. I haven't had the heart to tell her that my powers are getting stronger again, that I keep stamping out little pink flames at the worst times. I'd nearly burned her cottage down the other night, and she had no idea.

"Leave the masks to me, little bird." I wink, leaning into her touch. "Let's just go and lose ourselves to the festival."

"It might just be the one party my mother won't be at," she chuckles, closing her book and setting it aside. "How could I say no to that?"

She hasn't mentioned it much, but the Mockingbird disapproves of our courtship wholeheartedly. I'd walked into the clearing to catch the tail end of one of their arguments. The Mockingbird had clammed up and left but not before I heard her words.

"You are meant to marry a noble, daughter, and I will not have you ruining your reputation by gallivanting off with that man."

"I don't want to marry a noble, mother. I've made up my mind. I love the Flamingo, and that's all there is to it. I've never been worried about my reputation."

"And what about my reputation, hmm? You think anyone will feel safe telling me their secrets now?"

"That's what this is about, isn't it? It's not about my reputation at all. You're only worried about yourself."

They'd both heard my approach then, and the Mockingbird eyed my form, the tattoos swirling around my skin, and dismissed me with a harrumph before striding away into the trees. I'd glanced at Doe only to find her smiling warmly at me, her hand outstretched. I'd taken it without any hesitation. The Mockingbird might not approve, and Doe might have to listen to her complaints, but I'm a selfish creature. I want the Dodo bird for as long as she'll have me.

Hopefully, it's no less than forever.

"What does one wear to a Heathen Festival?" Doe asks, moving forward to straddle my lap.

I clasp her waist in appreciation, always happy to hold her close. I press my lips to the skin above her dress, right over her heart. "Something easy to push aside," I mumble against her skin. "The Festival can get heated."

"Now that sounds promising," she says, threading her fingers into my hair. "We still need to finish our tryst in the maze. It would be fun to have another chase between the hedges."

My chest rumbles, and I capture her lips with mine. "Always teasing, little bird. One day, it'll come back and bite you in the ass."

"Oh, I hope so," she purrs, and I end up giving her a preview of what happens at the Heathen Festival when emotions run high and the monsters come out to play.

DODO

I stare at the dress I'd picked out, shifting around to see the movement in the mirror. Flam disappeared to go fetch us some masks, so I took the opportunity to get ready. Since we've been together, for months and months now, I've avoided the color pink like a plague. To me, Flam is more than the single color, and I always want to remind him that I see all of him, but tonight, I want to remind the Flamingo that he can be whoever he chooses, even at a festival celebrating his beast.

The dress flows to the floor in gentle waves, fuchsia colored just like Flam's eyes. I leave my feet bare; there will be no need for shoes at such a festival. I leave my hair down around my shoulders, my feathers out to add decoration to the dress. My shoulders and neck are bare, the dress cut to reveal without revealing. The best part is the high slit that goes up the length of my left thigh. Flam always likes when they do that.

"I've gotten us masks . . ." Flam strides in through the doorway, and his voice trails off when he sees the dress I'm wearing, his mouth dropping open.

"Do you like it?" I ask, lifting my leg from the skirts to show off the split. His eyes go right to the skin revealed, to the tiny chains that jingle on my ankles with the movement.

"Like it?" He strides forward, cupping my chin and tilting it up. "I ought to strip it from your body and have you right here," he growls.

I laugh, leaning forward to press a soft kiss on his lips. "Then we wouldn't make it to the Festival, and I really want to see what it's all about."

Flam groans before threading his fingers through mine and tugging me out of my cottage, but not before he reaches through the silks of my dress and strokes a finger along my thigh. *I will most certainly be getting it later*, I think with glee.

"What mask will I be wearing?" I ask. Instead of answering, he reaches into a box and pulls out a large mask, far more intricate that I expected. When I realize what it is, I laugh. "Really?"

The mask is mainly black, gold accents tracing beautiful patterns in the leather. Feathers ring the outside, and it will completely obscure my face. The mouth is open in a grotesque grin, a forked tongue splitting the teeth. He found me a Jabberwocky mask, out of all the options.

"I thought it fitting, no. After all, you'll be attending with the only Jabberwocky in existence."

"Ah, but you're not all Jabberwocky," I tease, taking the mask from him. "I will gladly wear your namesake, pretty bird." I look at him. "And what mask will you wear?"

Flam reaches into the box again and pulls out another mask, holding it up to his face. I laugh, shaking my head. "What do you think?"

"I think the Cheshire Cat is going to skewer you!"

Flam wears a mask with a striking resemblance to the Son of Wonderland, the very aggressive and prone to violence Son. The mask is so dark it's almost black, missing the grey of Cheshire, but the brilliant blue stripes leave no mistake who it's meant to be. The mouth is even open in a wide, exaggerated grin, a mockery of Cheshire's cavalier attitude.

I hope Cheshire is in attendance. I can't wait to see his face.

We enter the Heathen Festival just as the stars come out to dance, to find it's already in full swing, many of the masked guests intoxicated on the Hatter's tea. So many wear faces of other creatures, horrifying monsters, and yet it doesn't unnerve me. After all, none are more threatening than my own Flamingo.

The King and Queen sit on a dais, watching the festivities, the only ones without masks. When the Queen's eyes meet mine, she motions me forward, her gaze flicking to Flam to let me know she means him, too.

"The Queen has asked for an audience with us," I whisper, tugging Flam towards the stage.

I can feel Flam's confusion as strongly as mine, and I hope it's not to warn us away from each other the same as my mother has been doing.

With creatures laughing and being overly raucous around us, we step before the King and Queen and bow low, holding the position for a moment as our station demands, before standing tall again. The Queen wears a blood-red gown embroidered with intricate monsters and beasts. The King wears an outfit in a similar color.

"What can I do for you, Your Majesties?" I ask, my fingers twitching in Flam's. I reach up and push my mask above my eyes, so they can see my face. Flam does the same on his side.

"Dodo," the Queen says affectionately, and I smile at her. "Your mother has been talking to me lately, about you and our very own Flamingo."

Flam's fingers tighten in mine the smallest amount, the only sign of his discomfort. I know it bothers him that so many are against our coupling, but I remind him daily that I don't mind; that I love him no matter what.

"Good things, I hope." She meets my eyes, and I know it's very much not good things at all. No, my mother has been telling the Queen her concerns about everything, it seems.

"The Mockingbird has a reputation to keep. She's worried about what this means for herself, and she's a very good friend of mine."

I nod my head, my jaw clenched. This conversation feels as if it's going to go in a terrible direction. If the Queen orders us to stay away from each other, we won't have a choice. We will have to do as she bids or flee Wonderland completely. And it's no choice really. I'd choose Flam over everything. There are other worlds we could find comfort in.

The King leans forward and eyes Flam closely. "I've sensed your powers growing stronger, Flamingo. Are you keeping control?"

"Yes, Your Majesty," Flam answers, but he hesitates a moment before his words. I will need to address it later. He thinks he's been hiding his little mishaps from me, but the silly man forgets my senses are as strong as his. I can smell a flame long before it turns into an inferno.

"Good. If you have need, you may come to us. We only wish to help you control your powers, so that you may continue being an asset of Wonderland, rather than a threat."

"Understood, Your Majesty."

The Queen smiles, and I brace myself. Here it goes. She's going to demand we separate, tell us it's too dangerous, that we shouldn't be together.

"Dodo," she begins, and I clench my jaw. "I want to give you our blessing."

The festival guests are drowned out behind me, the world growing silent at her words. "I'm sorry, what?"

She laughs, looking towards her husband. "I'm giving you our blessing to continue as you are." I stare in open-mouthed shock as she stands and steps down from the dais. "Doe, I've watched you grow into the beautiful woman you are. I knew you would never be happy with the nobles your mother paraded you in front of. The Mockingbird has high aspirations, but she forgets that you have your own path to travel, rather than her own." She lifts our joined hands and clamps hers around ours, her warmth seeping into our bones. Flam stares at her in surprise; he must have expected the same as I did. "Anyone with eyes can see how much you are meant for each other. The Flamingo and the Dodo bird." She grins.

"Are you saying that you approve of us together, even knowing what I am?" Flam asks, confusion heavy in his words. "Why?"

The Queen releases our hands, but she doesn't move away. "When your mother came to me all those years ago, claiming she had fallen in love with a Jabberwocky, I thought she was mad. What sort of woman fell in love with such a monster?" Flam flinches at my side, and I squeeze his fingers in reassurance. "And then I realized that only the most special of women can love a monster and remind him that he's not a monster, at all. Why was your father a monster? Because he had not found love, and although he was not able to ultimately control his powers, he proved himself capable of the most basic of emotions, and the most important. He loved your mother with his whole heart, no matter the devastation his instincts caused." Tears spring to my eyes at her words, and I move closer to Flam. "Before you let your worries get in the way, or the Mockingbird keep intruding, I want to give you our blessing because there is no better pairing in Wonderland. You make each other better, and that's what love is." She turns and steps back onto the dais. She raises her arms, and the music pauses, all eyes looking towards her. "All hail, the Flamingo and the Dodo bird on this most holy Heathen night!" she cries, and cheers go up around the garden.

I look over and meet Flam's eyes, tears threatening to spill from mine. He doesn't wait for them to fall. He jerks me to him and kisses me as if there's nothing else that matters, as if we've just been told that nothing can come between us. And perhaps, we were told exactly that.

Flam breaks the kiss and meets my gaze, all of his fire swirling in his eyes. "Marry me?" he asks. "Let's make it forever."

Cheers go up again at his words, and I grin, pressing my forehead against his.

"Yes, pretty bird," I whisper. "I'll marry you."

The Heathen Festival is never so joyous as that moment, and when we all howl, it's in celebration of the night.

But the night doesn't end there, and I should have known that we wouldn't be accepted into the folds of Wonderland so easily. The Heathen Festival always ends with a hunt through the trees, when all manners of creatures hunt their mates and send up a howl in celebration. Sex is a large part of the festival, and while you don't have to hunt only your mate, most do so. I know Flam will only search for me, and my excitement can't be hidden as we stare at each other, waiting for the horns to blow. The prey runs into the forest first, getting a head start. The hunters go at the second horn, and then it's a dance of laughter and celebration.

"Catch me if you can," I purr as the first horn blows. I have the pleasure of seeing Flam's eyes light with fire as I sprint into the trees, ready for the chase. This is my favorite part, and I didn't realize I would enjoy the idea as much as I do. There's something about awakening his primal side that makes my heart rate skyrocket and fall in love with him a little more.

The music doesn't penetrate the tree line like it did in the gardens. The only sounds that reach my ears are that of the other "prey" running through the woods alongside me. My mask feels heavy on my face, but I leave it on as the tradition dictates. Tonight, we are all beasts. Tonight, we are the heathens.

I run for two minutes before the second horn blows, letting the "hunters" follow. I grin, knowing Flam will be on me in no time. I never cheat and shift to my Dodo form. I'd never be caught that way, and I'm very much looking forward to the moment of capture.

I'm lost in my thoughts as I run, anticipating Flam coming up behind me, so I don't realize that I'm running into an ambush until it's too late.

I burst into a small clearing, right into the arms of a dozen creatures, all male and armed with weapons. I scream, and a few other "prey" howl, thinking that I've been captured by my mate already. I start to shift, but someone shoves something down my throat, making me gag and breaking my concentration.

"Fucking whore of a bird," someone snarls, wrenching my arms around. I fight against them, and it takes all but one of them to hold me, but there's too many. And then Flam comes barreling through the trees, panting hard, a severe snarl on his face. He would have known my scream was for his ears alone.

"Release her, and you won't die," he says calmly, contradicting the rage on his face.

"Both of you should be put down like your whore of a mother and her monster," the lead man growls. When he lifts his mask above his face, I recognize the warthog from the night we first met. "So we decided we're going to do it ourselves if the King and Queen won't do it." He pulls a long filet knife from his hip, and my eyes widen when he turns towards me.

"Take another step," Flam warns, eyeing the warthog.

Warthog—his name escapes me—grins, and I know he'll die tonight. I jerk against the men holding me and send one of them stumbling. I meet Flam's eyes, and I feel a small amount of his power bleed into me in answer to the question in my gaze. He doesn't have the full power of the Jabberwocky when it comes to the sharing of powers, but he has enough that I can feel the moment I start to glow, the moment I grow strong enough to send all the men stumbling away as I sprint for Flam. But the warthog is faster than I prepare for, and his knife slices right along my side. I fall to the ground in a heap, clamping my hand over the deep wound.

Flam roars when he sees me fall, and I don't have a moment to process what's happened before he's in his giant form, so fast I never hear his bones pop. The transition will wear him out, doing it that quickly, and he'll kill far more than just the men in this clearing if his powers all release in his rage. There are other couples out here, other innocents that had celebrated our joining.

"Flam," I cry, reaching for him, but my fingers miss him as he slithers forward and swallows the warthog whole.

It all turns to chaos after that, pink flames springing up around the clearing as Flam takes out man after man, shredding them to pieces, setting them aflame, killing each and every one who touched me. He's so lost in his emotions, that when the last man tries to run into the woods crying for mercy, he rips him to tiny pieces, and he doesn't do it with any ounce of mercy. They all die because they dared to touch me, to threaten me, to attempt to take on the Flamingo and his mate.

A roar rattles the air as he turns around, his eyes so bright that I can tell that Flam is letting instincts take over, and he will destroy this whole wood because everything is a threat.

"Flam!" I cry. "You have to stop!"

KILL! KILL! KILL!

His voice vibrates inside my skull so loud that I clamp my hands over my head as if that'll help. I scream in pain, and flames erupt around me, dancing along the skirts of my dress. My scream grows shrill when the flames touch my thigh, and they sear my flesh with a loud sizzle.

The flames die instantly, as if by magic, and Flam stands before me again, nude, panting heavily, panic in his eyes.

"Doe." His words are a ragged whisper when he drops to his knees and hovers over me, afraid to touch, afraid to hurt me more.

"I'm okay," I console him, but I'm not. I'm bleeding from the wound at my side, my thigh wears the burn from his flames, and my head feels as if I've been crushed.

Flam gently scoops me into his arms, but it still causes the pain to shift in my body, and I cry out. "I'm so sorry," he whispers. "I'm so sorry."

He repeats that mantra all the way to the castle, and I repeat mine. "It's okay."

But it's not. It's not okay, at all.

Chapter 8

FLAMINGO

I pray to Wonderland and anyone who will listen, that Doe isn't harmed permanently, that she forgives me, that she remains safe. I take her to the only place I know that offered help, the only place I know that we won't be met with disgust.

The King had offered to help me should my powers become too much. They were too much the moment I was able to harm Doe. I sprint inside the castle, the festival music still playing in the garden, screaming for help. I've never been so afraid in my life.

One of the butlers comes running, and I roar at him to get the King and Queen. He runs away in fright, and I hope he does what I ask. I collapse on the marble floor, Doe in my arms as panic fills me. I press my lips to her forehead and push as much power as I'm able to into her body, wishing that the power came stronger from my father. It's the first time I've ever wished to use a power my father gave me, and the irony isn't lost on me that it's to save the love of my life that I harmed in the first place.

Doe sighs, her eyes opening to meet mine. "That's better," she whispers. I keep pushing more power into her, until I can feel exhaustion dance at the edges of my vision, and still, I push more. "Flam, stop."

"I can't. I have to heal you."

"Flam," she bites, harsher than before, and I focus on her gaze. "That's enough. I will heal the rest of the way. You'll kill yourself."

The wound on her side is closed the smallest amount, not healed, but not bleeding. The burn on her thigh is still puckered and angry, the tatters of her skirt around her. "Your thigh will scar if I don't heal it."

"Then, let it scar," she sighs, wrapping her hand around mine.

"I'm so sorry," I repeat again, and she shakes her head.

"You were defending me."

"But I couldn't stop. I wanted to destroy the world."

"And yet, you didn't," she whispers, smiling.

"Only because of you. Next time, I might not be able to stop."

"Then we conquer that, too."

The King and Queen come rushing into the room at her words, both wearing outfits far more casual than I've ever seen them. I have a moment where I feel out of place, as if I shouldn't be seeing them this way, before I remember the dire situation I created. "What's happened?" The Queen shouts, panicked when she sees Doe laying in my arms on the floor. "Who caused this?"

"I did." I raise my chin, determined to take any and all punishment.

"No," Doe growls, pushing to sit up. She flinches with the burn but otherwise, remains strong. "I was ambushed during the hunt by a group of creatures who decided we should no longer be allowed to live."

The King's face morphs with anger, but it's not near as scary as the Queen's. "And where are these miscreants now?" She turns to the King. "Summon Cheshire."

"There's no need." Doe clenches my hand hard. "Flam took care of them."

Understanding passes the Queen's face when her eyes pass over Doe's body, taking in the injuries. "The wound on your side?" It's mostly healed now, but it's still very apparent there was a severe wound in the flesh.

"A knife that I got too close to."

"And the burn?"

Doe bites her lip. "It was an accident."

"I lost control," I say, interrupting. "My rage took over, and I couldn't control my powers. Doe was burned by my flame."

"And you came for help," the King nods. "We've prepared for this moment." He snaps at one of the butlers who rushes forward. "Please, grab the box on my desk, the one with the pink glow."

"You've prepared?" Doe asks, tilting her head.

The Queen steps down and grabs a bottle from a table filled with them. This one contains the phosphorescent glow of the mushrooms that grow in the forest. She kneels down besides us, and I gulp, unused to seeing her in such a position. She puts some of whatever is in the bottle on her fingers and gently dabs it at the burn on Doe's thigh. Doe hisses in pain, and I hold her tighter, shame filling me even more. I harmed my mate, and I'll never be able to forget that. "You know," the Queen begins, "I'm not as blind to things as some people think I am."

"What do you mean?" I ask, watching as the butler returns with the box the King requested.

"For example, I know my son is in love with the Hope Bringer, and that he plans to announce their courtship at his coronation." Doe gasps at the information, but the Queen continues. "I know my son thinks I won't approve, because of the expectations I've set on him. I also know that I will smile when he stands up for who he loves and tells all of Wonderland. Can you imagine his face? So much strife for the boy."

"What does that have to do with us?" Doe hisses again when the Queen adds more ointment.

"You see, I know many things, things the Mockingbird doesn't even have knowledge of. I know that Flam has been hiding how strong his powers are from you, and I also know that you already know he's trying to hide it."

Doe smiles and glances at me.

I frown. "You knew?"

"I knew." She chuckles a little bit between her hisses of pain. "You sometimes forget my senses are as strong as yours."

I hang my head, ashamed I'd kept the secret.

"There's no need to be frightened, or ashamed of your powers,"

Her Majesty reminds, closing the bottle and reaching behind her for a towel. The King steps forward then and kneels beside his wife. "Which is why we took precautions the moment you were born."

He opens the box and a small necklace lays inside, a tiny vial on the end of it. It glows brilliant pink, the colors of my mother.

"Your mother made sure you would be protected, and before she left this world, we discussed an enchantment that could seal your powers until you're strong enough to control them. This is only a temporary fix, and something you only need while you're adjusting. Once you gain control, it can also be used to temporarily break any enchantment, but the enchantment will return when the power wears away."

"This is your mother's gift to you," the King adds, "and your father's. We were able to create the enchantment because of his knowledge. Until you're ready, you can wear this, and it will prevent any more mishaps."

Emotion chokes my throat as the King places the necklace around my neck. The effects are instant, the feeling of erratic energy beneath my skin fading into a dull nuisance. For once, I relax, a sigh on my lips. "Thank you," I whisper. "I can never repay you."

"There's no need for repayment," the Queen shakes her head. "I only ask that when you marry each other before all of Wonderland, that we can be in attendance. Everyone should celebrate this occasion, and I know our darling Dodo bird would prefer something far more secret and smaller. Sorry, dear."

Doe laughs, looking up into my eyes and placing a chaste kiss against my lips. "Deal," she says.

"You still want to marry me?" I ask, eying the burn on her thigh, the place where a scar will always mottle her flesh.

"Silly bird," she whispers. "It's too late to get rid of me now. You're stuck with me."

"Forever?" I ask.

"Forever."

The Queen wraps her arms around us in a hug, and I've never felt so light, all because a Dodo bird walked into a party, and refused to tell me her name.

DODO

I stare in wonder at the dress I'm wearing, my reflection far more elegant than I ever expected. I've read in some of my books that brides wear white or red for their special day. Wonderland has no such traditions, and I would never wear either of those colors as they belong to the monarchies. So what does a Dodo bird wear to marry a Flamingo?

She wears her own colors.

The dress I'm wearing appears black at first, or at least very dark. But the moment I move, shifting the material, all the colors of the rainbow shimmer, sparkling in the light. Tiny jewels encrust the bodice, glittering bright and forming designs in the shape of feathers. The skirt has similar jewels along the hem, dancing as I move. When I walk down the aisle, I'll shine so bright that the guests might have to shield their eyes.

My hair has been left down, gentle curls in the dark tresses. One of the Queen's maidens came in and painted my face, a beautiful design curling around my left eye, declaring the monumental day.

Today, I'll marry Flam, and we'll become husband and wife.

I take a deep breath and pick up the ceremonial skull on the table. Every bride carries the aged bone in their hands as they walk down the aisle. It's a declaration that we will love each other until death. It's an old tradition, one that the Queen offered that we could forgo, but I understand that this wedding is about far more than just Flam and I. We love each other completely even though many thought Flam incapable of love. This wedding will show them all that love is more powerful than their judgement.

A knock on the door draws my attention. When it opens, I smile tightly, the Mockingbird stepping inside and closing the door behind her. Our relationship has been strained since our wedding was announced, and I haven't spoken to her since. Every time she's come to me, she's had something terrible to say, or some judgement to add. I used to think my mother was above such things, but I learned that no one is immune to such thoughts. I just hope that she isn't here to beg me again. I can never get that sight out of my mind, of the woman who raised me begging me to think of her reputation before my love.

The Mockingbird turns and meets my gaze before she takes in my appearance. She looks at the dress and the skull, and tears spring to her eyes. I can't tell if they're happy or sad.

"Are you sure you want to do this?" she asks.

I clench my jaw and turn back to the mirror, studying the dress again. It really is beautiful and everything I could've ever imagined. I'm anxious to see what Flam wears, to see if he chose his normal leather pants, or if he's dressed for the occasion as well. I'll be happy either way. Flam is Flam, no matter what he wears.

"I'm not discussing this with you again today." I stare over my shoulder in the mirror, watching my mother's face carefully. I'm tired of her warnings and her judgement. The Mockingbird is supposed to be neutral. She isn't supposed to interfere. She certainly shouldn't be in here on the day of my wedding spouting off such things.

She's silent for a moment, wringing her hands in front of her. "You look beautiful," she whispers, and I turn around to face her.

I watch my mother with sad eyes, before I reach out for her, hoping she accepts my hug. She comes to me in a flourish and wraps her arms around me, holding me tight.

"Will you come?" She's never said if she'll be attending the wedding or not. I hope she will, but I also understand if she doesn't. I also know that our relationship will never be the same if she continues to look at Flam as a monster. He's not just some beast. He'll soon be my husband.

My mother nods her head, and I smile, leaning back. It's an olive branch, the first step in our relationship being repaired. Perhaps, one day, she'll come to love the man Flam is, instead of judging him for his lineage.

The sounds of an organ playing alerts us that it's time to head to the ballroom, letting everyone in the hall know they should take their seats. The Queen arranged the entire wedding, decorating each and every bit of the castle for the day. She insisted that everyone should be invited, that all should see the romance of the era. I'd seen flowers in every color, jewels dripping from the ceiling. Her majesty had spared no expense, and while neither Flam nor I are nobles, you wouldn't be able to tell it from the decorations.

It's customary for the bride and groom to gift each other after they speak their vows. My gift for Flam is a book—something he will, no doubt, expect—but I can't wait to see his face when I hand it to him. I tuck it into my skirts and open the door. My mother leaves before me, giving my shoulder one last final squeeze of encouragement, and I follow her towards the ballroom. I'm nervous, but the closer we get to the double doors I'll enter through, the calmer I get. It's as if I can sense Flam on the other side, waiting for me, and his presence alone keeps me from panicking at the sheer number of guests I feel coming from inside the room. There really will be a lot of creatures watching our wedding.

"I love you," my mother says when she grabs my hand and kisses me on the cheek. "I just want you to be happy."

"I will be," I assure her. "I've never been happier."

She nods and leaves me at the doors to go around to the guest entrance. I take a deep breath and brace myself for the doors to open. I clasp the skull in my hands and tip my chin up. This is it. This will be the most important moment of my life so far. I'm marrying the Flamingo and starting a new era in Wonderland.

The organ changes tempo and starts playing a dark song of love and sacrifice just as the double doors swing open, and I'm met by hundreds and hundreds of gasps. Thankfully, not all of Wonderland can fit inside. The reception will take place out in the gardens so that everyone can join in, but there's still easily five hundred people in the ballroom. I don't even notice when they all start whispering as I take a step forward, and then another, my eyes riveted on the man waiting at the front of the room for me.

Flam isn't wearing his normal clothing. No, he's far more dressed up than I'm used to. He's wearing an intricate tailored suit, the pants lined with gold. The coat has similar designs, two tails draping down the back. The whole suit is in his signature color, a brilliant, amazing pink. He grins when he sees me, his eyes shimmering with fire and happiness. I swear I see moisture there, but he keeps it contained for now.

Slowly, I walk down the aisle, my steps measured, drawing closer and closer to him. When I finally reach the dais, he reaches down and takes my hand, helping me up the steps, before we face each other. I keep the skull clenched in my left hand.

"You're breathtaking," he whispers, the words almost a growl.

"So are you." My eyes trail down the suit again, and I chuckle when I realize he still doesn't wear a shirt. No, my Flamingo still shows off all of his tattoos proudly. The necklace the King and Queen gave him rests against his chest, glowing softly in the light.

"We are gathered here today to join these two creatures in heathen matrimony," the Queen announces, her voice echoing around the ballroom. I raise my brows, and Flam winks. Normally, the ceremony would say in "honored matrimony," but the words have been changed. I can't say I don't like the new version. "The ceremonial skull has been presented. Please place both of your hands over it." Both Flam and I hold the skull between us, and I take a deep breath. "The skull is a symbol of your everlasting love, that you will cherish each other long after death, and carry each other into the Here After. Do you, Dodo, solemnly swear that you will hold his hand whether into the dark, the light, or the Here After, as long as you shall exist?"

"I do." I grin at Flam, his eyes dancing with his own excitement.

"And do you, Flamingo, solemnly swear that you will hold her hand whether into the dark, the light, or the Here After, as long as you shall exist?"

"Fuck yeah, I do."

I giggle at his words, ignoring the snorts of those who don't approve in the crowd.

"Then, it is time to exchange your vows and your gifts." The Queen takes the skull from us, and we link our hands together. "Dodo, you will go first."

I clear my throat gently and meet Flam's eyes, a small smile on my face. "Flam, when I first saw you at the Dancing of the Stars, it was to find you brawling, blood already on your knuckles. And then you turned, and your eyes found me, and my entire world shifted. Everyone scattered when you stalked towards me, but I was so curious." I pause for a moment, biting my lip, squeezing his hand gently. "I didn't know it then, but I already loved you, blood on your knuckles, fire in your eyes, and the dancing stars behind you. So, this is my vow to you." I take a small step forward, bringing us just a little closer. "I will always be there to walk through your fire with you. I will not shy away from your nature, and I will hold your hand when it becomes too much. I will run a little slower during our chases, so you can catch me sooner." Everyone laughs, including Flam. I reach into the pocket of my dress and pull out the black leather-bound book. Gold swirls decorate the cover, along with the words embossed there. Flam looks down at it in surprise, taking the book with gentle fingers. "We will write our story together, and when we perish, we will do that together, too. Flamingo, son of the Flamingo and the Jabberwocky, I give my heart to you," I finish. Flam looks down at the book again, reading the words inscribed there. "The Flamingo and the Dodo Bird." I'd had it made by the best book binder in Wonderland. It'll stand the test of time and remain behind long after we're gone.

Flam tucks it against his heart and meets my eyes, a small tear trailing down his face, his emotion getting the better of him. I reach up and wipe it away gently, before standing on my tiptoes to kiss him gently.

"Flamingo, it's time for you to exchange your vows and gift," the Queen says, her voice cracking. When I glance at her, she's wiping away her own tears hastily.

Flam takes a deep breath. "I don't know if I'll be able to top that," he teases, handing the book to the king. He takes both of my hands in his and meets my eyes. "Doe, you looked at a monster and saw a man. The moment you walked away from me at that first party, refusing to tell me your name, I might add," laughter from the audience, "I knew without a doubt I wanted to marry you. But I didn't think anyone could love me the way you do. I didn't know what love was until you bashed me over the head with your words and told me to stop being an idiot." I grin, my own eyes welling. "I used to watch my mother and my father, watching how much they loved each other even though the odds were against them. I didn't understand then, but I do now. A wise woman once said that when you love a monster, they aren't a monster at all." The Queen sniffles, and my first tear falls. "Little bird, you see the best parts of me. You make me better. You make me whole, and I will spend the rest of my life reminding you of your beauty, chasing you when you run far too fast, and loving you with my entire being." He reaches inside his coat and pulls out a small narrow box. When he opens it, I see a pen nestled inside, but not just any pen. Trapped within its chamber, I watch brilliant pink flames dance, trapped and always burning. "You'll need something to write our history together," he whispers, and I take the box with shaking fingers, tears dripping down my face now. "Dodo, daughter of the Mockingbird and the Crane, I give my heart to you."

I don't wait for the Queen to claim we're married before I throw my arms around his shoulders and press my lips to his. The ballroom erupts in cheers, the shouts and well wishes echoing like thunder in the large room.

"Please welcome, the Flamingo and the Dodo bird, husband and wife!" the Queen shouts.

"Tea for everyone!" I hear the Hatter shout, and another round of cheers go up. I chuckle against Flam's lips, so completely happy, I can't imagine ever being happier.

We celebrate for three days, and each day, I fall more and more in love with the Flamingo. The first time I write in the leather book, I speak about the first time we met, and the love that transcended judgement, prejudice, and the odds. When Flam asks me what I'm doing, I chuckle and drop my flaming pen. I shove him away and sprint into the trees. I only look back over my shoulder once, a wide grin on my face.

"Catch me if you can, pretty bird." And then I shift. We run together in our beast forms, happy, unaware, lost in each other's love.

And that's the way I would have kept it, if only I'd had the chance.

Chapter 10

FLAMINGO

"The King and Queen request your's and the Dodo bird's presence."

I look over at Cheshire where he stands in our clearing, his expression anything but pleasant. "They make you the messenger boy now?"

"Apparently," he growls. "Do you receive their message?"

"If I say no, will you punish me?" I tease, knowing full well that the cat hates that he's been chosen. I can't say I blame him. Watching the things the Sons have gone through, the madness that has stolen across the Hatter's gaze, the anxiety in the White Rabbit, the hate in Cheshire, I've never been more thankful that I hadn't been chosen for some greater purpose. I prefer to remain neutral, just as my mother always had.

"I'll fucking eat you, bird. Don't test me."

We both know that Cheshire couldn't harm me. I don't need to be punished for one, but for another, I'm stronger than the Cheshire cat. At least, for now I am. He may grow stronger, but I'll always still have the beast in me. The thing is, Cheshire has a beast inside him, too. Perhaps, one day, we can test out that theory.

"Message received. I'll be along shortly after I grab Doe."

Cheshire Fades away without another word, and I watch the empty spot sadly. That one just feels like turmoil and chaos. I should ask Doe if she would like to spend more time with the Cat and his sister. The Hope Bringer seems like she'd become fast friends with my wife.

"Little bird," I call into the cottage.

"I heard." She steps from the doorway and wipes her hands free of the paint she'd been working with. "I'm ready."

We walk to the castle hand in hand, not rushing but not moving slow. We've been summoned, which means we're not being called as friends. We're being called as subjects of Wonderland.

The audience room is free of soldiers and butlers, unusual, but it's the grave faces of the King and Queen that really put me on edge.

"Your Majesties." Both of us bow at the same time before straightening and waiting for their words.

"I'm sorry to call you here on such short notice, but I need you to go on a trip." The Queen steps down from her dais and stops in front of us.

"We can leave immediately."

She shakes her head. "No, only you will go, Flam. Doe must remain here."

I glance at Doe when she squeezes my hand, already sensing my hesitancy. "I'm a big girl. I survived perfectly fine before I married the big bad Flamingo," she teases. "I'll be alright."

"Doe, I need you to ask your mother about some rumors, and if she's had any word of a prophecy."

"Yes, Your Majesty."

"And Flam, I need a moment with you alone." The King nods his head at Doe, and the Queen gives her a gentle smile as she bows. She gives my hand one final squeeze before she turns and leaves the room.

"Is something wrong?" I ask, keeping my voice low. I can only assume whatever task asked of me will be dangerous.

"Not yet. But it might be." The King sighs and runs his hand over his face, exhaustion clear on his eyes.

"Is this about the coronation?" The Prince is to hold his coronation in four days. The celebrations will be large, and thanks to the Queen, we also know that the Prince plans on declaring the Hope Bringer, Cheshire's sister, as his own Queen. It'll be a scandal and chaos, but we already know the Queen is actually fine with the idea. Wonderland, however, might have other thoughts.

"It's not." The Queen frowns. "We have reason to believe that a threat is coming to Wonderland. The Caterpillar is being tight-lipped, but we know there's some sort of impending doom coming. We need you to gain control of your powers. We know it's been a few years since we gave you the enchantment, and your control is growing, but we need it to be faster in case you're called upon to fight for your world."

"What would you have me do?"

"There is talk of a man who can help you, one in a different world. He goes by 'The Wizard,' and we believe he can help you gain control quickly. White will help you travel there. You'll unfortunately be gone for at least a few weeks, but we will make sure Doe is protected in your absence. We wouldn't risk this if we didn't think it was imperative."

"I understand." I don't like the thought of being apart from Doe for so long, but my monarchy is asking me to step up, and so, step up I shall. "Will I have time to tell my wife goodbye?"

"Yes. White will come to you tomorrow morning." The King steps down next to his wife and claps me on the shoulder. "We're depending on you, son. Go find The Wizard and then come back home. And please, don't speak a word about this to anyone. We don't want to cause a panic."

"Yes, Your Majesties." I bow and back away, leaving the room, my chest already hurting for the good-bye.

DODO

"You're leaving for a few weeks?" I ask, frowning at Flam as we sit in the clearing outside of my cabin. "And you can't tell me where you're going?"

Flam clenches his jaw. "I want to, little bird. I really do, but I told them I wouldn't speak of it. Trust me. When I return, I'll tell you all about the adventure that I went on."

"You'd better," I chide, shaking my head. "My mother didn't know anything about a prophecy, either. Apparently, the Caterpillar is being extra secretive."

"Something is going on," Flam nods. "I don't know what, but it's something big. Are you sure you'll be alright while I'm gone?"

"Of course." I lean forward and press my lips against his briefly. "Go on your adventure, complete your task, and then come right back home to me."

"Deal," he whispers, and then we say good-bye in the best way possible.

WHITE SHOWS UP BRIGHT AND EARLY THE NEXT MORNING. I WATCH Flam disappear into the trees with him sadly, but not before we shared a long kiss, only breaking apart when White cleared his throat. The Time Keeper has the patience of a warthog.

The moment he's gone, I already feel alone. It seems I've come to rely on the Flamingo far more than I realized. I miss him so drastically that I attempt to lose myself in a good book. It's pointless really. Nothing takes my mind away from him.

Two days later, I'm driving myself mad with boredom, and I set up my easel outside to paint. I've barely began to brush red paint in a long line before my mother bursts from the tree line and frightens me so badly that I drop my brush and knock over my table. Her hair is wild, her appearance far more unkempt than I've ever seen her.

"Get your things. Now!" she whispers harshly.

"Mother, what's going on?"

"I'll explain later. You need to grab anything you can't live without, and we have to leave this world."

"I can't leave. I have to wait for Flam."

"If we don't leave, you won't be alive to wait for him," she bites out, and I freeze, staring at her in horror.

"What do you mean?" She doesn't wait for me to start packing my things. She drags me inside the cottage and starts shoving my paints and some books into a bag. "Mother? What's happening?" I start to panic. I don't know what's going on, but it can't be good, not for my mother to be acting as she is. She's usually so composed, no calm.

She stops for a moment and meets my eyes. "Alice has returned."

I relax. "That's all?"

"She didn't come back alone. No one knows, the only reason I do is because the trees whispered in my ear. She's a much bigger threat than anyone suspects."

"That's impossible. She can't do anything."

"We have to leave. No one else knows what she hides, and she'll be coming for me. She'll know that I hold the secrets."

"We have to get to the King and Queen," I reason. "They can help us."

"They can't, sweetheart." She turns and meets my eyes. "When I told you that I hadn't heard any prophecies, I lied."

"What?"

"There's a prophecy, but I thought we had more time. If we don't leave, we will die, and Wonderland will follow."

"We can't just leave them all!" I cry.

My mother shoves the door open, and we step outside. I pause, a chill running down my spine. The Mockingbird stands in front of me, her hand holding me back, as if she's strong enough to protect me. Whatever my mother had been frightened of, we're too late. We didn't move fast enough.

"Hello, Mockingbird."

I stare in horror at the woman sitting high on a massive beast, a wicked smile on her face. She's dressed in a bright-red dress, armor on the sleeves, the color of the monarchy, and the Queen's crown sits on top of her head.

"What have you done?" I whisper, but she hears me.

"You must be the Dodo bird. We've never met, but I heard all about you from your mother when I was a child. She said you were beautiful." Alice glances down my dress, at the paint splattered on my fingers. "You're not as beautiful as I expected."

"What do you want?" my mother asks, her shoulders shaking in fear.

"I think you know what I want, old bird." She tilts her head to the side. "I'm not ready for my secret to get out. I can't have you blabbing your mouth."

"I won't say a word," my mother reassures her, and I frown. We must tell everyone immediately, warn everyone. "You know how well I can keep a secret."

"I don't believe you." Alice glances towards me again. "Your own daughter doesn't look like she agrees. Did you already spill my secret to her?"

"No! Leave her out of this! She doesn't know!"

"There's only one way to be sure." She snaps her fingers, and beastly-looking creatures dressed in armor come from the trees, swarming around us. I don't know what any of the creatures are, what Alice has made them. "Capture them."

I start to shift, preparing to spirit my mother away from here. I'm the fastest in Wonderland. I can get us out of here as long as I shift. Something slams into my shoulder hard, but when I look down, expecting a wound, there's nothing there. I wrinkle my brow in confusion, and when I move to transform again, my eyes grow heavy, and I start to drop.

"I can't have you escaping," Alice says, but her voice sounds fuzzy to my ears as I collapse to the ground. My mother screams, but after that, I hear nothing else.

I float in a sea of darkness, confused, and all I see is brilliant fuschia-colored eyes.

Flam, where are you?

"WAKE UP!" SOMEONE SHOUTS. I JERK UPRIGHT AS ICE COLD WATER splashes down on me, sputtering at the agony. My arms are tied behind my back, my shoulder aching from the odd position. Alice stands in front of me, a grin on her face. "Finally," she purrs. "The fun is about to begin."

Beside me, I can see the Hatter strung up against the wall. He isn't moving, and my heart gives a hard throb. He can't be dead, not really, not as a Son, but still the sight threatens to send me into a panic.

"Where's my mother?" I ask, my voice a hard croak.

"Oh, you'll see her in a moment. We're about to join her."

Alice's soldiers surround me, their faces smooth and without emotion. Then one opens its mouth, and I jerk away in horror, but they hold tight to me, making sure I'm marched right behind Alice. We don't stop until we're in the gardens, and I gasp at the blood everywhere. A slaughter must have happened between the moment she came and now, because it's everywhere. Grotesque creatures, many we celebrated with during the Heathen Festival swarm the gardens, boisterous laughter coming from their group. They're amped up, feeding on the violence Alice is supplying them.

Beside the Queen's ornate throne stands Alexander, but when he turns, I realize he's no longer the Prince I know. His face is mottled with red roses, his one remaining eye empty. Whatever Alice has done to him, I can't count on help from his hand. On the other side of the throne, stands White, his arms folded behind him as if he's comfortable, but I can see the tension in his shoulders, as if he's fighting an invisible battle. His eyes dart to mine as I'm led forward, and the tendons on his neck stand out harder. No help there, either. In front of the throne, my mother kneels, her arms wrenched behind her back same as mine. She's sporting a black eye, and anger fills me at the sight. The Mockingbird isn't violent. She isn't capable of such things. I'm thrown on the ground beside her, and the creatures around us go wild.

"Now that everyone is here, let's begin."

"Please. You don't have to do this," my mother cries. I glance at her, at the other wounds on her skin. "Just let my daughter go. She doesn't know. She doesn't know!"

"I don't care. Get rid of one, get rid of the other. It's a precaution, nothing more. Don't take it personally."

My mother starts to cry then, and when she turns and meets my eyes, my own tears leak over my lashes. We're going to die here, and I'll never get to see Flam again. I fight against the restraints on my wrists, but it doesn't do any good. They're too strong. I can't save my mother. I can't save myself.

"God, the crying is annoying. Someone take care of her."

I scream when the creatures surround us, but they don't touch me, not yet. They lift the Mockingbird into the air.

"Let my daughter go!" she screams. "Let her go!"

I snarl, fighting harder against my bonds, and feel them loosen. "Don't you touch her!" My left hand frees, and I stumble to my feet, attacking the nearest creature. He falls to the ground when my claws slash across his throat. My bones start to pop, and I shift, far faster than I've ever done before. It's a risk, exhaustion dancing at my senses, but I can't allow Alice to stop me again. I barrel through the creatures, knocking them away from my mother, biting any who get too close in half. We're going to get out of here. We must!

Alice sighs. "Stop them, you useless twits. You're ruining my fun."

"Mother!" I scream, standing in front of her as protection. "Get on my back."

She scrambles up as fast as she can, her fingers wrenching at my feathers, but I grit my teeth against the pain. She wraps her arms around me, and I turn, preparing to dart into the trees, but her hold loosens, and I feel her begin to slide. "You have to hold on," I scream, but she's not listening. Her body slumps from my back, and I'm not quick enough to catch her. When I turn to her body, I scream.

"Oh, I'm sorry," Alice purrs. "Did you need that?"

My mother stares at me with lifeless eyes, a small sword protruding from her chest. She's gone, so fast I had no chance to save her. I scream in pure rage and sprint towards Alice. She doesn't move or look frightened at all as I bear down on her. Someone loops a chain around my neck, jerking me backwards, but it isn't strong enough to stop me. "You will die for this!" I snarl, throwing off the creature, but another chain wraps around my throat, and another, and another, until I'm being dragged to the ground with a snarl, roaring my agony, my eyes glancing at the lifeless body of my mother. "I'll shred you to fucking pieces!"

Alice smiles. "I see you're not as proper as your mother tried to make you. Silly thing about mothers, they never quite do what they promised. They never protect us; they don't quite love us like they should. They're useless, really."

"Don't think that your mommy problems are my own," I snarl.

"Were your own." Alice laughs. "You don't have a mother anymore. And neither do I."

Something wraps around my throat. When I look down, I see a red glowing string. The creature that tied it gets too close, and I slice him in half with my beak, snapping at any others who are too brave, who think me subdued. Alice only claps her hands with glee at the sight, and then I'm being tied down to the ground in the center of the gardens, blood beneath my face, my eyes on my mother as Alice addresses the beasts around me.

"Let's see if a Dodo bird tastes like chicken, shall we?"

The first feather they pluck from my hide brings a scream of agony ripping from my throat. The first kick brings stars to my eyes. White never moves, never steps up to help, and I cry out for Flam over and over again, but he can't hear me because he isn't here.

No, he can't hear me in another world.

We will write our story together, and when we perish, we will do that together, too.

I'm sorry, I think. *I'm so sorry I won't get to keep my promise....*

Alice's laughter is all I hear.

When another feather is yanked from my skin, I scream, and scream, and scream.

Grief is the price we pay for love.

A VERY MAD WEDDING

KENDRA MORENO

It's time for a new Reign to begin...

Chapter 1

I watch a pair of frog creatures hang up flower decorations along the walls, trying to ignore that some of the flowers have faces open in grotesque rage. Once picked, they're no longer a threat, but the sight of them still skeeves me out even after all the time I've been in Wonderland. White bounces around the tearoom, dictating where each decoration goes, what has to be done before the ceremony. The colors of the décor are mostly black and purple, the Hatter's colors, but soon, I will have a color of my own. Wonderland will decide it for me. I'm hoping it's not red or white. I can't bear to wear those colors after everything we've been through. I won't be the new Red Queen. I'll be the Empress. I take a deep breath.

Today is not only my wedding, but also my coronation.

All of Wonderland will come to witness my marriage to the Hatter, and the crowns placed upon our heads. Well, my head, anyway. The Hatter refuses to wear anything but his top hat. I'm a little relieved by that, that he isn't going to change just because the threat to Wonderland is over and that he'll be an Emperor. I refused to take the crown as well, but Hatter said I have to at least wear it for the coronation. After that, he promised to strip me of my royalty and treat me like the Hattress I am. His words, not mine. I'm most definitely looking forward to that.

"Clara?"

I turn towards Jupiter as she strides up to me. She's not dressed in her formal wear, but that's okay. Neither am I. The ceremony is hours away still, but I should be getting ready. Jupiter's bright hair is loose and wild around her, an endearing trait that I know White likes as much as I do.

"Hi," I mumble, biting my lip. I've been caught. There are, no doubt, some women waiting in a room somewhere to do my hair and makeup.

Jupiter, though, isn't stupid. She's far from it, so smart that I sometimes wonder what we would have done without her. The Hope Bringer is a whole other creature. Wonderland couldn't have chosen a better person for the job.

She eyes the robe I'm wearing, my loose hair and clean face, and smiles.

"Are you nervous?" she asks, holding out her hand for mine. I take it without hesitation. We're sisters of a sort, not by blood, but by circumstance. I only wish Cal and Cheshire could have stayed, but I understand why they didn't. Cal has more responsibilities than just Wonderland; she has a brother to raise. I know they'll come back, but I miss them while they're gone. I'm looking forward to their arrival for the wedding. White assured me that they would be on time.

"About the wedding, no." My answer is honest. I'm not nervous about marrying the Hatter. I'm excited. I've waited for this day since the moment I fell down the rabbit hole.

"About the coronation, then." Jupiter smiles and starts to tug me towards the preparation room. I smile at her gratefully and follow behind. "What makes you nervous for it?"

"Only everything. Girl, I'm about to be crowned an Empress of an entire world. I am woefully underprepared and not suited at all to the job."

When we reach the preparation room, Jupiter smiles at the women waiting there, one with gorgeous antelope horns, the other sporting goat legs. "Would you mind giving us a few minutes to talk please?"

"Of course." They both curtsey and leave the room.

"See, that!" I point out once they're free from the room. "I don't want anyone bowing to me, or curtseying."

"So, then make it a law when you're empress that no one needs to bow before you," Jupiter shrugs. "You'll be the ruler. You can make the rules."

I sigh. "That's a very good point. It still doesn't mean I know what I'm doing."

"Does anyone know what they're doing when they're called for a higher purpose?" Jupiter grins. "I certainly didn't know what I was doing when I fell into Wonderland, or when I started slipping into dreams, or when we found out I'm the Hope Bringer. Hell, I still don't know what I'm doing. There's no Punisher here at the moment. That means it's up to me to defuse any situations that spring up. So, consider this me defusing you."

"Damn." I laugh, scraping my hair out of my face. "Now I feel like a bomb."

"You should. You're a strong, independent woman. Because of you, Wonderland is alive."

"Not only me, though."

"But you were the first, and you might not realize it, but without you, it would have never worked. You're the glue that held us together, that made Cheshire see the light, that helped me rescue White when Alice took him, that raised your sword at the final battle. You are our glue, and now you get a fancy title for it. Just consider this a promotion."

Snorting, I shake my head, but a small smile pulls at my lips. "But how am I supposed to be ready? How do I know when I am? And how do I know I'm not making some massive mistake?"

The smile on Jupiter's face falls, and I realize I've touched a nerve. I'm tempted to tell her never mind, that I'll figure it out myself, but I can sense she also wants to talk about something hurting her, so I reach out and take her hand again, before we take a seat on the small couch.

"I used to have a sister, a twin." Jupiter doesn't look me in the eyes. "Actually, she's the only reason I ended up in Wonderland. Before she died, I promised her that I would go on an adventure, so when she was gone, I packed up everything I owned and moved from the east coast to California."

"What happened to her?" I whisper, squeezing her hand in reassurance.

"Neptune was different, always addicted to something. At first, it was books, then boys, but then the wrong boy introduced her to drugs. I didn't notice until she started lagging at softball practice. And then I started finding the drugs hidden in her room. When I asked her about it, she said it was just a passing fancy, that she was just experimenting. But she never stopped, and it only got worse. The last time I saw her, she called me to come over. I didn't know it at the time, but she was saying goodbye. My sister was a firm believer in the universe and told me that I would have adventures while we grew up. She never said we." She turns sad eyes to me. "She never said we. Now, I know she always knew that she was going to die young. After she made me promise to have adventures, and I left, she committed suicide."

The words "I'm sorry" almost spill from my lips, but I know from my own experience that those are the worst words to say. They only cause more pain.

"And the promise she made you keep sent you straight to White," I clarify, pulling Jupiter into a hug. "Have you told him that?"

"We've discussed it. White thinks that Neptune had some of the powers of Absalom, that she saw things. If she would have told me, then I could have helped her. But it's my mistake that I didn't see something was wrong with my twin. That's my point. We don't know if we're making mistakes, and if we do make one, that it isn't some preordained nonsense that leads to something better. You're gonna make mistakes, Clara. There's no doubt about that." She meets my eyes. "The point is, you won't be alone when you make them. You have a whole family behind you. Something I'm eternally grateful for myself."

"Thank you," I whisper, taking a deep breath. "For sharing your story and helping me to clear my head."

"Anytime," she grins. "If you need me to start making nerd jokes or to tell you the entire table of elements, I'm your girl, too." The wink she throws me is all awkward and completely Jupiter. She's a breath of fresh air, and it's easy to see why White is so in love with her. "Now, let's get you ready for your wedding."

The ladies come in when Jupiter calls for them, and they start bustling around my hair, wrapping it up into a fancy updo that I never could have achieved myself. A string of glowing crystals is threaded through the locks, casting a soft purple glow.

"Let's see the dress," Jupiter claps, reaching for the large bundle hanging from the door. When she opens the bag, she gasps. "It's glowing!"

"Hatter said something about being infused with the mushrooms' phosphorescence." I know Jupiter will appreciate that piece of information. When she strokes a finger gently down the dress and checks it for the essence rubbing off on her—it doesn't—she sighs.

"Remind me to ask Hatter how it was done. That's a very neat trick."

With the help of the two other women, they manage to get the dress on and laced up the back until I almost can't breathe. When I look in the mirror, I sigh. While I don't want my color to be white, the base shade of the dress is of that color, but the glow from the mushrooms gives it a blue glow that kind of dances around like it's covered in glitter. With a dropped-waist skirt that poofs out around my hips and a sweetheart neckline, it really is the wedding dress far greater than any of my dreams. And I get to marry the Hatter in it.

Just as I'm turning to check out my butt in the dress, the door opens, and Cal strides in. I choke. "You're in a dress!" I exclaim. I don't know why I'm so shocked. She looks gorgeous in a dark-blue formal gown, short in the front but long in the back. She's wearing her black-leather jacket over it, and her combat boots stand out beneath it. She's certainly still dressed in her style.

"Of course, I'm wearing a dress," she laughs. "I'm coming to a wedding and a royal coronation. I had to get a little fancy." She strides forward to hug me first before doing the same for Jupiter, and suddenly, it's a little hard to swallow.

It's been a year in Wonderland since the final battle, longer probably in the real world, and we still haven't told Cal and Cheshire about the newest problem, about Neverland.

"Cheshire and Attie are waiting outside with the other guys. The decorations are morbidly awesome by the way." Cal grins. "I can't help but appreciate the nasty little assholes being used in the flower arrangements."

"I'm glad someone likes them," I moan. "I really could have gone without so many beady eyes looking at me when I walk down the aisle." We all laugh at that, none of us losing any love on the carnivorous plant life of Wonderland. "I can't wait to see your brother and Cheshire. I've missed you all."

"We missed you, too. I'll tell you all about it when you get a moment to breathe. There's a particular story of Cheshire getting into a fight with the washing machine that I can't wait to share." Cal stands up like she's about to leave, and I panic. Now, I need to tell her now.

"Wait!"

Cal turns, a smile on her face. "What's wrong?"

"I have something I need to tell you."

"Whatever it is, I'm sure it can wait until after the ceremony." Cal grins. "I gotta go make sure Cheshire and Attie stay out of trouble. The two of them have started playing pranks together. Let me tell you, I've never been so nervous in my own home as I am when those two start getting ideas in their heads. Would you believe they Saran wrapped the toilet on me?"

I smile, letting my anxiety go until later. "What did you do in retaliation?"

A wicked smile spreads across her face. "I Saran wrapped their motorcycles together. Took them hours to get it all off."

She laughs and leaves the room, leaving Jupiter and I to chuckle over their antics.

I look in the mirror again. "I'm not looking forward to the conversation," I sigh, glancing at Jupiter.

"Neither am I. But it's better to come from us, and she knows that there will be a whole host of people making sure he's safe."

"Will he be safe, though?" I ask, biting my lip. "None of us know much about Neverland. I only know what the storybooks say, and I doubt it's anything like those. Wonderland sure wasn't."

"White won't talk about it. I don't know if it's because he doesn't know, or if he just genuinely is frightened of what he knows."

"It's just a new obstacle we'll tackle together, right?"

"Of course. We totally got this."

I wonder what it means when even the Hope Bringer can't calm my nerves with her words, when her enthusiasm doesn't ease my heart. No, something bad is coming, and unfortunately, Atlas will be a large part of it.

Someone just has to tell his big sister first.

Back at home, the bride's father walks her down the aisle and gives her away, but I no longer have a dad, and this isn't the regular world. In Wonderland, the bride has the option to walk with whomever she likes, whether it's a single person or a whole train of people spread out behind her. I considered asking Cheshire, because outside of Hatter, he felt like the next logical choice, but I decided not to when I saw him so comfortable with Cal and Atlas. Whoever walks me down the aisle would have to stand at the front with me, as a sort of Man of Honor. After debating for a long time, I realized that it's okay to make the journey alone. Besides, my dress is far too poofy for anyone to actually walk beside me comfortably.

The song that plays as the wide doors open to the tearoom isn't something I recognize. The tone is different, the cadence bright and happy and still somehow dark. Leave it to Wonderland to make me feel as if I'm both marching into battle and getting married at the same time. The Hatter's table isn't in the center, moved away until after the festivities. Instead, the entire expanse of the large ballroom is filled with tree stumps for guests to sit on, each one filled. It's decorated as if the outside came in; a small rolling mist even flows along the floor, giving everything a romantic, and a creepy, feel. Candles add another level of ambience to the area as every pair of eyes turn to watch as I step inside the room. In my hands, I hold a skull that Hatter swore was part of some sort of ceremony. I asked who it belonged to, and he shrugged his shoulders.

"Honestly, I don't think anyone remembers at this point." That had been his answer. So, now I carry an unknown person's skull in my hands as I walk up the center aisle, my eyes on Hatter.

The Hatter doesn't look much different than he does normally, although he's wearing a mesh shirt beneath the more ornate purple jacket he wears. He still wears his combat boots, although he might have shined them up a little, and his top hat still sits precariously on his head. His face lights up as he watches me step down the aisle, heading right for him.

He doesn't wait for me to make my way up to the stage set up at the front, like I was told he should do. He swoops down the steps and runs right up to me, the crowd gasping at he ignores all sense of tradition. Hatter never cared for such things, and there are no laws anyways against the slight. I laugh with glee when he picks me up and swirls me in a circle regardless of the large dress. He doesn't waste time before he throws me over his shoulder, rather roughly, and sprints towards the stage. If I wasn't wearing a floor-length gown, I'd worry about flashing everyone. I just barely keep ahold of the skull as I wave at the guests in delight, almost upside down. There's a mix of laughter and sniffs of disdain from the crowd, and it feels kind of like when an older generation thinks the younger one is insane. Funny, that even in Wonderland, there are those who look down on change. I hear Cal and Atlas whoop in excitement at the proceedings before Hatter steps up on the small stage and gently sets me on my feet again.

"Are you in a hurry, Hatter?" I ask, my face red with laughter.

"To marry you? Absolutely!" He grins, tipping his hat. "Can't have you changing your mind."

I hold out the skull with my own grin stretching my face, and he clasps his hands around mine. I really do love this man.

Because there is no current King and Queen, our wedding is being overseen by the next best person, the Time Keeper. White grins at us as he stands there in a weird version of a pope outfit. I think it's a joke, at least I hope so, because the black robe and funny looking hat are a little ridiculous. I don't even know how the hat stays on his head. It's decorated with skulls and gold thread, some jewels added for good effect. It has to be heavy. His ears are spread to the sides of the hat, making the sight even weirder.

"We are gathered here today to join these two creatures in honored matrimony," he reads from a piece of paper in his hand. The handwriting is rough and hastily scribbled; I wonder how he's even able to read it. "More like mad matrimony. Since when is anything we do honored?" I laugh even as Hatter scowls at the Time Keeper, but White continues as if he doesn't see the hard look. "The ceremonial skull has been presented, the poor sap. Please place both your hands over it." He looks up to where our hands are already clasped and clears his throat. "Right, then. Uh, the skull is a symbol of your everlasting love, that you will cherish each other long after death, and carry each other into the Here After." He raises his brow. "Well, however that works with Hatter. You get the point." White looks up at me, a gentle smile on his face even after all the joking. "Do you, Clara Bee, solemnly swear that you will hold the Hatter's hand whether into the dark, the light, or the Here After, as long as you shall exist?"

"I do." I smile up at Hatter, glad that there's at least some similarities between a wedding in my world and his. There's something satisfying about saying those words.

"And do you, Hatter, solemnly swear that you will hold Clara's hand whether into the dark, the light, or the Here After, as long as you shall exist?"

Hatter's lips stretch across his face, so wicked that I shift on my feet. "I do, backwards, forwards, and upside down." He wiggles his eyebrows at me, and I chuckle, looking back towards White for the next part.

"It is time to exchange your vows and gifts." White frowns. "Umm, I assume Clara goes first. Someone didn't write anything on my notes about that." He reaches forward and takes the skull from us, tossing it into the crowd. A creature shouts with glee after catching it and holding it aloft. I'm pretty sure White wasn't supposed to do that, but I choose not to worry about it right now.

Meeting Hatter's eyes, I take a deep breath and thread my fingers through his. "Hatter, I didn't fall in love with you." There's a moment where I can tell people don't understand, but I continue as if they aren't even there. "That makes it sound like it was an accident, and I very much love you on purpose. I believe that there is fate and destiny in this world, and that Wonderland likes to have a heavy hand in all that happens, but I also believe that we're fated to do the things that we would choose to do, anyway." At his encouraging smile, I continue. "Since the moment I fell into Wonderland and met a certain Mad

Hatter, I knew my life was about to change, although at the time, I wasn't sure if it was for better or worse. Now, standing in front of you, the danger of Alice gone, with the opportunity to love you without limits, I make these promises to you." I let go of his hand to reach into the hidden pocket of my dress, where I have the ring. Hatter told me that it's tradition to exchange a gift at the wedding, but when I explained the ring exchange in my world, he'd been far more excited about the idea. The ring I pull from my pocket is mostly gold, a thread of twisting purple and black metal running through the middle. Slowly, I slide it onto his ring finger, and he swallows, his eyes watching the movements. "I promise to love you until I'm no longer able to open my mouth and tell you, and even then, I will still love you from the depths of my soul. I promise to always embrace your madness, to accept everything that comes with being a Son of Wonderland. I promise to love you, to respect you, and to keep you by my side forever, because I would simply go mad without you. I promise that if you ever slip so deep into the madness that you can't find your way out, that I'll be the beacon to bring you home."

There's an audible sniffle, and I when I look at White, he scowls. "Stop looking at me," he hisses. I laugh and turn back to Hatter, my smile so wide, my cheeks ache.

"Above all, I promise to be your wife, your Clara Bee, and anything else you ask of me, because when I look at you, I understand that love is both a hurricane and a warm summer day, that it's both terrifying and perfect. One side can't exist without the other, and I choose to never exist without you again."

"Hatter," White growls, skipping the actual line and gesturing wildly at him. I try my hardest not to laugh at his obvious distress about being touched by my words.

Hatter doesn't even seem to notice White's problem, his eyes riveted on me and nothing else. "Clara Bee, if there's a point I start to rhyme, I'm sorry, but I know you won't care because you're perfect in every way for me. When I first learned of the prophecy, of a woman that was meant for me, I thought it was utter madness. Until you arrived, and my heart beat so hard, I thought Alice had surely done something to the organ. You didn't back down from the frightful world. You rose up to the challenge and took on everything that Wonderland asked of you, including one very Mad Hatter. Now that I get to stand here and make you my wife, and my Empress, there are some things that I need to get off my chest and promise you." Gently, he reaches up and takes off his top hat. He runs his fingers along the inside and pulls out a little pouch before handing the hat off to White. When he dumps the ring from the velvet, the sparkle makes me blink, and I blanch when I see the size of the purple stone on top. The metal wraps around the stone, and I realize with a start that the black metal forms skulls, the perfect representation of the Hatter. "I promise that if my madness ever gets to be too much for you, I'll tell you to thump me upside the head to bring me back. Although, there are certainly other ways you can distract me." I laugh as he slides the ring onto my finger, the weight of it both odd and yet comfortable. "I promise that I'll always look at you as my equal, and that I will be by your side for anything this world, or any other, throws at us, whether prophesied or a surprise. I promise that I will help you lead this world in the best way I know how, and when you stumble, I will be there to keep you from falling. If we do fall—which will inevitably happen because I'm the Mad Hatter, after all—we'll fall together, and then we will help each other stand again. If there ever comes a time where we must walk into the darkness, I promise I will hold your hand there, and that I will lead you back into the light." There are, obviously, many more sniffles from the crowd now, including some from myself, and I struggle not to cry. It's futile, and the tears start to spill over my lashes, anyway. "And, finally, I promise to love you with all the madness in my soul. I'm yours completely, for as long as you'll have me," Hatter says, his voice husky with emotion. "And when Wonderland deems it my time to move on, when we must walk into the Here After together, I'll love you even then, because even death can't take away what I feel for you."

Hatter pulls me into his arms, and I gladly go into them, wrapping myself around him and holding him close.

"Wait, there's still more to do," White interrupts. "Before you two get carried away and forget there's a whole crowd here watching you, we need to do the coronation part, too. Someone please get the crown."

Jupiter stumbles from her seat and moves up the dais to a small box. When she lifts it and walks towards us, I pull back and meet her eyes. "It's alright," she whispers, winking at me. "Just a trinket, nothing more."

But she's a total liar because when she opens the box, it's much more than a trinket. The crown is filled with crystal-clear stones, each one so pure-looking, any jeweler would probably weep when looking at it. It won't have any color until I'm officially crowned, and Wonderland assigns me one. Apparently, every monarchy must come with a label; there's so many little things that the creatures of this world have no control over that it makes me a little sad. Maybe I can be that change.

Jupiter lifts the crown from the padding inside and looks at White expectantly. Hatter kisses the back of my hands and then steps back, letting me stand for a moment on my own. Clearing his throat, White flips his wrinkled paper over.

"Turn towards the crowd," Jupiter whispers in encouragement, and I follow her direction, clasping my hands in front of me and meeting far too many eyes. I tilt my head up, trying to appear as regal as an empress should be, but I'm certain I just look odd and unqualified.

"A new era is starting," White begins, his voice booming in the quiet room. "And with it, a new reign is crowned. History has ways of becoming, Wonderland has ways of deciding, but this reign will mark the moment that both are in agreement. Clara Bee, do you swear to uphold this world with your reign, to bring it prosperity, luck, and peace? Do you swear to keep your arms around Wonderland and do what must be done to keep this land safe?"

I take a deep breath in through my nose. Am I ready for such a sacrifice? Because that's what this is. This isn't just some pretty crown and a title that I won't have to touch. This is a huge deal, and I refuse to be anything like Alice. It's harder to rule without fear, but far more satisfying to rule with love. Can I love every creature of this land, and earn their respect in return? Am I ready?

My eyes dance over to the Hatter as everyone waits for my answer. I expect an encouraging smile. I don't expect a playful wink. There's a glitter in his eyes when he glances at the crown that tells me he's imagining me wearing the piece and nothing else, and I can't help the quiet laugh beneath my breath. I may not know if I can handle this world, but I certainly know I won't be alone for it. With the Hatter by my side, nothing can seem so impossible.

"I swear," my voice rings out into the room, and a hundred smiles meet my own.

"Then, by the power invested in me by some weird twist of rules and fate," White announces, a teasing lilt in his voice, "let's crown the Empress."

Jupiter steps forward then, the crown cradled in her fingers. She's shorter than I am, so I bend my knees a little, giving her better access to lift up and place the crown on my head. My first thought is about how heavy the metal and jewels are, how the weight already puts strain on my neck. The crowd murmurs, a few claps and quiet cheers trickling out, but it all descends into silence when a light so bright flashes in front of me that I have to squeeze my eyes shut from the pain. The room grows still, and when I peek from between my lashes again, I realize that no one else is moving, frozen as if in ice.

"Clara Bee," a tinkling voice that is both a single sound and a million, says, and I jerk as if I was slapped. "I am so proud of you."

I look closer at the brilliant ball of light in front of me, even though it's painful, and see the vague shape of a woman. I can't make out any other details, as if she purposely keeps herself hidden.

"Who are you?"

"I am all," she says, the light throbbing.

"You're Wonderland?"

"In a sense."

"Then, I have a bone to pick with you," I snap, stepping forward. "This world is not a toy. You play with emotions and prophecies as if we're nothing more than a dollhouse. Your hand in everything needs to stop."

Tinkling laughter is my answer, and I scowl. "I knew you were perfect the moment you fell down the Rabbit Hole, Clara Bee. And I know you will make a great Empress. This world needs your spine and your love."

"So, that means you'll stop?"

The light lashes out, blinding, and the pain burns my retinas. "I did not say that. I am still a goddess, Clara Bee, and an Empress has no place giving me orders."

"Then why are you here?" I snap, "If all you're going to do is throw your might around."

"To give you your color, Clara. I had to look at your soul to find it, and what a wonderful color you are."

The light begins to fade, spots dancing in front of my eyes until it blinks away completely. The next second, everyone starts to move again, and they look around in confusion. Cal is the first to notice it, standing from her seat with her mouth hanging open. I look down at my dress, at what used to be white, to see the brilliant yellow of the sun, of the light the Goddess had used as punishment. The crowd gasps at the realization, that the transformation happened without them seeing, all except for Cheshire. He stands from his seat, a solemn look on his face as he meets my eyes, and I wonder if he'd been frozen at all during the time. He nods his head the barest amount, and I know, he's met the goddess before, has dealt with her, and it makes me feel a little better that I'm not alone in that. Cheshire understands.

"The color of happiness," Hatter mumbles, coming to stand beside me, threading his fingers through mine. Together we face the crowd, a united front, Hatter in his purple and me in my newly added yellow.

"Introducing!" White shouts, and the hall grows quiet, "Clara Bee and the Hatter, wife and husband," he pauses for dramatic effect, and I almost roll my eyes. "Empress and Emperor of Wonderland."

When the crowd erupts in cheers, I hear the TICK, TICK, TICK of a clock. Curious. So very curious. When will the ticking stop?

The celebration afterwards will be written in the history books. All the creatures of Wonderland converge in the Hatter's clearing. Music and shouts fill the air, and many dance in the center space left for such a thing. I'd had the pleasure of dancing with Hatter right away, all eyes on us as we sailed around the clearing as if we were flying. Then Hatter had announced "Tea for everyone!" and the partying erupted. We were just now getting a breather after the many creatures came to give us their congratulations, each one smiling brightly as they clasped our hands. The words, "Long live the Yellow Reign" danced on their lips. The line still makes me laugh, a tiny bit of immaturity slipping through, but no one seems to mind. I'll have to have a talk with Hatter about changing the words a little.

Out on the dance floor, I watch as Atlas twirls around with a few of the Wonderland creatures, a woman with deer antlers playing his partner. Doe and Flam dance around as if they float on air and laugh as Atlas and the woman try to keep up with them, all their heads thrown back with genuine laughter. I grin when Atlas throws up his hands and starts doing the chicken dance at them, mock insult on Flam's face.

Atlas isn't the same fifteen-year-old boy he'd been last time he was here, however. No, he's older.

"I can't believe Atlas has grown so much," I tell Cal, who sits across from me at the table. All of us sit together, away from the party a little, watching the festivities, but there are things that need to be discussed, things that need to be said. "It's only been a year since you three left."

Cal and Cheshire look at each other, a comfortable ease between them now that hadn't been there before. The time away has done them good. "It was four years for us."

White and Jupiter sit to my right, the latter shifting in her seat with unease. We know the news we must share won't be happy, not at all, and I dread having to say it at all. Hatter sits on my left, his hand in mine, our fingers hardly separating the entire night. "We have something to tell you," I say, keeping my voice low. My eyes find Atlas again on the dance floor, now doing the sprinkler, and I smile at the now nineteen-year-old, but it disappears when I meet Cal and Cheshire's gazes. "We've received a message from another world."

Cheshire scowls. "Of course, you did. What bad news doesn't start with that line?"

"It's from the Daughters of Neverland," Hatter continues as if Cheshire didn't speak, knowing the longer we let this go on, the worse it'll be. "They're in trouble, and they're asking for our help."

"Okay. Neverland," Cal breathes, running a hand through her hair. "And what does that have to do with us?" Her eyes dance between us, trying to piece together the puzzle.

I sigh. "There are four Sons of Wonderland."

"Okay." Cal's frown deepens but Cheshire stiffens beside her, already knowing where this is going.

"The Protector of the Here After," I point at Hatter, "The Time Keeper," I pause with a nod towards White, "the Hands of Justice . . ." I look towards Cheshire.

"And the Berserker," Jupiter whispers, her eyes looking anywhere but at Cal, her fingers twisting over and over each other.

"Atlas will be tantamount in helping Neverland," Hatter adds, a frown on his own face. He doesn't like this any more than I do. We've all grown fond of the young Berserker.

Cal already started shaking her head the moment the words came out of Jupiter's mouth, but now she shakes it so hard, I worry she'll make herself dizzy. "No. Absolutely not!"

"It's too late," Cheshire whispers, anger dripping from the words as he wraps his arm around Cal. "He was chosen before, and no one could have known he would be needed again so soon."

"I'm not letting my little brother go alone into another strange world! He's only nineteen! He just got settled into college."

"He doesn't have to right away," I say, meeting Cal's eyes. I understand her pain, of not wanting Wonderland to have a hand in her brother's life in such a way, but Cheshire is right. It's already too late, and if he doesn't go, a world might perish. "You can still go back to your world in the meantime, but when Neverland calls and when the time is right, Atlas will have to go to Neverland. Some of us can go with him. Not all, because some will have to stay here."

"The Empress won't be able to leave," Hatter says, meeting my eyes, "And neither will I. If I'm not here, the dead cannot cross. Everyone else will be able to cross over and help."

"And what is this threat that they're facing?" Cal asks, her face hard, needing to know as many details as possible.

"We don't know. We only know that they wouldn't have asked for help if it wasn't dire," White finally speaks. "I hold the key to their world, and have been there once, a long time ago, but I haven't been able to figure out what the threat can be. It has to be something that came after my time there."

"Fantastic," Cal grumbles.

Atlas runs up from the dance floor then, laughing, his hand on Cal's shoulder as he tries to pull her in. "Come on, sis!" But then he sees the matching expressions on our faces, and his own grows hard. His shoulders straighten as he meets my eyes, and I see the man he has become, and who he will grow to be. Atlas is every inch the Berserker our world needs. "What's happened?" he asks, his voice strong.

> "Sons of Wonderland lost,
> Triad of love understood,
> Enter now—the Berserker stood."

White's words hang in the air for a moment, lingering with long forgotten prophecy. Atlas nods his head in understanding, knowing when he was chosen, when he'd picked up that weapon in the armor room before, that something would change, and that he would be given a role.

"I'm ready," Atlas says, his eyes hard.

"You won't be going alone." Cal stands and stares us all down. "We'll go together when the time comes."

When Cal, Cheshire, and Atlas left the first time, Attie had left his Berserker weapon behind, saying he wouldn't need it in his world, and he'd been right. Was there a reason a fifteen-year-old needed that thing hanging in their bedroom? Definitely not. But now, the need is here, and Attie is no longer a child, but a man. Change is coming, and a new world beckons, despite our wishes. We'll face it together, just like Cal said, but at that point of this new adventure, Atlas will stand tall, the forgotten Son of Wonderland, the Berserker.

Attie raises his chin, preparing himself for what will, no doubt, be a new battle, one he will be a large part of. His words are strong when he speaks, and I know that Neverland has no idea what's in store for it, that the Daughters won't quite know what they're getting when they asked our world for help. "Second star to the right and straight on 'til morning, right?" He grins. "I guess someone better bring me my axe."

It's time to go to Never Never land. . . .

ACKNOWLEDGMENTS

There are so many people I feel I need to thank for this final installment of the Sons of Wonderland. Most know that this isn't the end, not completely, and because of everyone who has picked this up, that's possible. When I first started this writing thing, I never expected to find so much support in the book community. As writers, we're told writing is a solo endeavor, but I've found that's hardly the case. Writing, especially in the indie community, takes a whole group of people to achieve your goals, from family, friends, beta readers, Editors, cover designers, Proofreaders, Formatters, ARC readers, and finally the readers, everyone is just as important as the other.

To my family -- my husband, son, parents, and family that supports me every step of the way -- Your support means the world to me. Without your encouragement, I would never have pursued writing to begin with. Shout out to my mom for telling everyone she can that I write "weird shit". You make my day every time you brag about me to someone.

To my friends -- Katie Knight, Poppy Woods, and Mallory Kent -- none of this would be possible without you. This year started off in the worst way possible, and only seemed to add more and more on top of it. Y'all kept me sane, and when my motivation lagged, you told me to get my ass in gear and write. Thank you for making me see what I was doing.

Thank you Ruxandra Tudorica for always making amazing covers for this series. You always seem to get my vision and then make it a million times better. Thank you to Michelle Hoffman for editing and Dani Black for Proofreading. You make sure to remind me to take out the million repetitive words I always include. Thanks to Nicole for always making the interior of my books so gorgeous. You're awesome! Large shout out to Maria Vela for writing the small poem used in A Very Mad Wedding. It worked perfectly and I'm so glad I got to meet you in person.

And finally, thank you to all the Readers who continue to pick up my books and support me along the way. Without you, none of this would be possible, and I wouldn't be able to continue on to another adventure. I hope you like this one, and to make up for the two sad stories, I made sure to include two happy-ish ones. Sorry, but not really.
Next time we meet, we'll be in Neverland.

ABOUT THE AUTHOR

Kendra Moreno was born and raised in Texas where, if the locusts don't drive you mad, the fire ants and sticker burrs will. Iced tea, or aptly called straight sugar, fuels her for battling the forces of evil and washing the never ending dishes her son dirties. She has one husband who listens to her spin tall tales constantly without fail. Although he doesn't always know what she's talking about, he supports her like a pair of expensive compression socks. Kendra has one son who will one day read her stories. For now she's teaching him books are meant to be cherished and not destroyed. Her two Hellhounds keep her company while she writes. If she isn't writing, you can usually find Kendra elbows deep in anything from paint to cookie dough.

**Find out more on Kendra's website
or join her Facebook Reader Group to stay up to date
on all things Kendra.**

kendramorenoauthor.com

facebook.com/kendra.morenoauthor.7
instagram.com/writingbeast90

ALSO BY KENDRA MORENO

Sons of Wonderland:

MAD AS A HATTER

LATE AS A RABBIT

FERAL AS A CAT

CRUEL AS A QUEEN: SONS OF WONDERLAND COMPANION BOOK

Anthologies:

Cupid's Playthings:

SUPERNOVA

At World's End: An Apocalypse Anthology:

WINGS OF RAGE

Falling For Them Anthology Vol. 4:

FOUR PARTS SUPER

Falling For Them Anthology Vol. 5:

PHAROAH-MONES (COMING SOON)

Steampunk Reverse Harem:

CLOCKWORK BUTTERFLY

Dark Fantasy Reverse Harem
From Poppy Woods, K.A. Knight, and Kendra Moreno:

SHIPWRECKED SOULS

Daughters of Neverland:

VICIOUS AS A DARLING (COMING SOON)

Continue on for a preview of Clockwork Butterfly and a hint of Shipwrecked Souls...

CLOCKWORK BUTTERFLY
AVAILABLE NOW ON KINDLE UNLIMITED

Chapter One

"That's it, little machine. There you are."

Vic stared at the tiny mechanical creature on the workbench in front of her, concentrating hard as she tinkered with the small gears. She had been working on the project for days, a distraction from her father's anxiousness and her own excitement. Word still had not come of the news they have been waiting years to hear. Vic did not have the patience for such things.

Her cat, Gear, lay on the workbench beside her, watching with fascination as the butterfly wings flapped with the movement of the cogs. The soft grind of his own gears, those that made up his hind quarters, filled the small workroom. Vic had found him as a kitten, brutally beaten by some miscreants who had run the moment she had stormed into the alley. Steam had risen behind her, lending to the demon image they no doubt pegged her with. It added to the terrifying sight she had surely made, a woman dressed in trousers and a tunic, a pair of spectacle goggles on her head, grease smeared across her face. The puffs of steam that regularly came from her leg certainly helped. Vic was an odd woman for her time, raised around machines and preferring them to the boring social nuances of other human beings. Gear had become her companion after she had nursed him back to health. His hind legs had been mangled beyond repair, so she had built him new ones. The fact that they both had prosthetic limbs drew them closer, similarities and all that.

Gear purred when Vic reached over and scratched him under the chin, happy to steal some of her affection from the machine sitting under the magnifying glass. The newest tinker was a machine smaller than Vic had yet accomplished, a mechanical butterfly. As she wound the gears tight and leaned back, she held her breath expectantly. The tiny, stained glass wings began to flap, gently at first before speeding up as the apparatus began to run.

"We did it, Gear!" Vic exclaimed, lifting her goggles onto her forehead.

She pushed the magnifying glass out of the way and watched in excitement as the butterfly's wings flapped faster before rising into the air, the wings mimicking those of the real insects. The wings had taken some ingenuity. At first, she tried a fine layer of silk but found they were too porous. Eventually, she had found her answer in a micro-thin layer of stained glass. The result was a dazzling display of multicolored beauty, closer to a butterfly than she could have ever hoped.

Gear sat up and watched, enraptured with the moving parts. The butterfly took off into the air, and Vic clapped happily. The tiny machine fluttered around the room, sending glittering colors around the walls when they caught the light. It moved closer to Gear, clicking, teasing. Gear's tail whipped from side to side as he glared at the offending thing, agitated instantly at its incessant fluttering. Before Vic had enough time to truly celebrate the tinkering feat she had pulled off, Gear reached out his paw and batted the machine from the air. It immediately stopped fluttering and fell straight to the floor with a tiny clank.

"Oh no! Gear, what have you done?" Vic chided, squatting down and scooping up the butterfly. One wing tried to move again, but some of the pieces in the mechanisms were bent at wrong angles. She sighed, placing it back on the workbench. "Naughty Kitty." Gear just meowed in pride before laying back down, keeping a close eye on the machine in case it took off again. "This is going to take ages to repair."

Vic was just beginning to straighten out one of the cogs, the smell of grease and lubricant strong in her nose, when the door to her workshop burst open, startling her and making her drop the tool she had been holding. Her father rushed into the shop, tension across his shoulders. At first, she thought he might be upset or angry with something she had done or forgotten to do, so she immediately attempted to smooth things over.

"Father, I haven't been in here that long, I swear."

He waved her words away, a bright smile crossing his face.

"Both you and I know that you have been in this workshop since the moment you rose this morning, but that is not why I am here."

"It's not?" Vic asked dubiously. Her father was constantly trying to convince her to mingle with other people. He thought it was good for her social skills, and though he was not adamant that she act like a lady, he wanted her to have every opportunity if she so chose. In reality, social events made her feel like a bumbling fool when the other ladies looked down their noses at her, commenting on the state of her hair or her lack of petticoat. Dresses were not a favorite of hers, and so each moment wearing one made her feel terribly uncomfortable. The men were worse, coming up and asking her to dance every five minutes. She wanted to have a conversation, not waltz and listen to the men drone on and on about their accomplishments or assets. She particularly did not like having her feet stepped on. A lot of men were terrible dancers. One day, Vic hoped she could tell a man about her accomplishments, and he would actually listen with interest. Alas, she seemed doomed to end up a spinster. She did not mind so much. She would always have her machines. But her father would think it his fault if she did not join society as their station dictated, being the child of Lady Jenica. He had felt guilty a lot since her mother died, as if he was failing to give her the opportunities their station afforded them.

"No, my dear! I have received a letter!"

"A letter from who?" she asked, her own excitement growing with the obvious emotion leaking from her father.

"The High Council of Sciences and Exploration!"

Vic jumped from her seat,

"Well? What does it say?" She held her breath.

Her father stood there for a moment, letting the anticipation grow before he finally spoke.

"We have been fully funded!"

"No!" Vic laughed. "You are jesting."

"I swear it! Read for yourself." Her father passed the letter into her hands, and she scanned the document.

"That is the Queen's seal," she whispered.

"That it is."

"What does this all mean then? You are leaving?"

Vic was sad she would not get to see her father, but this had been his dream since she could remember. He had been fighting his entire life to get funding for an expedition to the Amazon rainforests where there were legends of a temple, the Temple of the Rising Sun. Those legends spoke of a great fire opal protected inside, potent enough to act as a power source capable of fueling dozens of cities at once. This was her father's moment, his dream come true. She would not hold him back.

"This means we are both leaving."

"Have you gone mad?" Vic asked, staring at him in confusion. "Would I not be in the way?"

"On the contrary, I have been tasked with picking the crew for the journey. I am in need of a Master Tinker, if you are interested."

"If I am interested?" Vic wrinkled her brow. "Of course, I am interested! When do we leave? What do I need? How long is the trip?"

"Patience, my dear. All in due time. For now, let us celebrate!" Vic could not stop the excitement that coursed through her body. She jumped up and down as her father offered his elbow. Her leg hissed and clinked at the pressure, the shocks absorbing the impact. She scratched Gear under his chin one more time, dropped some food in his half empty bowl, and looped her arm through her father's.

"Let us make haste," her father told her. "I have a lot of work to do."

Chapter Two

The next few weeks went by in a flurry of activity. Vic worked with her father to arrange for the letters to go out, requesting the service of certain renowned tradesmen. Vic was amazed that letters went to the Americas and, one in particular, to Germany. She had heard great things about Bram Schmitt, the up and coming German inventor. Letters had already begun to arrive with answers, and she was pleased when he was among those who had accepted.

Vic had her own preparations to make for the expedition. Three years ago, at sixteen, she'd garnered the attention of a local Master Tinker. He'd taken her under his wing, and at first, it had been something she was proud of. Until she began to work with him, that is. Master Frederick was a drunk, and a sordid one at that. He could be found most days passed out in his shop, a bottle of whiskey tucked under his arm with his snoring rattling the window panes.

An opportunity that started off as an honor turned into Vic running the entire machine shop. Master Frederick's patrons came because they knew she could fix their machines. She did her job, and she did it well. While Master Frederick had never taught her the things she had expected, she had learned so much more. Running a tinker's shop was the greatest experience, even if it took her a while before she was running it well. It helped that the Tinker Shop was a short ten-minute walk from her home.

Vic opened the door to Fred's Tinkering and immediately wrinkled her nose. The smell of whiskey and stale musk were heavy on the air. The scent of urine also permeated the shop, a rather terrible habit of the Master Tinker. She had heard he had once been the greatest Tinker London had ever seen. She was not quite sure where that man went, but the lump of flesh currently dry heaving over a bucket certainly was not him.

"Master Frederick," Vic spoke. "Are you well?"

"You're late," he groaned, waving his hand at the work table against the wall. There were various machines piled up: a typewriter, a steam-powered horn, and some other machine she had not seen before.

"That is what I am here to discuss with you," Vic started, keeping far away from Master Frederick as he heaved again. She had been the target of his vomit one too many times. She had no desire to repeat the event.

"Just get to work, girl. The patrons do not pay you to talk."

Vic frowned down at him, her anger getting the better of her. No, the patrons did not pay her to talk. In fact, they did not pay her at all. Master Frederick paid her a measly salary when he felt like it, and only if he did not piss it away on whiskey and the brothel. She straightened her spine and lifted her chin.

"No."

Master Frederick stopped heaving long enough to look at Vic. His cheeks were ruddy, and sweat was coating his skin and soaking into his clothing. His hair hung in strings across his forehead, dirty and unkempt. She was not sure when the last time he had bathed himself was, but the smell told her it had been far too long.

"What do you mean 'no'?" he growled. "I don't pay you to stand around and look pathetic."

"I am afraid I have to take my leave from my position, Master Frederick. My father's expedition had been funded, and I have been signed on as the Master Tinker." Vic shifted in annoyance, her leg giving off a small puff of steam at the movement. His eyes fell to the leg with a sneer.

"You're a cripple and a woman. What in the devil would make them think you would make a good Tinker?"

Vic raised her chin impossibly high. Master Frederick was often rude when he had been drinking, and it seemed this time was no different. It was a wonder he was ever sober enough to sign her on as his apprentice. The old fool would have gone under long before if he had not done her that service.

"I believe I have proved my worth during my time here, Master Frederick. I am taking the opportunity presented to me. I thought it prudent to inform you I would no longer be coming into the shop to do your work."

"Your job won't be waiting when you come back," he sneered before heaving into the bucket again. Once he caught his breath, he talked into the bucket, his voice a muffled echo. "I can find any other incompetent fool to take your place."

Vic nodded her head.

"It is a shame you feel that way, Master Frederick. I will take my leave now." She turned towards the door, but her eyes fell on the steam-powered horn. "The bell is cracked," she pointed out, a courtesy. The crack was miniscule, hardly apparent in the right light. With his eyes seeing double, it was doubtful he would find it. If it went unfixed, the horn would have a fuzzy sound when played.

"Good riddance." He dropped the bucket and slouched down on the floor. He pulled the bottle of whiskey towards him and took a long swig. Vic sighed. Some things never changed. It was likely he would not remember the conversation tomorrow. She grabbed a paper and pen from the workbench and scratched out a note for when he was sober again. She included the fix of the horn. Then she pushed through the door and breathed in air that was blessedly free from the smell of human disappointment.

London was not the cleanest city, the smell of horse droppings and steam coating your tongue long before you ever got a breath of clean air, but it was home. And Vic would be leaving it for the better part of eight months. She was excited for the adventure, and at the same time, she would miss the Queen's land dearly.

Since Vic would be leaving the city for so long, she thought it necessary to stock up on essentials she would need for the journey, including ordering a shipment of her favorite gear oil from the local shipyard. There were many vendors that sold the oil, but there was a rash of them adding water to the oil in an attempt to add to their coin. It never worked. Water and oil did not mix, and if one looked into the barrel, they would know instantly. Unfortunately, a lot of Tinkers did not think to look until the shipment arrived at their doorstep, and they found themselves in the possession of oil they could not use. Vic had stayed clear of anyone that was rumored to sell the tainted oil and instead went to the only man she trusted.

"Paolo," she exclaimed, walking into the shop close to the shipyard. Airships came and went around her, the hums of their propellers and boilers not quite masked in the small shop. Paolo had come to London, as a child, from Italy. His father was an abusive drunkard that his mother risked running from. She had left everything she had known to give her son a better life, and it had worked. His mother lived with him, a wife, and three children, and Paolo was one of the most successful vendors in London.

Paolo looked up from where he was marking in his log books—a task Vic had no urge to ever take on—and grinned at her.

"Victoria," he exclaimed, opening his arms. She immediately stepped into his embrace, accepting the warm hugs he was famous for. He smelled like oil and the metallic sting of metal, the best combination.

"You know I prefer Vic," she admonished, pulling from his embrace.

"I know. I just like to tease, is all. To what do I owe the pleasure?"

"I have a rather large order for you, I am afraid."

"That Master Frederick working you to the bone again?"

Vic grinned.

"Actually, this order is for me." She pulled a bag of coin from her belt. "I am the Master Tinker for my father's expedition."

Paolo clapped his hands.

"It is about time, no? Congratulations, Vic! You deserve it every bit." He looked down at the pile of coins, and his eyes bugged. "How much are you purchasing?"

"Eight months' worth of gear oil."

Tears sprang to his eyes, and he pulled her back into his arms.

"That is enough to pay the rent twelve times over. You have taken care of my family by bringing this order to me."

"I would never trust anyone else, Paolo. You are the best at what you do."

She meant it. Paolo mixed the oil himself, making sure the balance was always right for proper lubrication. There was no one else who did what he did.

Paolo kissed her cheeks, excitement in his eyes, before grabbing his notebook and writing down her order. After he took the details of the delivery address and date, he grinned at her.

"Stay there. I have something for you," he said, but before he could make his way to the back, the bell above the door chimed.

A man walked in, not many years her senior, dressed in a grey double-breasted sack suit. Vic immediately noted him as higher class than the men she usually dealt with. He did not once look her way as he pulled his gloves from his hands and walked up to the counter.

"Are you Paolo Ricci?" he asked, his voice rich and cultured. He was most definitely high class. Vic unconsciously smoothed down her trousers, noting the small smudges of grease on her sleeves she never seemed to be without.

"Yes, sir. What can I help you with?"

"I am in a need of an order of box gears, and see that it is delivered by tomorrow."

"I'm afraid that won't be possible, sir. It will take me at least a week to procure your order."

"Are you the best-known vendor, Paolo, or not?"

"Yes, sir, but—"

"Then I expect the order on my doorstep by tomorrow evening. See that it is done, or I will make sure everyone knows you are nothing but a fraud."

Paolo's face went white.

"Excuse me?" Vic interrupted, furious at the man's treatment of her friend. Class did not give a man permission to act a fool. "That is no way to speak to him."

The man turned towards her voice. His amber-colored eyes took her in, from the boots on her feet, to the trousers, the corset, and the goggles strapped in her hair. His expression immediately changed, his whole demeanor evolving into a smooth, dignified viper.

"What is a beauty like you doing in a dingy shop such as this?" he asked, his voice a purr.

"Paolo is the best vendor in the city. No one else could get you gears that fast, and that is exactly why you came to him. Perhaps you could use a little more class when addressing him rather than act like a boar," Vic said, holding her head high.

The man waved away her words and stalked towards her, stopping when they were merely inches apart. It was completely inappropriate for a man to be so close to a woman other than his wife, but Vic did not have delicate sensibilities. She was as stubborn as they came, and she refused to back down from this man, no matter his status.

"What does it matter how I choose to talk to my inferiors, Little Tinker?" His voice was soft and seductive.

"The true merit of man is not measured by his class." Vic met the eyes of Paolo who was watching carefully, waiting to see if she needed any help. "It is measured by how he treats his inferiors." She flicked her eyes back towards the well-dressed man in front of her. "Paolo will get your shipment as fast as possible, like he always does, and you will respect him."

"And if I do not?" he asked, tilting his head to the side. His eyes dropped to her lips and she fought against the sudden skip in her heartbeat. She was not attracted to this fool. She refused to be.

"Then I will make sure there is not a crate of box gears in this entire city."

The man's lips curled the smallest amount, and he inclined his head.

"Mr. Paolo, as soon as possible would be splendid." He dropped a large bag of coin on the counter, much more than his order cost. "I will await the delivery anxiously."

He turned back towards Vic and smiled.

"Good evening, Madam Tinker," he said, bowing and tipping his bowler.

Vic raised her eyebrows at the man.

"Good evening, Sir Boar."

The man laughed and headed for the door, pulling on his gloves. At the last moment, he turned back and touched his cheek.

"You have a bit of a smudge just there."

Vic wiped her hand across her cheek. Indeed, her hand held the telltale streak of grease, and she sighed. The man shot her one last appreciative glance before stepping out into the cacophony of airships and steam-autos, disappearing quickly in the crowd.

CLOCKWORK BUTTERFLY
AVAILABLE NOW

SHIPWRECKED SOULS

Three sisters.

When sirens come of age, they are given a single task—sink their first ship. Leucoisa, Ligeia, and Lorelai must fulfill their destinies to prove their place in society.

One mission.

Shipwreck Souls is a coming of age tale with twists and turns that will leave you *breathless*. When a ship is out to sea and a siren is near, no one is safe.

Come join the sisters three on their quest to discover who they are. Sirens were always meant to sing.

It's time to paint the seas red...

Made in the USA
Columbia, SC
04 May 2022